5

# SOMEBODY'S

# NOBODY

## HELEN AITCHISON

Write on the Tyne

ISBN: 9781739488277 (Paperback)

Cover image & design: Jarmila Takac (Instagram: @jarmila.covers)

Published by Write on the Tyne
www.writeonthetyne.com

For Joanne and Carl

# Chapter 1: The Past

'Dad, please?' the child begged, voice cracking as they stared at the man who was supposed to protect, nurture, and inspire them. Albert groaned at his child as they blinked back tears, their small hands in tight fists by the side of their skinny frame. Closing and opening his eyes several times to focus, Albert lay sprawled out on the battered brown sofa as the weak autumn sun cracked through the dusty terracotta curtains. The child had cried a million rivers, but nothing ever changed.

'Dad, please, please, stop drinking.' The last two words were sobbed out as saliva bubbled in the corner of their mouth; lips red and cheeks flushed with emotion.

They looked down at their care-giver, grimacing at the face of their father, who dissolved a little more each day. An empty bottle of whisky lay discarded on the floor. The smell of the woody honey tones lingered in the air, mixed with the pungent odour of soiled clothes and sweat. The scent that had become the nauseating fragrance of their neglected home. A desperate plea, the child remained stood over their father, searching his watery and bloodshot eyes for reassurance. He smacked his dry, cracked lips together, craving some moisture from his arid mouth. Surely, he could see the pain in his youngster's eyes? The tiny ten-year-old stood, bent over, mouth contorted with fear, despair, disgust. A child being dragged into an adult's world.

Albert let out a croaky cough. 'Tomorrow kid, tomorrow I will,' he slurred, before closing his eyes. Moaning, he turned his head away, sliding it across the brown cushion that was once cream. Dismissing his duties, he immediately fell back into a drunken unconsciousness.

The child stood, shaking. Their breathing irregular as they bit their lip and placed their small hands over their ears. Eyes fixed on the snoring lump, a glazed stare, willing for their father to jump up with a new, sober motivation. Instead, the child was taunted by the empty bottle of whisky that lay on a blue carrier bag by their small, socked feet. It was loved more than they were — the poison of their childhood. Exasperated with defeat, they knew tomorrow was a promise their father could never keep.

An only child, they remembered when their mother was diagnosed. Albert said Mam was poorly, but would be okay and surely Dad wouldn't lie? They clung to that sentence, thinking everything would be made better through warm, creamy chicken soup, buttered bread, and sweet, milky tea. Mam would be fine, she just needed to rest after collapsing at work and being in hospital. The doctors had operated; taken away the badness. Albert had said so.

When Albert had to go back to work at the ship yard in Wallsend, Grandma helped. They had made themselves small and quiet, popping in to see Mam a few times a day as she lay like a pale mannequin in her bed. Kissing her soft forehead with tenderness and holding her hand like a porcelain bauble as the other hand held a drawing, designed with love and made just for her. The tired smile on Mam's face etched onto the mind of her only child forever. The grieving started long before Mam died and never stopped.

Soon Mam could do very little and the nurses would visit daily and then twice a day. The team of professionals were kind and had warm faces, with laugher lines and chubby cheeks. They wanted the nurses to envelop them and cuddle them tightly, like a fluffy dressing gown. They craved comfort that Mam could no longer give and that Albert never showed. Instead, he showed affection increasingly for the sour alcohol he consumed nightly as he hugged the bottle, shouting orders over the TV.

He didn't talk about Mam, about what would happen after. Instead, they went to bed each night frightened their precious mother would be gone in the morning. A time bomb. The thoughts created a pot of sickness that lived permanently in their stomach. One morning, it became reality and life got even worse. They could still remember the day Mam got taken away by the undertaker and those days leading up to the funeral where they had to breathe underwater. The burning of their vomit on the morning of the funeral and their paralysis sitting in the cold church, surrounded by a blur of solemn faces.

Their first, scarring experience of death, watching their beloved mother disappear behind a velvet maroon curtain in her wooden tomb. Crying all around them, muting the noise of their own. But the internal screaming never stopped — even when Grandma held them tight as Albert sat, head in hands, whisky as his aftershave. Mam was gone and an axe had left a welt in their world that would never heal.

The death of their child showed on Grandma and Grandad's aged faces. Lines on their foreheads; deep and furrowed like estuaries leading to an ocean of grief. Sadness etched on their down-turned mouths. Eyes red, raw with melancholy, as dark circles became their permanent make-up. They didn't receive much comfort because Grandma and Grandad were dying inside themselves.

Life was irreversible because Mam was gone and even though he was alive, Dad had already begun killing himself. They continued at school, blending in, like a tree in the forest — but now they were the child with the dead mother. They saw Robyn, the school welfare support officer, once a week. It was the only thing they looked forward to and felt like it could help, alongside the cutting, which had become the release they needed.

They were allowed a sweet from the glass jar that sat on her desk. Like a jewellery box of tasty gems, they would think about what sugary delights may greet them each week. Bright posters decorated the wall, depicting waterfalls and beaches and a cosy sofa with soft blankets welcomed them, alongside squidgy balls to squeeze when upset. On week four, Robyn handed them a notebook. This wasn't the usual thin, blue, stapled school book where a little black box on the front read 'Name' and 'Class'. This was a real adult notebook — mint green with white swirls all over the glossy front cover.

'This is for you. I want you to write a journal,' Robyn had said, her voice soft. She explained it was their personal diary — a place where they could privately document their thoughts, feelings, worries, and achievements each day. Robyn explained it may help to put down feelings on paper and reading over them in a few months' time to see if they felt better. They thought it was one of the most brilliant ideas they had ever heard and that day, they believed Robyn may be the best person alive. They wrote in their diary religiously each day.

But the excitement of the journal and its contents soon dissolved as the entries became more desperate, lonely, and melancholic. Yet still they documented their daily thoughts, almost like an obsession. A secret compulsion no one else could read.

For the first year after Mam died, they tried to help Dad. Attempted to make him smile and laugh, and be good at home and school in the hope he would return to the father he had been. The pressure felt like they were walking up a mountain and could slip at any time. They found solace in Robyn; she was medicine for their heart. She would tell them they were doing well. That Mam would have been proud and that Dad had his own grief, but in time, things would be easier.

Time didn't make things easier. Support from Robyn ended when they moved to high school two years after beginning to work with her. Another loss. Their wound became further infected, creating a poison that spread, consuming them. Producing a despair that led to anger, hate, resentment, and a promise that they would do all they could to make sure no child ever felt the way they had.

Life continued, well, existence did. Eventually, Albert lost his job. He was ringing in sick and wouldn't admit to being an alcoholic. Never properly sober; constantly topping up. He had always been a big, respected man. Now pitied, no one could reach out far enough to rescue the drowning drunk. Albert was driving around Northumberland under the influence, in a bubble of blind selfishness and risk. Each time Dad got into the car, they were terrified he would kill someone. Thoughts of him ploughing into a bollard and killing himself crossed their mind frequently. This felt terrifying and desirable in equal measures, like eating an insect covered in luxurious chocolate.

When Albert lost his job, they were almost fifteen years old. It had been over four years since Mam had died. Part of Dad had died alongside her. The rest of him, no doubt terminal. They had been an adult for a long time. Too old for social services to do much. Instead, they felt like a fly in a spider's web, trapped, and life with Albert was something they were even more desperate to escape.

Years later, Albert lay in the hospital bed, the last hours of his life ticking by. Looking briefly at his eyes full of pity, it was still hard for them to register any feelings except negative ones towards their father. They had heard all the excuses and lies spewed out of his rancid mouth that never took responsibility. Said so easily, with no consideration for their needs or pain. As a child and adult, they couldn't even mourn the loss of their own mother; Albert polluted it with his own wants and weakness. Something that should have made him love and protect his child more, had turned into a selfish catalogue of destruction, alcoholism, and neglect. But they were no longer a child.

Now an adult, standing over the bed, watching the final demise of the man who created them. 'You never got that help. You never did change,' they wanted to shout. The love, compassion, and hope held for so long had eroded over the years. Feelings rotting like wood left outside against the elements. Pleas, begging, threatening him to get help; all wasted. In the end, they cut him out. There was nothing else for it and part of them began to live again, maimed but managing. Albert never bothered anyway.

No cards on birthdays, no Christmas presents. No interest in them, as a child or young adult. Just the gifts of crippling worry he inflicted. Albert wasn't even worthy of the title 'father'.

He lay in his clinical bed, in and out of consciousness. Dosed up on morphine for the pain, tucked in tightly, as if already in his tomb. The pale blue blanket folded immaculately as he lay unmoving. An old man, aged before his time. They rubbed their neck and let out an exasperated sigh. There was no one left to miss him.

Not wanting to visit, everything in their head said not to. But somewhere in their heart, they wondered if they would get the acknowledgement, the sorry. A little healing for the pain that had become part of them. Moving slightly in the plastic padded hospital chair, they looked at their watch. They had been there an hour and only once had Albert opened his eyes to his child. A desperate half smile, they had looked back at him, blankly. They just wanted to hear him say it. But as the minutes ticked by and his life clock began its final countdown, it seemed they would never get the apology.

Pushing themselves up from the arms of the chair, they clenched their fists, annoyed with themselves for thinking this could have been redemption. They left the hospital ward quietly, without saying a goodbye. They vowed to make people listen. They would not be permitted to make the mistakes Albert had. They would not allow others to die slowly with those who love them becoming more and more destroyed. Polluting the lives of people who only want love and respect. They would make people listen, and listen by force if needed.

# Chapter 2: Stuart

Stuart whistled as he pushed open the heavy blue door, inhaling the familiar smell of the centre in Crosley, Northumberland. His venture, his creation, his calling. The comforting aroma of mustiness combined with disinfectant smelt like home to him and a place of security where he and his team could help others. Switching on the hall lights, a smile spread across his thin face. The community centre of Homeless Helping Hands still filled Stuart with gratitude each day.

Stuart had experienced dread in his jobs before becoming the 'Second Stuart' as he referred to it. Now the 'Third Stuart', re-birth sounded a little grandiose for his liking, but the concept was the same. The Third Stuart lived that dream job life as the CEO of charity, Homeless Helping Hands. Granted, he had crawled away from the gates of hell to get there, but here he was. For over three years, every day, Stuart had woken, grateful to be alive and ecstatic to get to work.

At his most chaotic, six years ago, Stuart had no lifeline. With few services to turn to and even fewer people, he self-harmed, begged, slept rough, and sofa surfed — existing in a haze of alcohol-fuelled oblivion, tinged with the sobering reality of loss and hopelessness. There was no listening ear, no safety net, no helping hand. His life became an assortment of blue light services, following the demise of his marriage to Sharren, and subsequent loss of his job at the local supermarket, loss of his home, and loss of his dignity.

Stuart moved to his brother's sofa and had already begun sliding into the bottle of alcoholism. Hiding it at first; his own sympathetic companion. Then, as addiction got its grip around him — like a mouse caught in a trap — he stopped giving a damn who saw him or what people thought.

Alcohol was the only reliable thing in his world, yet his worst enemy. It had crept in, a poison, drip by drip, becoming his lifeblood. An abusive, toxic tormentor. Asking for help just felt like more of his masculinity was getting eroded. A failure as a husband, as a manager, as a brother, as a man.

Soon, Stuart was polluting Johnny's life, his kid brother, who he should always protect. After one alcohol-induced incident too many, the stitching had come undone, and Johnny asked him to leave. Even in the haze of drink and being soiled with bodily fluids, Stuart still saw the look in his brother's eyes. The look of absolute, undiluted disappointment.

The council housing team arranged a place in a hostel run by a charity called Next Steps. Stuart arrived at the hostel, to smiles from staff, nods from other residents, and a stare-down from a bald guy who thought he was the lead of G-wing at HMP Northumberland. A friendly voice led the way to the office while Stuart's eyes glanced at the worn floral carpet and magnolia walls with scuff marks, as he wondered if he could ever get back to the man he was. Stuart stayed at the supported accommodation until he did actually move on to the 'next step', but he almost lost his footing permanently, dozens of times during the journey.

His catalyst for change presented itself in a roundabout, destructive way. Stuart and another resident had been begging outside the local supermarket. Taking up position, people tossed the odd coin at them. Some avoided eye contact and played with their phones. Others gave a look of disgust. Stuart didn't care. He had some drink in him, the sun on his face, and was sitting with the only friend he had in the world.

Then his world was macheted when he saw her. Sharren, walking towards them. Panic rose in Stuart. His ears pulsated, and he felt faint. Heart rate accelerating; his mouth became dry as he moved his backside on the ground. Sharren noticed him; the man she had loved for two decades, begging. And shame threatened to knock Stuart out with a force more powerful than a punch from the world heavyweight boxing champion.

It was Stuart's catalyst for change. Only it got worse before it got better as he began unravelling further, buying street Valium from a local dealer. He'd never used Valium, or 'blues' as they were called. Only the odd joint, a few dodgy painkillers or sleeping tablets now and then. With the pills in his pocket, he walked to the nearest supermarket that he wasn't barred from and stole two bottles of vodka to make a cocktail with his drugs. Sitting in a secluded spot in a local park, with each sip of vodka and each pop of the blister pack of Valium, he felt release. Tears of regret, heartbreak, and relief fell. But he knew it was for better times, and part of him felt no fear at all.

Two days later, Stuart woke up in ICU at the hospital. Opening his eyes, he closed them again tightly, hoping it was a dream. His mouth felt like sandpaper, his tongue, sore. He looked around his medical nest — tubes and monitors sprung from his body like branches of a tree. Stuart felt like a muddy puddle and he wanted to trickle down the drain and disappear.

'Shit,' he croaked as a smiley nurse approached.

'Hello, lovely. Nice to see you awake,' she beamed, as if talking to a toddler waking from a nap. 'I'll get you some fresh water and the doctors will pop and see you soon.'

On day four post suicide attempt, Stuart was staring into space, his mind numb. He heard an annoying jingling as a man came closer to his bed before stopping and glancing down at him. Tilting his head, Stuart returned a gaze at the noisy offender; a punk-like chain hanging from his belt hoop. Stuart rolled his eyes, hoping he wasn't some sort of new-age vicar.

'Alright? I'm Craig. I'm not a doctor. You can probably tell. I'm from Next Steps Outreach Team.' Craig raised an eyebrow and Stuart made a humph noise. 'Can I take up ten mins of your time to explain what I do?' Craig asked, a warm smile on his round jowly face.

Pressing his lips together, Stuart moved slightly in his narrow hospital bed. 'Why not? I'm not exactly going anywhere, am I?' he said sarcastically.

For the next few minutes, Craig explained he had been in hospital too, after a mental breakdown, becoming homeless, and trying to take his own life. Stuart nodded, listening intently to the random bloke.

'Next Steps helped me get somewhere to stay temporarily, then somewhere more permanent. I got back on my feet, got the right help for up here.' Craig tapped his head. 'And now I see that ironically, trying to take my life, saved my life.' Craig winked.

Stuart sat up a little, wincing as he did so, his eyes remaining fixed on the stranger sharing his story.

'I started volunteering with Next Steps, did a shit load of training and then got this job. That's my sales pitch mate.'

Craig put his hands up, shoulder height, palms out. 'I can help you however you want. Support you, listen to you, be your voice if you need me too. But only if it's something you want.' He tapped the pocket of his utility trousers and squashed two fingers in before pulling out a little card. 'Have a think. Here's my card. I'll pop by in the morning.'

Stuart blinked, realising he had been holding his gaze on Craig. A stranger telling his own story sounded like an epiphany. 'Thanks,' was all he could muster, unsure if he was going to cry.

That was *the day*. The moment Stuart's existence ended. The moment he began to live again as the Third Stuart. With support from Craig, he left hospital sober and on the right meds. It took Stuart almost eighteen months to feel recovered, both physically and mentally. He volunteered with local charities and networked.

Stuart developed an extra layer of skills, an intelligence, and empathy to work with excluded, disadvantaged folk. He wanted to do more, and Homeless Helping Hands was born. Now he ran his own day centre and had the evening outreach providing food and clothing to those who wouldn't, couldn't, or weren't quite ready to come indoors or access help. Stuart never thought his life would turn out like this, but he had never felt so fulfilled.

# Chapter 3: Lorna

Lorna sat in the rush-hour traffic, smiling and tapping the steering wheel to the beat of a song. Even being in traffic with the tooting and stop-starting, she was happy, knowing that she was heading home to James and their new home. Both almost thirty, they'd been living together for three months, after a year of blissful dating. It still felt new, sparkly, and sexy.

'You're so high maintenance,' her best friend, Chantelle, joked in the past about Lorna's dating antics. Lorna was set on her ideal and wouldn't compromise. She had encountered a stadium full of liars and disappointments over the years; it was time she got the happy-ever-after she deserved. James and Lorna had exchanged messages on a dating app and their initial meeting in a local bar felt like destiny. When they bought their first home, Lorna was more in love than ever.

Eventually, she drove into the quiet street and pulled up on the drive of their two-bed semi. Angus, her Border Collie dog, appeared at the window, steaming up the glass with his gaping mouth. As she opened the grey composite front door and stepped into the hallway, Angus fussed around her, his tail wagging ferociously.

As she began making dinner, Lorna reflected on her life. The stability of her relationship and new home with her dream man made Lorna crave more. Working at Fentons, a local haulage company, she wanted a career; job satisfaction through helping people — perhaps now was the right time.

'Voila!' said Lorna, placing a plate of curry and rice in front of James on their white dining table thirty minutes later. Her hazel eyes remained on him, waiting for a response.

'Looks great,' he replied, inhaling the spicy aroma and eagerly grabbing a crispy poppadom as he shook his floppy hair out of his face.

Lorna sat opposite, flashing a smile as she picked up her fork and dug it into the gold-coloured rich sauce. 'How was your day?'

'Yeah, alright. We talked about setting up a five-a-side team between some departments. I think it would help keep this down.' He grinned, tapping his stomach before shovelling a fork full of rice and fragrant curry into his mouth.

'I love you just the way you are.' She reached over the table and touched James's forearm, as she thought of how many hours it would absorb from their couple time.

The next day, Lorna sat outside Fentons on her lunch break after chasing up emails most of the morning and thought about her career. She was young and had many transferable skills. Running a hand through her long, light brown hair, she tried to see the positives of a career leap. Now she had James and their house, what was she really waiting for? She knew the answer to what was holding her back. Fear, rejection, the emotional element of working with people rather than mainly systems.

She sighed. Perhaps James's football could be a good thing. She could look to volunteer in the community when he was out. Maybe something local could help her decide the right fit for her career wise. Standing from the bench, she pushed her broad shoulders back as if to drop the negativity off them as she walked back into the building.

The following night, after dinner and walking Angus, the couple sat on their navy blue, L-shaped sofa covered in a large cream fleece. The TV played in the background as the pair scrolled through their phones.

'Hey, this looks interesting.' James held his phone out. 'They're looking for volunteers at Homeless Helping Hands in Crosley. It says here even an hour a week would benefit the people they support. You would be great at that.' A smile grew on his face as his eyes widened, awaiting Lorna's response.

Lorna took the phone, eyebrows raised. Reading the advert, jolts of excitement ran through her. She could talk to anyone and liked to help people.

'Why not call them, find out a bit more?' James shrugged and leant over to Lorna, kissing her cheek.

She stared at the phone and nodded. 'Yeah, maybe. Maybe I will.'

That Saturday, Lorna drove to meet the manager of Homeless Helping Hands. Approaching the area, she bit on her bottom lip, wondering, *would she be good enough? Would they like her? Would she emotionally cope with such a role?* Pulling up outside the old building that looked like a church, people were congregating. It was lunchtime, and she had been invited to the centre at its busiest time. Lorna checked herself in the visor mirror, smoothed her hair, took a deep breath and got out of her car. Receiving a few smiles, she walked through the noisy crowd, her black chunky-soled boots crunching on the gravel path as a middle-aged man came out of a door and greeted her. Skinny, with a bird-like face, he was around five foot ten, the same height as Lorna. He had thinning black hair and was wearing a T-shirt brandishing the charity logo.

'You must be Lorna?' He flashed a smile and held out his hand. 'I'm Stuart, great to meet you.'

'Hi, nice to meet you,' she replied, shaking his hand.

'Come on in.' He raised his arm as he turned, beckoning her to follow.

Lorna pushed her lips together and followed. Walking through the door Stuart came from, she entered a large hall with parquet flooring and thick, lined red curtains hanging like sentinels at rows of windows. She wrung her hands lightly, glancing around as she walked. Feeling every part the stranger as eyes followed her, she absorbed the old building; a sofa area and brightly filled notice boards on the white walls. Lorna smelt comfort food; lasagne and garlic bread. Inhaling, she relaxed slightly as she followed the centre leader, receiving a few smiles and nods that helped her shyness retreat, like snow melting with the sun.

The centre hall was filled with tables as music played and voices churned. There was a feeling of camaraderie in the crowd as hungry people took a seat. Lorna relaxed a little — it felt like a community. Reaching a small office, Stuart unlocked the door.

'Here we go. We can have a chat without the hustle and bustle.' Stuart gestured Lorna into the small room that housed three office desks, a kitchenette, filing cabinets, and an old-looking printer. Mismatched computer chairs accompanied the desks and in the corner were two blue semi-padded chairs that looked like they were donated from a bank twenty years ago. Despite the lack of style, the office felt welcoming.

'Take a seat,' Stuart pointed to the chairs and smiled. 'You want a tea, coffee, water?' He held the kettle under the tap.

'Water is great, thanks.'

Stuart nodded and reached for a glass from one cupboard, filled it from the sink, and passed it to Lorna. He took a notebook from a desk, then sat in the other semi-padded chair opposite her, dropped the notebook to his lap, and clapped his hands together. Over the next twenty minutes, she answered questions and talked about her work experience. It felt natural chatting to Stuart, but she kept it professional. Stuart nodded, making notes. He explained the service, being open about his own recovery, and Lorna listened intently, feeling inspired and motivated.

'Let's show you around then.' Stuart slapped his thighs before getting to his feet.

Lorna followed Stuart back into the main hall, watching as he strolled around with ease. Speaking to the odd person. A wave, a tap on the shoulder, or nod as he introduced Lorna. They reached a door off the side of the main hall and Stuart pushed it open.

'Team, this is Lorna.'

Two faces turned around from a kitchen and storage area, and said a warm, 'Hi,' in unison.

'Where's Mo?' asked Stuart, just before a middle-aged, bald guy popped his head around a door.

'I'm here. Nice to meet ya.' He nodded to Lorna.

'Erm, hi everyone,' Lorna said, pulling at the sleeves of her jumper.

'This is the day shift team. We have more helpers for night time outreach. It would be great to have you on board.'

Stuart grinned, holding his palms up.

Lorna wasn't expecting an offer to volunteer with the service there and then, but knew already that she wanted to be part of something so accepting and caring.

'Wow, thanks so much. I'd love to join the company,' she replied, blushing slightly.

That night, Lorna was like a firework, bursting with excitement to tell James about her new role with Homeless Helping Hands.

'I'm so proud of you, babe,' he beamed. 'I know how much this means to you and how great you'll be. It may lead to a complete career change.' He hugged her tightly, and Lorna felt his support soak into her.

Lorna knew she was doing the right thing. It was time for her to use her skills and develop as a person. It could be what had been missing all these years.

# Chapter 4: Mo

Mo had been attending the Hallington recovery group once a week for the past three years, since the week he knew he had hit his real rock bottom. That's the thing with the disease of addiction — once on the destructive road, the minor car crash and collision are never enough to halt the misuse. It has to be rock bottom; the lowest depth of hell, where the only way is up or six feet under.

Mo wanted to help others in need and did so through his day job at Homeless Helping Hands, where he worked. Thanks to Stuart, he was working with people in need and Mo felt he made a difference every day. There were always some ungrateful people; that was life. However, for the majority, who wanted help and to help themselves, he offered a role model and a listening ear. With the work at Homeless Helping Hands, his recovery group, and seeing his son Mason twice a week, life was good. Better than good, it was marvellous and somewhat of a miracle from where he had been three years ago.

He felt almost complete. Then in walked new member, Annie Joyce to the recovery group last week. In the following days, Mo felt giddy thinking about her, bubbles expanding in his stomach like bread rising in the oven. But accompanying this was haunting panic. He had been hurt over the years by people meant to love him. Let down most of his life; part of him felt relationships always ended, often with guttural pain.

It was the following Tuesday night and Mo was on his way to the Hallington recovery group. After years in the chaos of addiction, he relished his routines. Some people reached for the stars; Mo was happy just to have the sight to see them. That evening, as he walked into the group, Annie was talking to a member. A smile with the warmth that could melt an iceberg, framed by her round face, dotted with freckles and wrinkles that made her look like a beautiful painting. She raised her hand halfway to Mo, her other hand touching her bouncy auburn curls. He smiled, hand on his bald head, trying to play it cool when inside he felt like a teenager wanting to ask a girl out.

Mo got a cup of tea and dunked a few biscuits. He reached for more before he heard a voice and turned.

'Another biscuit?' Annie stood in front of him, smiling.

'What can I say? I'm a growing lad,' Mo answered, tapping his stomach, his eyes creasing behind his glasses.

He looked around the room and the feeling of dread smacked him. *Shit,* he thought, spotting Lance Cole, a Homeless Helping Hands centre user. Lance grinned and Mo gritted his teeth, swallowing anger. He visited a recovery group out of Crosley to avoid people who used the centre. Taking a seat, Mo saw a smirk form across Lance's face. He would give him the benefit of the doubt, but already it felt wrong. *How dare Lance come to this group? He knew Mo was in recovery and attended groups. Lance had no bloody intention of giving up the drink.* This was something more, something malicious, and as the group started, Mo was getting angrier by the minute.

# Chapter 5: Lorna

'I got the job!' Lorna shouted out from the kitchen. Angus darted in, mouth open, tilting his head. James followed, ran to Lorna, and hugged her.

'Get in, you're amazing!' He kissed her on the lips, then held her out, his chocolate brown eyes looking at her.

Lorna had interviewed for a full-time job at Homeless Helping Hands after Stuart had secured a grant. She felt a buzz surge through her as James's smile filled his face. But immediately there was doubt and concern that she wasn't good enough for a demanding role full time, despite having volunteered there for almost three months. She took a deep breath and smiled, watching James, who was celebrating by dancing around the kitchen as Angus moved alongside him, tongue hanging out.

She could handle it and had James now. Lorna pushed the uncertainty to the back of her mind and handed in her notice at Fentons the next day, burying the tiny seed of doubt in her head about her capabilities.

On the morning of starting full-time at Homeless Helping Hands, as she drove to work, Lorna's stomach spun like a washing machine. Despite her clammy hands and wavering confidence, Lorna was certain she could make a difference, helping folk to keep on the right path. She soon pulled up to the centre and parked, noticing the back doors were open for food delivery.

Starting at 9 am today, her shifts would include early morning work and evening outreach. She liked the thought of the variety, but also felt anxious about ensuring time with James. Lorna knew she invested too much emotion in James. She would make herself almost physically sick, ruminating on what would happen if he left her or if he died. Scars of rejection run deep. Her train of thoughts that was heading in a negative direction was interrupted by Stuart's voice as he came through the double doors into the kitchen.

'Welcome, officially,' he said, eyes wide and hands together, as Lorna turned around to face him.

'Thanks Stuart, I'm really excited.' She smiled, but her thumb nail instinctively travelled to her mouth.

Lorna went straight to help Dot, who managed the kitchen, and the fast pace of the centre made the shift pass quickly. On the drive home, stuck in traffic, she yawned and rubbed a hand over her forehead. There was a lot to learn in such an important role of helping someone make life changes that was different to volunteering. Lorna would do her best. She knew she could help people turn their lives around. Missed opportunities in the past would become the right chance. She could bring hope to the hopeless and help the helpless, of that, she was sure.

The next week, Lorna did outreach in the food van. Teamed with Stuart, they visited a regular rough sleeper, Charlie.

'There you go, Charlie,' Stuart said as he served Charlie casserole and pitta bread.

'Thanks mate.' Charlie shuffled off to sit on a bench.

Charlie was a regular, both to outreach and the centre and seeing him the last week, Lorna had said hello a few times.

Ex-army, he served in Afghanistan, and Stuart told her he was the carbon copy of someone he had seen too often. A squaddie with a backpack of trauma and PTSD. Charlie was the blueprint of the fallen soldier and had been on the streets for four years. Setting up camp under a local bridge, he engaged with the service sporadically. The average age of death for a homeless man is forty-five-years-old and Charlie was already older. *Maybe he was tired and ready to come indoors*, thought Lorna that evening.

Stuart mentioned him in and others using the service during the team case management the following day. 'Donald hasn't been engaging well with his probation worker and is at risk of being recalled.' He tapped a finger over his mouth. 'Lorna, could you try to engage him? Mo can't work with him. They don't get on, shall we say.' Stuart looked at Mo, who was slightly flushed.

'That's cos he's a plastic gangster.' Mo crossed his arms.

'I know, and sometimes people just don't get on. The past and all that. It's nothing you have or haven't done, mate,' Stuart replied with a reassuring smile before turning to Lorna and waiting for a response.

'I'll see if he is around at lunchtime.' Lorna nodded and scribbled his name on her notebook.

'He should be, pet. He seldom misses Curry Wednesday,' laughed Dot.

Lorna smiled before Stuart continued, sharing positive news of a few people including a woman, Beth, who was looking likely to have her child return to her care and John, a regular, who had begun volunteering with Next Steps.

'I'm concerned about Lance. He seems to have become overly assertive since helping out with meal set-up.' Stuart scratched his head and Lorna noticed Mo was tapping his feet, arms across his chest. 'I don't want to take that off him. But he's commented about people and called me an arsehole yesterday. We need to monitor.' Stuart rubbed his neck.

Mo shook his head, removed his glasses, and began wiping them with his jumper sleeve.

'Lorna and I talked to Charlie last night.' Stuart glanced at Lorna and she leant forward slightly in her seat, fully engaged. 'He's been in more recently. He may be ready to come inside. It feels like we've been working with him, or maybe against him, for so long.' Stuart smoothed his dark, thinning hair. 'Lorna, can you chat with him, please? A new face may help.'

She nodded. 'Of course.'

Five hours later, Lorna arrived home from her walk with Angus as James's car pulled onto the drive. His face displaying his handsome smile, that she struggled to return as Angus bounced around, excited to see him.

'Hi, my favs,' he said, getting out of the car and grabbing his sports bag from the back seat then patting Angus on the head.

'Hi,' she replied flatly, putting her key in the front door.

James followed inside and reached out to touch Lorna's shoulder. 'What's up, Lorn?'

Lorna shrugged. 'I'm really annoyed with what someone using the centre said today. A bloke called Lance.'

James shut the door, placed his bag on the hallway laminate floor, and pushed his brown hair from his face. Lorna took her trainers off, sliding them with her foot to the side of their striped rug and sighed, rubbing her hands together.

'He said a woman who'd been assaulted shouldn't have

dressed the way she did, and was always pissed, so probably made it up.' Lorna shook her head. 'I was so annoyed. I had to walk away.' Her nostrils flared and James tutted, eyebrows raised. Placing his arms around her, he mistook her demeanour as upset when inside Lorna felt fury rising.

In the shower, Lorna ruminated on her day as the hot water ran down her scalp and over her shoulders; washing away the smell of sausages and cigarettes from work, but not cleansing her mind of the dirty mark the day had made. Her shift had gone well until Lance had started acting up — jealous of limited attention as all the team were busy, he behaved like a chimpanzee fighting over bananas. Lorna had been speaking with Charlie and he talked about a son who lived on the other side of the river in Gateshead. She hadn't pushed it, but was keen to find out more tomorrow. *Little steps,* thought Lorna, *made for large milestones in change and recovery.*

The next morning, Lorna made a note in Lance's case file. Other outbursts were documented along with a note written by Mo. It stated that Lance had passed out in the disused bus stop shelter a minute or so walk from the centre on several occasions over the last week. Closing his file, Lorna rolled her eyes.

Within the hour, lunch preparation had begun. Lorna yawned and stretched in her office chair before getting up, and going to help the team. Walking to the kitchen, she inhaled the smell of food as she glanced into the hall. One worker, Liam, was unstacking chairs. Lance was whistling a tune as he set the tables, carrying plastic jugs of water and juice. Looking up, he saw Lorna approaching. *Was that a smug smile she saw on his face? How dare he.* Lorna walked past him, without interacting, as she stomped towards the kitchen, pushing her shoulders back. Entering the kitchen, Dot spun around with a smile as she poured pasta into a pan the size of an old tin bath and promptly gave Lorna instructions to help, taking her mind off Lance.

Twenty minutes later, the hungry folk of Northumberland arrived. Lorna stood in the hall, greeting people. Charlie soon made an appearance, getting in the line for lunch, but there was no sign of Donald. Lunch was served to forty people then most began to leave. Lorna approached the table where Charlie was sitting alone, cuppa in his hand, reading the daily newspaper. She cleared her throat and he glanced up.

'Hey Charlie, how you doing?' Lorna pulled out a chair on the opposite side of the table.

'Not bad, ta. How ya settling in?' He smiled and put his cup down, callused hand shaking.

Lorna nodded and smiled. 'Good thanks, I'm loving being here full time. It feels nice helping people. It would be good to see how we can help you. Perhaps with your son, Tommy?'

Charlie moved in his seat and coughed. 'Er, I'm not sure. I haven't seen him for years. Not since, well, you know...' His eyes turned to the floor. He rubbed his straggly beard with weathered hands as a few seconds of silence passed.

'Since you and his mam split up?' Lorna asked, leaning forward slightly, palms up.

'Yeah, and since I hit the drink. He'll be thirty-two now. I have been thinking about the past recently.' He swallowed. 'I do want to make amends. But I'm scared.' He let out a sarcastic laugh. 'Stupid, ain't it? I've been in combat, but scared to phone my own kid.' Charlie tilted his head and sniffed.

Lorna nodded. 'Well, maybe we could reach out to him. Show him how well you're doing?'

Charlie remained silent. Lorna pressed her lips together, feet tapping under the table. 'What are you scared of? That he won't want to know?'

Charlie nodded, raising his hand to his head.

'Perhaps we could give him a call together?' She shrugged.

'I haven't got his number,' Charlie sighed. 'He used to manage an IT firm, Techno-go. Perhaps he's still there?'

'We could Google the number and try it?' Lorna couldn't hold her excitement as she clapped her hands.

Charlie pushed his body back into his seat and bit his lip. 'Erm, I don't know, it's a lot to take in. I'll have a think. But thanks. I'm gonna have a tab.' Charlie stood up and left.

Lorna deflated immediately. *Why would he not want to connect with his son? She would help him, make him see it was important,* she thought to herself as a wave of disappointment washed over her. Lorna went to the office, disgruntled but reminded herself that people need time to see the right path and she must be patient.

For the rest of the day, Lorna deliberated on her conversation with Charlie and how much she wanted him to reach out to his son. Chatting with James over dinner, she became more frustrated with his blasé response of telling her she can't make him meet his son. Lorna knew this, but she wanted to help Charlie and she wanted to help Tommy. Help him get the father back he lost to alcohol and mistakes. All those missing years. They both had a chance many don't get. Charlie could erase some of the damage he had caused, make amends. He owed it to Tommy and, in a way, after trying to help him, Lorna felt he owed it to her.

'Next Wednesday!' Lorna said to Charlie the next day. A grin decorated her face as she placed the phone down.

Charlie smiled back, like a nervous school child.

'It's amazing you have this chance, Charlie. Tommy will be so pleased. He can become your reason to stop drinking.' Lorna's hazel eyes fixed on him. She knew that with her help, Charlie would be the first of many people changing their ways and repairing the damage caused.

His eye twitched as he scratched his head.

Lorna leant forward and slapped her hands on her thighs. 'I'll be there. I can sit a few tables away in the café, give you space,' she said quickly.

'Erm, thanks. I hope I'm enough for him.'

Lorna pushed her shoulders back and placed her hands on the table. 'You have a lot of making up to do, Charlie. But at least you're starting. That's what Tommy needs.' Lorna tilted her chin up and nodded. She would be the plaster to help these broken families heal before it's too late. People could make amends; repair the damage they've caused their families.

Lorna planned how the event would go in her mind over and over. Years of resentment and lost hope — beginning to heal. Charlie choosing happiness as his new substance and his son returning into his life. This was why she wanted to work in the field, to help people rectify their mistakes, and as the day got closer, she could think about little else.

Discussing the 'reunion of the year' with James, he'd annoyingly told her not to get too emotionally involved in case it went wrong. Lorna was angry he would try to extinguish her enthusiasm to reconnect a family. But when she went to bed that night, she couldn't help but ruminate on what would happen if it didn't work out the way her mind played the reunion.

# Chapter 6: Mo

Lance hadn't returned to the Hallington recovery group for a few weeks, and Mo was relieved. He'd gritted his teeth that first evening Lance showed up, speaking little whilst fuming inside. Annie had noticed, but Mo said he had a bad stomach, and that's why he was quiet. Her concern had just made Mo grow fonder of her and they had begun chatting over text messages.

He would picture her smiling, her mesmerising blue eyes and auburn curls cascading around her soft face. Mo liked her and he knew Annie liked him too. He might have been out of the race for a long time, but he still knew how to run. At fifty-two, Mo was a good-looking bloke, despite age taking his hair and his long-distance sight. He may not be Jason Statham, but he had an appeal, even after three decades of substance abuse.

Mo had remained professional at work, focusing on clients who were doing well and engaging with help, despite Lance becoming pest of the month in and out of Homeless Helping Hands. Lance always seemed to have something to stick his nose into, like a rat around bags of rubbish. Mo had been able to keep out of his way. Until that lunchtime.

'Watch out, arsehole!' was shouted in the queue for food.

Mo looked to see what the kerfuffle was about, to witness Lance arguing with another regular. 'Right, pack it in, lads,' he said, calmly walking over.

Lance spun around, glared at Mo, and curled his lip. 'You

can piss off, chasing a shag around like a dog with two dicks. You couldn't get a whistle off a boiling kettle with a face like that,' Lance shouted, pointing at Mo.

People in the queue began to laugh. Mo's body stiffened as he felt his temper start to blow up like a balloon.

Lance looked Mo up and down. 'I reckon sweet Annie fancies me,' Lance slurred, making a kissing sound as he puckered his lips. He waved his hand as if to waft a persistent wasp away and narrowed his eyes at Mo.

Rage heated inside Mo, engulfing his composure and professionalism. 'Lance, out now!' he shouted, as Lorna glanced between Mo and the rest of the room. Staring at Mo, Lance pushed his shoulders back.

'I said get out!' Red-faced, spittle flew from Mo's mouth as he got within arm's reach of Lance, eyes fixed on him.

Lance's eyes widened, shocked at the response. 'I'm fucking going, but I'll be telling Stuart about this.'

Lance puffed his chest out, trying to remain defiant, before turning and wobbling out of the centre. Mo followed him to the car park. Lance spun around, jumping from the unexpected approach. They stood, facing one another. Mo sneered as he shook his head.

'Bring my private life into this centre again and you'll be sorry, Lance,' he spat before turning around.

'I'm watching ya,' Lance hissed to Mo's back as he returned into the centre, shaking with anger and adrenaline. Taking deep breaths was all Mo could do to not punch the centre door.

The next day, Mo met Annie at a café. Sharing a pot of tea and a huge piece of red velvet cake, being alone outside of the recovery group highlighted their connection. Annie had that giggly, flirty charm that felt like the early morning birdsong. For those few hours, they were in their own snow globe, sprinkles of glitter coating them. That night, as the world slept, Mo lay in the darkness thinking about Annie, his past, and future. The possibility of adventure, like the feeling of stepping off a plane in a new country. But Mo wasn't too much of a hardened man that he couldn't admit to himself his fear of falling in love.

He'd survived prison, with some extremely dangerous men, but emotions were a tougher fight than physical attack. Despite the intoxication of love, being emotionally vulnerable terrified him. A love that could leave him like it had in the past. And that's what kept Mo awake in the end — the absolute terror of losing something that had only just started.

Donald, who used the centre, and Mo had a history around addiction and offending, serving time together eight years ago. A history Mo was keen to forget. Donald was a weasel, and his latest stint at His Majesty's pleasure had done little to change him. Instead, Donald had come out thinking he was Crosley's Walter White and Mo suspected he was planning, if not already mobilising drug deals. Stuart knew their past and reminded Mo that he was a professional and had to conduct himself like one. What with Lance and Donald lurking around, Mo felt like a volcano threatening to erupt.

Two days later, crowds gathered at the centre as breakfast started. Mo spotted Lance skulking around, observing. Donald hovered about, mingling from group to group, playing the 'big I am'. After the breakfast rush, Mo went outside for a cigarette. Autumn held a chill in the air and the trees were lipstick shades of red and purple. Leaves danced across the yard in the light wind. Sitting on the wall, Mo closed his eyes.

'Alright big lad?' interrupted his moment. Mo's eyes opened to see Donald standing smugly.

'Aye,' he nodded, keeping the conversation brief. 'You?'

'All good in the hood, man.' Donald replied, clicking his fingers in the air.

Mo rolled his eyes; Donald the plastic gangster.

Noticing his dismissive body language, Donald stepped towards Mo. 'Still think ya better than everyone, don't ya, Mo?' Donald turned his head to the side and spat on the ground. 'Well, it only takes a few words to tell this lot you ain't no reformed character,' Donald said, leaning into Mo's space.

'What you talking about, man? I know you've been in and out of the nick more times than a gambler visits the bookies, but some of us have actually got clean and stopped being scumbags.' Mo sneered the last word. His nostrils flared as he took a deep breath, anger bubbling up to his throat.

'Ya smug prick, Mo, I'll bring you down.' Donald leant over and reached for Mo's collar.

'Piss off,' Mo shouted, jumping up and stepping away. If he wasn't at work, he would have punched Donald in the face.

As Mo spoke, he saw Lance come outside. *Bloody magic,* thought Mo, that was all he needed. Dot popped her head into the yard, seeing the confrontation. Mo stood, breathing heavily, ready to go back into the centre against his instinct to have it out with Donald. Exhaling deeply, he straightened his shoulders and relaxed his jaw.

'We all know you've not changed, ya sneaky shit,' Donald sneered, goading Mo with his hands in a c'mon motion.

'You're a loser, Don.' Mo's hands formed fists by his side.

Stuart and Dot burst outside. 'What the hell is going on?' Stuart asked with limited authority his nature allowed. His question was answered with silence. It felt like Mo was back on B-Wing after a fight with Donald.

Stuart turned to Mo; his face flushed. 'Get inside.'

Mo did as he was told, fists clenched so tightly he thought he would surely draw blood. Breathing deep, his temples pulsated as he walked into the centre. A lecture from Stuart began and Mo sat, biting his lip and nodding for ten minutes.

'Mo, going on like that, it's just not recovery. There'll be repercussions. For now, head home. We'll talk tomorrow.'

'Thanks, Stu,' said Mo, head down as he got up to leave, feeling wounded.

'And Mo, look after yourself,' added Stuart, with concern Mo recognised as that used for people accessing the centre.

Flopping on his battered, black leather sofa, Mo questioned if this work was right for him. *Could he ever escape his past? The leeches using the service would always know about his private life and pick away the scabs of his past.* People who knew him from old; the stains on his soul. He sighed flatly before he lit a cigarette. Something had to give. Each time he felt he was climbing to the peak of his happiness mountain and doing positive work with people at work, some bastard would pull him back down.

The people who wanted help, Mo thrived on them and got a buzz like no drug had given him from seeing their achievement and stability. But the minority with sabotage as their main agenda, well, they had to be stopped. 'They fucking have to be stopped,' he said aloud to no one as he ran a hand over his bald skull and sucked on his cigarette.

# Chapter 7

Lance had been an abusive whirlwind for a few days and as the day progressed, he had returned for food or fights, topped up by extra units of cider. His body stunk as much as his attitude, but cycles of binging were as common as mail being delivered at Homeless Helping Hands.

That day, Lance had been in the centre mouthing off and being vile, offending people using the service, being abusive to all, including the staff. An insult to the help he had been offered on repeat, he was collecting enemies by the hour. His behaviour had resulted in Stuart temporarily barring him from the service and Lance left the day centre, slurring swear words and insults at him as he stumbled away.

As closing time approached, it was dark but mild for mid-October. After locking the centre, everyone dispersed, saying goodbye. They hung back, a film reel of an idea playing on repeat in their head like it had the last few days. The idea of revenge so the nasty piece of work that was Lance Cole might think twice about opening his mouth in the centre again. The ungrateful drunk had been offered help; and a hell of a lot more than they'd been offered as a child living with their alcoholic dad, Albert. An innocent child who had needed and deserved help for so long; deserted. Lance was just another Albert.

Everyone left in the direction of their home, waving to one another as cars moved. They waited momentarily, not enough to rouse any suspicion, then drove out of the car park slowly. Pulling over in the next street once all were out of sight, they exited their car. CCTV cameras surrounded the day centre, but not the street and green space around Homeless Helping Hands. However, there could be some household cameras, so they pulled up their hood. Placing their gloves on, they rushed, in the dark early evening, to the disused bus shelter on a quiet country lane — a minute walk from the centre where Lance had been drowning his sorrows recently.

Sniggering, they clapped their hands lightly and tipped their head back as they arrived to the sight of Lance sitting inside the bus shelter on the concrete floor, leaning against the stone wall. An empty bottle of cheap cider lay by his feet as he slept off his bender. A showering of pity fell on them before a gust of anger pushed it away. Lance had been a poisonous, spiteful bastard for the last few weeks. He had upset many people at the centre and had not once apologised. His vicious mouth and dismissive attitude reminded them of Albert and that left a sickness in their stomach that no medicine could cure. Lance needed to learn a lesson, and they were his teacher.

They glanced around quickly. It was almost pitch black on the country lane — only the dim light of the houses on the other side of the lane giving a soft glow. Bending down, they gagged from the scent of sweat, cider, and dirt. Lance's fleece jacket had its pockets unzipped, and they sat open like two wide mouths as his body slumped against the brick. They said his name, seeing if it would wake him, but leaning in, they could hear snoring. He was flat out like a baby, only Lance was far from cute, innocent, and precious.

Kicking his foot gently, there was no stirring. He would be

soundly sleeping off his food and multiple bottles of cider. They grimaced as they tried not to breathe in his revolting scent. Edging closer to Lance, they poked a gloved finger into his pocket. They pulled out a squashed hand-rolled cigarette. Frowning at the state of it, they fished into their own pocket and pulled out a lighter — a great tool to carry to start a conversation, or in this case, a fire! They stared at the lighter for a few seconds, the custard yellow of the plastic casing blurring around the edges through their gaze. Shaking their head, they let out a little chuckle, remembering where they were and what they were there for.

Looking around, they held the lighter to the cigarette, watching it burn through slitted eyes, before throwing it onto Lance's thigh. Mesmerised, they were back, looking at Albert on the sofa as he lay, a useless lump, passed out. Begging, pleading for him to stop — words to ears that never listened. They shivered and let out their held breath. Blinking rapidly several times, they turned and dashed away, leaving the cigarette burning into Lance's trousers.

Their heart pounded walking to their car; the adrenaline fuelling their speed and they felt they were almost walking on air. Driving home, their head pulsated with what they had done and what may happen to Lance. A voice drifted into their mind saying it was wrong, that Lance needed help. It was quickly stamped on by the reality — Lance Cole had been offered help and declined it with abuse and blame before turning on the pathetic pity. The parasite hadn't helped himself. He was another Albert and had to pay. They nodded slowly, a smile creeping on their face as they turned the radio up and began to sing.

# Chapter 8: Lorna

Lorna arrived early for her shift. It was the day Charlie was meeting Tommy. Concern about it not happening rolled around in her stomach like the aftermath of a dodgy takeaway. Walking into the office, she caught the tail end of a phone conversation Stuart was having, as Mo made cuppas.

'Right, okay. Thanks for letting us know. Please send our well wishes,' Stuart said quietly as he paced the already worn carpet tiles. Putting the phone down, he rubbed his jaw.

'What's up?' asked Mo, taking the milk from the fridge as Lorna took off her burgundy coat.

Stuart puffed out air. 'It's Lance. He's in hospital. Third-degree burns to his legs. Sounds like he fell asleep with a cigarette in his hand. Needs some skin grafts, but by all accounts, he's been very lucky.' Stuart put a hand to his dark hair.

'Shit,' Mo muttered, remaining on the spot momentarily with two cups in his hands.

Stuart glanced at Lorna. Her eyes widened. 'That's awful.'

Stuart nodded and his team could see the road map of worry etched on his face.

Lorna spent the next hour trying to catch up on admin in the office, whilst intermittently getting up and checking the centre hall to see if Charlie had arrived. On what felt like her fiftieth time scanning the room, she saw Stuart talking to people. Lorna tilted her head, beckoning him over.

'Stuart, Charlie's not here. Do you think he's okay?'

she said, voice strained as she glanced at the centre door.

'I'm sure he's fine, Lorna. He doesn't come here every morning, you know that. I'm certain he'll be in soon for the meeting with his son,' he said, smiling reassuringly.

She took a deep breath her feet tapping on the spot. 'I know, you're right.'

Just to make sure Charle was coming, she rang his mobile phone. It was switched off with no voicemail facility. Lorna shook her head, returning to the computer to try and do some admin. Luckily, Lorna was kept busy with several incidents, including an overdose on site, for the second time within a week. Stuart had suspected there may be dealing going on in the centre and a team meeting was arranged for the following morning. The panic of not seeing Charlie yet crept in again by 10:30 am, quickly interrupted by shouting from the back-yard. Staff went rushing out like prison officers would on a wing, to see some regular service users arguing with Donald.

'Hey, it's not bloody *Fight Club*, you dafties,' said Mo, interjecting in the altercation.

'And ye can piss off anarl, Mo. Got more faces than Big Ben, ye lad,' Donald sneered.

Stuart asked them to leave and after some more mouthing off, they complied. *No doubt, this had something to do with the recent atmosphere and drugs*, thought Lorna. She couldn't focus on that at the moment, though. Her priority was Charlie and their 11:30 am departure time. Ringing Charlie's mobile again, it was still off, with the annoying robotic voice telling her to call back later. Soon, 11 am arrived and there was still no Charlie. Lorna went to check outside, looking up and down the street as she bit her lip. No sign. Calling him again, the phone remained off.

'Don't you let me down,' she muttered under her breath as she felt her heart beating faster.

At 11:30 am, there was still no sign of Charlie. Lorna lectured herself, remembering not everyone was on time like she was, especially people who lived in chaos. Then it was 11:45 am — still no show. Lorna wasn't sure whether to scream or cry as she clenched her fists and her nails dug into her palms. After calling his mobile several times with no success, she had no choice but to wait as her hope escaped with each passing minute.

At 12 midday, and with still no sign of Charlie, Lorna realised she would have to ring Tommy and explain they weren't coming. After going into the toilet and sobbing into the sleeves of her jumper to muffle her disappointment, she took a few deep breaths and rang Tommy. He answered on the second ring, already in the coffee shop.

Lorna spent ten minutes trying to explain, apologise, and rearrange plans. It was no use; she knew what Tommy was saying came from his heart. His years of disappointment, the numerous chances. Gearing himself up for something, hoping it will happen, then the deflation of the selfish reality. Putting the phone down, it felt like her heart was breaking for Tommy. One chance, one effort by the man who had rejected his son for so long. Gone. It was all gone.

Lorna drove to work the next day with disappointment burning inside of her like charcoal on a lit BBQ. She had played it down to James but had a restless sleep, waking feeling like her mind had been burgled. She had even contemplated resigning, but realised how stupid she would sound telling Stuart she was resigning because Charlie didn't meet his son. The pain and frustration were real. She was wounded, and her heart hurt for Tommy. Putting on her best acting mask, she pushed the heavy blue doors of the centre open and walked to the office.

'You okay, Lorna?' Stuart asked gently, tilting his head as she entered.

She exhaled with force and spoke. 'I can't believe he's picked up again.' Lorna looked at her hands.

Stuart shrugged and half smiled. 'This is what Charlie does, Lorna. And all the other Charlies who use the services. They do well, they relapse. They do well again, they relapse again. I was another Charlie — we have to be patient. And we wait, helping, until they are ready to quit. Or, in some sad cases, their demons win.'

Lorna nodded and sniffed. 'Why don't people take the bloody help they are offered, Stuart?' She shook her head and sighed flatly. 'Some people never get a chance for help, then others decline with such ingratitude.'

'You probably feel let down? Like it's personal?' Stuart watched her as she nodded. 'It's not personal, Lorna. It's addiction.'

Lorna sighed, feeling patronised but knowing Stuart was coming from the right place.

The day passed quickly and towards the end of her shift, Charlie was still nowhere to be seen. Lorna thought about Tommy, another let down from his estranged father. She cared too much and hated herself for feeling out of control. Familiar, re-occurring feelings for Tommy himself, she was sure. Lorna decided she would call him.

'Tommy, it's Lorna again from Homeless Helping Hands.'
'Oh, hi, Lorna. How are you?'

*A nice reply from a nice man,* she thought. He didn't deserve this abandonment. 'I'm good, thanks. But more importantly, Tommy, how are you? I'm really sorry your dad never came to meet you,' she said gently.

'I expected nothing else, Lorna. He's a selfish man. He loves the drink more than me and put my mam through hell. Put me through hell as well.' He paused for a second before continuing, 'You know, hitting us and that. Blaming the army and anything else he could.'

There was silence, and for a moment, she could only hear her heartbeat pounding in her ear.

Tommy continued, 'I thought he might've changed. I wanted him to have changed. But it was wishful thinking, I guess. I'm just angry with myself for believing it may've been different, you know?'

Lorna could hear every breath of disappointment and re-gurgitated heartbreak in his voice. It felt so raw, like it was her own. She could almost see Tommy; deflated and as the boy he was when all the selfish, neglectful behaviour started from his father. Lorna felt sick. Sick with sadness, sick with frustration, and sick for the father Tommy lost.

# Chapter 9: Stuart

An air of tension, risk, and uncertainty coated Homeless Helping Hands. A storm brewing that threatened to let rip on the centre and the people accessing it. Usually, this related to drug dealing, a series of crimes, relationships, or just a volatile person using the service that caused a flood of destruction. Stuart had next week off as annual leave and was questioning whether it was wise to not be at work.

The radio played and Mo belted out the odd tune, inches away from Dot, looking into her face as he placed jugs of orange juice on a table. This was the side of Mo Stuart loved but his mood turned quicker than a light switch.

'Bugger off, you daft sod.' She chuckled at him as the others laughed and a few wolf-whistled to a blushing Dot.

Charlie came stumbling through the doors and Stuart immediately knew something was up. He looked like he'd been on a major bender or not slept for a week. His hat and coat were splattered with mud and his eyes were heavy.

'Charlie, nice to see you.' Stuart could smell stale alcohol and urine as he approached. 'Are you okay, mate?'

'What do you lot care?' Charlie slurred, his lip curling.

'Come on, let's chat. Lorna will get you some lunch.'

'She can piss off, anarl. Bossy little bitch caused all this,' Charlie spat, pointing toward a wide-eyed Lorna.

'Charlie, that's not fair. She's been trying to help you. We care about you.' Stuart tilted his palms out.

Charlie glanced at the floor, then back to Stuart. 'You might, that bitch doesn't. As for sly Mo, he's not changed.'

'Just sit there,' Stuart said, guiding Charlie to a table.

Stuart went to get a plate of food for Charlie. Passing a table, he heard the end of what sounded a heated conversation from Donald as another service user, Salvin Yanti, got up, saying goodbye to the table.

'Everything okay?' Stuart asked. Some people nodded and Donald said a confident yes then Stuart heard a commotion coming from behind him. He turned to see Charlie arguing with someone, the pair, inches away from each other's faces.

'Hey, hey!' Mo rushed over to the scene.

'And you, well, you can go to hell, Mo. You're as bent as they come,' slurred Charlie, eyes bulging. 'You're all in it for yourself, you lot,' continued Charlie, waving his hands. 'All your own bloody crazy agenda. The puppet masters, dictating what people should do.' He sneered and began pointing at the staff. 'I'm not in the friggin' army now. You can't tell me what to bloody do,' Charlie shouted, walking towards the front door. He turned as he grabbed the front door handle. 'I know all your secrets, you dirty, sly bastards,' he spat before opening the door and slamming it as he left.

The room was silent except for the radio playing quietly in the corner of the hall. Everyone waiting for a response. Donald got up and clapped and cheered, 'And the Oscar goes to...'

'Shut it, Donald,' shouted Mo, eyebrows furrowed on his red face.

Donald sat down, and the centre hall had a cold air of silence gust through it.

# Chapter 10: Mo

The day had started well, jovial even at work. Then the usual drunken, bitter lot kicked off. Mo still had to fight to shake off his past and stirrers like Lance and Donald didn't help. Jealousy spread around like the smell of a fart in the day centre. Even Charlie had become a troublemaker — and the three of them made the place stink, like discarded food rotting in the sun. Mo should have known he would never fully escape his past and right now, not only was it tedious, but it was pissing right on his rainbow and he was losing empathy by the hour.

On waking, he had a text message from Annie putting a bounce in his step. He had opened up to her about his past and she about hers. He was firmly in the cosy grips of infatuation. Alcohol numbed stuff; his past, his demons but now, Mo felt himself becoming addicted to Annie and he was terrified something or someone would destroy that. He kept grounding himself, trying to live in the moment as his recovery encouraged. It was hard and exhausting, like living with a constant cold.

That morning, feeling positive, he had arrived at work, helped with the daily tasks, and made a phone call with a client who was doing really well. Then drunk Charlie arrived, accusing all the staff of this and the other. Then Donald started. Anything to get the shit stirring going, that one. It was carnage and Mo felt a volcanic sized eruption building up in him yet again. He had sensed the seed of resentment growing in him over the last few weeks and knew it was because of the feelings of love he was developing for Annie and the poison of envy from others.

Donald was using new gossip like air freshener, spraying it everywhere he went to cover his own stink, and goading Mo with it. Where Lance lacked in balls, Donald more than made up for it. Both had a reason to want to see Mo's demise, and the bulk of it was jealousy. Others made remarks, in particular Charlie. Mo expected better from Charlie, but he had mentioned not letting a woman get between Mo and his son. An absolute nerve given Charlie was the catalogue model of a poor father. Charlie had laughed and Mo had felt tiny and angry. He wasn't going to sit back and let his happiness be destroyed.

The fire was raging in him and the true colours of people weren't just showing; they were bloody flashing everywhere he looked. Mo felt frightened he was losing control and his feelings for Annie were narrowing his vision. Love could provide the lifeboat and the wave to drown him.

Being with Annie felt like slipping into the finest robe. His whole body, warm and tingly as he gently kissed her lips, tasting remnants of coconut lip balm. Her touch around his waist felt like the security of a locked front door. Mo hadn't felt this for so long. He hadn't wanted to, or allowed himself to feel it. Until now. Their relationship was like a film, a perfect love story unfolding. Then, as soon as they left their snow globe sanctuary of just the two of them, it felt like the most magical feeling was getting poisoned by the envy and bitterness of people who he used to be like.

# Chapter 11: Charlie

It had been a fortnight of abuse to his body and mind, but drinking heavily had allowed Charlie to dissolve the pain and guilt he felt for letting Tommy down again. Charlie had tried over the years, perhaps not hard enough at times, but people didn't understand, unless they had been there. Addiction was a disease and the cure wasn't just an aspirin. Nevertheless, Charlie had failed his son again, and it was almost unbearable. Failure never got easier. Hurting people was painful and each time the alcohol won, it felt like the flame of fight in Charlie lost a little more of its glow.

He wished it had never been discussed at Homeless Helping Hands. They had made it a million times worse. Charlie didn't need the extra guilt. He already carried a sack full on his tired back. The staff at the day centre had pushed and pushed him with everything over the years. He questioned whether they were there to help or there to control people. Mo, Stuart, even Dot and Liam. Then bloody Lorna, with her need to do good. It wasn't their decision to make. His failure was because of their pressure building up in him like an overblown balloon until it popped. Rubbing his mouth, he took a swig of his alcohol as he sat beside the murky river on a shabby blue plastic crate.

The usual folk at the day centre had been interfering as well, thriving in other people's misery. The bastards who used any opportunity to push drugs. Charlie was as willing as a child at an ice-cream van, taking some cannabis at extortion-ate rates. He knew that Donald and his crew had taken advantage of him, but he was running out of options and needed his brain to be elsewhere; his thoughts to vanish like a magician's rabbit. Inevitably, Donald would keep his claws into him. He had seen it with others, the young ones mostly. A right Willy Wonka of the substance world. Along with vodka, the dope had worked. Charlie felt the dreamy void between sobriety and escapism. Where nothing much made sense and he could pretend reality was a terrible film he had switched off halfway through.

An hour later, Charlie returned to his usual resting place for the night under the bridge. It was sheltered and dark, with trees and vegetation around, seldom with anyone passing by. The concrete ground was hard and cold, but Charlie had adapted to it over the years and had a yoga mat and cardboard under his sleeping bag. By 5 pm, he had no vodka left. He had smoked one and a half joints earlier and finished the remaining half as he settled down in his sleeping bag. It would help him to drift off, even with a rumbling stomach.

Charlie hadn't been to Homeless Helping Hands that day after three outbursts in the last week and a temporary ban from Mo, in Stuart's absence. Mo had dished it out with the smugness of the Gestapo whilst Lorna played the sweetness act. He shook his head. They would be on outreach tomorrow night as usual. He would see who was there, get some free food, and maybe another sleeping bag as the November chill was creeping in. Charlie pulled his hat a little tighter over his head before zipping his worn, dirty fleece up to his neck as he tried to get comfortable in his sleeping bag.

He had almost dozed off when he thought he heard

someone say his name. Squinting, Charlie tried to open his eyes and use the dim light from the lamppost thirty metres away to focus. A face looked at him, smiling. Surprising given he'd pissed everyone off and verbally abused people the last fortnight as his alcohol train derailed. He wasn't happy to see them, but they were there and he might get something out of it. *What did they want, though? Maybe it was an apology coming.*

He licked his dry lips and cleared his throat. 'Um, hi,' he croaked, trying to pull himself to a seating position.

'Thought you might be hungry,' they said, handing over a soggy sandwich as they crouched down.

Charlie took it quickly and started eating, thanking his visitor with slight trepidation.

'Listen,' they continued, looking at Charlie, 'I know you've had a hard time lately and got some grief because of it. You caused it yourself, Charlie,' they shrugged. 'Some people can't or don't want to change. We're all like that to a degree.' They stared at Charlie, waiting for a response.

He swallowed a mouthful of the egg mayo sandwich and nodded apprehensively. He wasn't in the mood for a lecture, especially from this person — he was sick of the sight of them in all honesty. However, he knew if he played the game, it would go in his favour, eventually. Maybe the visitor was just here to give a lecture, make themself feel better. Maybe they were there to help him, to talk drugs and drink.

There was something about this lot that even though they were screwed up themselves, they liked to be sanctimonious. As if they knew it all, had been there, wrote the flamin' book! He placed a hand on top of his head, not knowing what to make of them; everyone had potential to be a rescuer and an enemy. They were all different shades of sickness.

'Here, I brought some cider.' They pushed the large plastic bottle towards Charlie as they stopped crouching and sat on the ground next to his sleeping bag. They grinned, unblinking, in a way that made Charlie feel uncomfortable, or maybe it was just paranoia from the dope. Charlie's head felt far from clear, but he was thirsty for alcohol.

'Not my usual drink,' he said, glancing at the empty bottle of vodka on the ground a metre away. 'But beggars can't be choosers,' Charlie continued with a light chuckle, as he wrapped a weathered hand around the bottle. He certainly would not turn down alcohol. Charlie opened the bottle, the hiss of the fizz escaping, and took a long swig. 'Ta. Want some?' he held out the bottle reluctantly, hoping they would decline — since this lot claim they don't drink.

'No thanks.' Their face remained straight. They glanced around before returning their gaze to Charlie and pulling their jacket tighter around their neck. 'So, are you going to sort this shit storm out that you've created, Charlie? Make it up to your family? Your son? The people trying to help you?' they asked, tapping their feet slowly on the surrounding concrete.

Taking another few swigs of cider, Charlie answered, 'It's not that easy.' He dropped his head, eyes moving to the floor.

They let out a snigger and Charlie jerked his head up, brow furrowed. 'What the hell do you know?' he snapped, wishing they would piss off. 'You're not me. You ain't walked in my shoes. You've not got a family who have rejected you. A son who makes you feel you are never enough,' he mumbled, with emotion coating his throat. He was sick of people judging him. *Who did this lot think they were?*

Letting out a hmph, they replied, 'I know more than you could imagine, Charlie. I've been there, you see. My so-called dad was a piece of shit like you.' They glared coldly at him, top lip curling.

'You what?' Charlie asked, mouth remaining open as he tried to sit up a little, but the effort was hard.

'My dad, Charlie. He let me down like you've let your son down. Time and time again.' They slowly moved their jaw from side to side. 'He chose the drink as his number one. He wasn't a father, not the way a father should be. Just a leech on society.' The visitor stared away, in the opposite direction. Shaking their head, they held their palms together, encased in black ski gloves.

There was silence for twenty seconds. Charlie swigged his cider and put his head back against the wall. He looked towards the trees and lampposts. The light blurred, as if a reflection in water. Rubbing his eyes, he tried to refocus as his jaw relaxed.

They sniffed up and jerked their head back to him. 'Neither are you, Charlie,' they said flatly.

Charlie tilted his head. 'Neither am I friggin' what?' He was rapidly losing patience with this condescending lecture.

'Neither are you a father,' they sneered. 'You're a selfish man, just like my dad, Albert, was. Putting the drink and your own pathetic needs first.' Their eyes bore into Charlie, filled with contempt.

Charlie swallowed, feeling panicked. This was harsh and not what he expected, even from a tough love approach. He looked away, willing the conversation to end and for them to leave. Despite the warmth and softness that the alcohol provided, this conversation felt unpleasant and unnerving.

'I'm sorry alright, that you had a shit time with it as well. That your dad had problems.' He moved his bottom slightly and took a swig of the cider — it was the only thing palatable about this situation and he wished they would just go away.

'The problem, Charlie, was Albert, my so-called dad. He was the problem, nothing else and fucking no one else,' the visitor said, through gritted teeth and an intense glare.

Charlie cleared his throat and looked down at the ground. He felt an assault of guilt about Tommy, like a whack from a baseball bat. But there was a disturbed glint in his visitor's eyes that frightened him. As if sensing his discomfort, a switch was flicked and they flashed a smile at Charlie.

He knew they were waiting for a response, a promise. Rubbing his mouth, he scrunched his eyes that felt so heavy. 'I'll get better. I just need to do things in my own time and for people to back off.' Charlie tried to sound convincing but assertive, a hopeful sign that he wasn't prepared to take any orders. The cider and the fact the visitor had given it to him could be something he could use in the future, should he have to. 'Why have you even brought this for me?' Charlie asked, pointing the bottle of cider in the direction of his visitor, but not daring to let it go.

'This should be your last alcoholic drink, Charlie. Before you get clean and get your act together. Embrace the help offered to you and sort yourself out,' they replied coolly, almost robotically, without looking at him.

Charlie was getting sick of the dictating of what he needed to do. He shrugged and gulped some more cider. 'What's the point? Tommy's a waste of my time. He wouldn't forgive me if I got awarded a bloody MBE.' He shook his head and released a sigh. 'Judgemental and harsh, like his mother. The drink is all I've got.' Charlie let out a sad chuckle, then a tiny yelp. He looked at the large bottle, its sides becoming fuzzy in his vision, and necked some more of his favourite medicine.

The visitor nodded, gaze remaining away. 'Well, time runs out at some point for us all. You only get so many chances.' Their gloved hand went into a fist.

Charlie had listened to enough now. This was his space and he didn't have to answer to anyone. 'Did you just come here to make me feel even more shit? You know, I've had enough of bloody lectures from everyone. Just bugger off, eh,' Charlie spat, wanting to show he was no pushover.

They chuckled, a strange, almost vicious laugh. 'Yeah, I'm away. I've got places to be myself. See you Charlie,' they sniggered as they got up and began walking away.

'Aye, get lost!' Charlie slurred under his breath as he took another swig of the cider, watching them disappear into the mist as their black outline vanished. Rubbing his eyes, the experience felt almost like a weird drug-induced hallucination. Glancing at the half-drank bottle of cider, he shrugged and gulped the rest of the alcohol in a matter of minutes.

He was angry and was going to do something about it the next day, but for now, he was content with his favourite reliable friend of alcohol, and to get some rest. Charlie soon felt the heavy weight of sleep encroaching on his body as the alcohol warmed and soothed him, helping him to switch off from his thoughts. Unable to keep his eyes open, like a plane door firmly sliding shut for take-off, Charlie surrendered to sleep.

Once in deep sleep, Charlie began having a vivid nightmare that he was under bottomless, cold water. He was struggling, feeling pulled down into the darkness. Trapped, he was trying but failing to reach the water's surface. He felt heavy, his whole body weighed down as if a brick was attached to every vein. Desperately attempting to catch his breath, he was failing, gasping, unable to burst through the murky water into fresh air and safety, freedom and to escape. Battling frantically to break through the surface of the oxygen-starving water felt so real. His panic increased as Charlie willed himself to wake up, but his eyes were almost cemented shut and his body felt paralysed.

He felt a sensation, rubbery, plasticy, touching his skin, his lips, then covering his mouth. A layer where air should enter his open mouth, preventing him from breathing. His mind blurring between reality and nightmare, consciousness and unconsciousness. Charlie tried again to open his eyes, but he simply couldn't — it was impossible. Painfully weighted down, it was as if opening them was like lifting a double-decker bus off the ground.

His whole body felt cripplingly heavy and saturated in darkness — no movement, no light. The weight increased on him; in his mouth, on his eyes, in his chest. His whole body sinking. He groaned, desperate to move, to wake himself from the nightmare. Despite trying to focus and using all his strength, he couldn't move. Couldn't rouse himself — his body turning to lead, muscles unable to move, frozen.

Panic soared through him, like flames on petrol, but he was mute and motionless, trapped in his body. He wanted to shout, scream, but his voice failed him. Then Charlie felt the trickle of warm urine spread across his crotch. As he gasped for breath in his murky reality, panic pounded in his head, almost certain to explode. Then it went dark and still.

# Chapter 12

They had said goodbye to Charlie as he lay on the floor in his dirty sleeping bag, hearing him slur ingratitude as they walked away, pulse speeding and anger fizzing inside of them like a shaken bottle of pop. The rage fuelling them, smothering any feelings of doubt about what had to happen. Walking away from Charlie, they didn't look back as they shook with anger, adrenalin, and nerves about the next part in their deadly plan.

Breathing deeply and slowly to calm their racing heartbeat, they wiggled their fingers in the padded ski gloves. Curling their top lip and baring their teeth like a dog about to attack, they began the walk back along the river route to avoid any CCTV. They were sick of these professional victims when the rest of the world struggled on, desperate, limping in pain. The Charlies of the world. The Alberts of the world. They needed disposed of.

And that's what they had to do. Putting Amitriptyline in cider that no alcoholic would ever decline — it was easy. Charlie had taken the cider like a baby taking a bottle of milk. He had guzzled it, not realising it would be his last as he spat out his lies, excuses, and false promises. He'd had a chance to apologise, but instead, Charlie just continued his pity party routine.

Their plan was to wait, making sure the sedative-laced alcohol would have worked on Charlie, before returning. Reaching the river, they walked into the vast greenery and crouched down, hidden in the bushes like a commando in battle, where they would sit for an hour while the sedatives drugged Charlie.

In that hour, the reality of what they had done and were going to do sank in. Thoughts ruminated, fuelling them. Keeping their temperature burning in the cold evening. It was really happening. All these years, they had waited for healing and for revenge against Albert, and now it had arrived. They could help end it for Tommy, like they had prayed to a non-existent God to end it for them, for what felt like a lifetime.

'Please let this living hell be over,' they'd pray at night to a God that never showed them any compassion. Instead, life became a carousel of repeated let downs. Of fear, neglect, and of an insatiable, toxic anger building up in them. Year after year, living two lives. One to the outside world; wearing a mask that stung, slashed, and distorted their face underneath.

They wore it well; they had been 'acting' since they were ten years old and life changed forever. Their facade was part of them; two sides of a coin. One side shiny, liked, treasured even. The other, dark, cracked, cold. Then there was the child inside them, who still dominated their thoughts, their unmet needs, their trauma. They needed, *they deserved,* the final therapy of vengeance against negligent, selfish fathers like Albert.

The fury and disgust never left, just diluted down when they were around people who were grateful and embraced help or helped themselves. These people deserved it. They were accepting a chance, a redemption. It wasn't too late for them and their families. The others; the liars and con artists — well, they deserved to be wiped out. They had waited for a chance to make things better for themself, for their inner child, and for all the other children who were living in pain, even as adults. The only way to achieve that was by eradicating the poison. But could they do it? When it came down to it? Could they end someone's life? They'd wavered all day, despite fantasising about it for what felt like forever. Then they remembered all those years at home with Albert and the years since. Never truly healing, despite the people-plasters around them. Days that felt like their mind, body, and soul was being slowly dissolved in acid — a torturous demise of each cell, each thought, each strand of hope.

Like Albert, Charlie had potential at the start to redeem himself for Tommy. But he had ruined it. Him and him alone. Now he had to pay and let his suffering son be free at last from the shackles of his selfish father that would never change. How many chances had Charlie had? Even going there tonight with the pathetic sandwich and revolting cider, they had opened dialogue to get Charlie to repent.

Another chance to make amends that he let float by. Countless opportunities he had dismissed and spat on as the knife sunk deeper into the heart of his son. He wouldn't change, didn't want to. Instead, spouting all the shit and excuses, pleas and desperation to get attention and resources that he threw back in the face of the people trying to help. It was twisted and perverse.

Charlie hadn't apologised. He didn't want to atone. Instead, he had made more excuses. Blaming the system, people, his family. Just like Albert had all those years ago and just like Albert, he chose alcohol. Charlie loved alcohol more than anything in life, right until the end.

'Tommy's a waste of time.' The words Charlie had slurred played over in their head as they sat motionless on the damp ground, waiting for Charlie to feel the impact of the sedatives.

Still, Charlie blamed everyone else for his behaviour. His own son had years of rejection, neglect, and dashed hope, and Charlie took no responsibility. Unbelievable. It was Albert, regurgitated. A carbon copy as if churned out in the same factory.

They were better off without Albert, just as Tommy was better off without Charlie. So, he had to go. It was doing the world a favour. Charlie had to be eliminated before he caused more hurt, more disappointment, and heartache. Shit had to be flushed away. It was as simple and justified as that.

However, reality was different to thoughts. Thoughts they'd had about Albert countless times — like an excruciating record stuck on one line of song. They had imagined revenge, and making the world a better place for years. They weren't a bad person; they knew that. They were a good person who had bad things inflicted on them. Fantasising, planning, obsessing about revenge, was one thing, but carrying thoughts out was another. Actually wiping someone out was completely different. And despite the years of ruminating, it still felt almost impulsive.

They waited, sat on the ground, covered by the bushes. The cold temperature was no match for the heat from their anger. Looking at their watch, they bit the inside of their lip. Rising from the ground, they trembled. *Could they do it? Could they actually kill Charlie?* Then they remembered how strong they were; Robyn had always said so during their sessions at school. They took a deep breath and continued walking back to where Charlie was. They were nervous, but it felt critical to complete their plan.

It was their job, their calling — to protect people, safeguard the real victims. And to heal their inner child that needed repaired. They had been patient and waited — the time was right. It was the only way. They had suffered enough all these years and he had to pay; Charlie had to pay because Albert couldn't.

On returning to Charlie's spot under the bridge that they had left an hour ago, they paused, lips pressed together. Glancing around, they fixed their eyes on the unconscious heap that was Charlie, ten metres in front of them. They began shaking with nerves. *If people knew, God, what would they think?* They snapped out of it. Surely, people would understand they had to do it — to stop the pain, for everyone.

Moving up close to Charlie, they froze for a moment. Time paused, the world became quiet and they were back in their family lounge by that tatty brown sofa, looking at their drunken father, passed out after another session with Jack Daniels. The smells of the woody whisky tones mixed with Albert's soul sickness omitting from his pores as the child in them watched helpless, hopeless.

A tear dropped from each eye, then a noise startled them out of their flashback. Jerking their body around, a collection of leaves whirled past in the light wind. They sniffed up violently and kicked Charlie's side with slight force. There was no response. At that moment, they got a buzz of adrenaline, excited like a gambler in Las Vegas. They let out a little chuckle, thinking they could kick him to death here and now, fuelled by the anger for all the Tommys of the world and for their own need for revenge.

Taking a blue plastic bag from their backpack, they let out the breath they had been holding and felt the pulsing of their heart in their ears as their eyes remained on Charlie. Straightening up, they scrunched their toes in their boots and took three deep breaths. *You can do this. You must do this*, they affirmed to themselves.

Glancing around once more, they pressed their lips together. Bending closer, Charlie still hadn't stirred. They leant in to his stinking sleeping bag and grimaced. His pathetic face peeped out of his bobble hat, visible only with the tiny shimmer of distant street lighting. Shaking their head they felt nausea, unsure if it was from the disgust of Charlie, excitement, or nerves. Their eyes met the blue bag resting in their hands, safe in their ski gloves. The flashback of Albert and his alcohol bottles strewn across their filthy lounge carpet burst through the door of their mind again.

Jutting their jaw out, they scooped the plastic bag over Charlie's hat, quickly glancing around to make sure there were still no passers-by at the desolate spot. Returning their gaze to Charlie, they paused for a second. Hands shaking, they took another deep breath. It absolutely had to be done, for the good of all. They repeated this message in their head a few times.

Looking down at scruffy Charlie, the drool on his face glistened in the dim light, repulsing them. A familiar sight that was forever etched on their brain by Albert and his self-indulgent, neglectful regime. He would lie soaked in his own urine, grunting like a pig, passed out from the constant absorption of alcohol. Sometimes food scraps on plates littered the floor around him. They had prayed so many times that the bastard would choke on his dinner or on his vomit as his body protested against the poison in his bloodstream.

Blinking, they shook their head. They needed to get on with it. The plastic bag had slid onto Charlie's head nicely, his body floppy with alcohol and the sedatives. They pulled the bag down, covering his pasty face, no signs of consciousness coming from him. Gathering the loose plastic of the bag around his neck, they held it tight in gloved hands and closed their eyes. Images of Albert flashed like a kaleidoscope on their eyelids.

Their body shook violently for a moment as they felt a release of the pain, anger, and resentment they had carried for so many long, hurtful years. It flowed to their fingertips, where they gripped the bag around Charlie's neck. They wanted to scream, 'Fuck you, Albert' but they had to remain silent, the drug of revenge pumping through their veins despite the lump forming in their throat.

Not sure what to expect, they waited for a possible struggle, gaining strength from what felt like a release of damaging emotions from their soul — like an enormous plug had been pulled from the bottom of a reservoir. Panic and excitement came in gusts of tremendous wind around them. *Was it the right thing to do? Yes, of course it was. Absolutely.* It was too late to stop, but they didn't want to, either. It had to end. He had to die.

*Dad, you selfish fucking bastard,* they thought, fighting the urge to scream. As tears escaped their eyes, they held the bag at the base of Charlie's neck, ensuring no air crept in to the plastic death trap. Charlie's leg twitched momentarily and he moved his head from side to side slowly.

'Fucking die, Dad,' they said quietly, eyes glazed over in a trance-like state. It was a weak struggle which — in those final moments fluctuating between elation, panic, and doubt — they were thankful for. Charlie grunted and his hand moved, possibly to try to weakly grab the bag, but his arms were slow, his energy dissolving. He gasped under the blue plastic of the bag as it was vacuumed into his desperate mouth as he frantically searched for air.

Then it was over. Charlie was dead and Tommy could heal. His father had been dying for decades. Now he could close the chapter on the toxic reoccurrence and move on. Just like they were one step closer to burying Albert somewhere in their brain that would forever be locked away and painless. One step closer to healing. The relief was invigorating. Shaking, they stood, legs wobbly. Gulping in air, plastic bag in one hand, they stared at their victim, who looked like a waxwork model, no longer a person.

This had really happened. The sense of euphoria was almost overwhelming; they weren't sure whether to laugh or cry. Their eyes glazed over as they glared at him, as if watching through the lens of another person. Then a gust of wind snapped them from their haze. For a second, they felt they may faint, their emotions cascading from elation to panic. Deliriously sick, they vomited a little in their own mouth. Swallowing the bile, they grasped their lips, feeling they may scream, as their whole body tingled.

'You're dead, Dad,' they whispered, unblinking eyes fixed on Charlie. Pulling up their hood, they shoved the plastic bag into their backpack and left — walking the journey back along the river to their car. It started to rain lightly as they hurried in the opposite direction of the bakery and its CCTV cameras. With every step, their heart pounded. Licking their lips, they tasted the sweat gathered on their philtrum — from the soaring anger and adrenalin that had caused an inferno in their mind, as they did to Charlie what they had wanted to do to Albert all those haunting years.

Rushing down a desolate alley, they hoped the dark,

wintery weather would minimise the number of people around the already secluded spot. They rushed along the same route they had walked an hour earlier when they went to talk to pathetic Charlie. To give him one last chance to apologise for the waste of space he was. The father who didn't deserve to be a father. They sneered at the thought of him and all the other Alberts before clamping their jaw teeth-shatteringly tight as a smile of satisfaction crept across their mouth.

It had been easier than they thought, well the first visit anyway. Greed made it simpler, as Charlie glugged the alcohol like there was no tomorrow. They chuckled at the irony; Charlie's tomorrows had ended as he gulped the disgusting cider. No thank you for anything anyone had done for him, no acknowledgement. No reflection. No remorse — just like Albert. They sniffed up and shuddered, speeding up their pace. For all the emotions and adrenaline pumping, they had a compulsion to write in their journal as soon as they got home.

# Chapter 13

They had spent a few days in a cycle of emotions. Guilt, denial, euphoria, and fear. Their violence was Albert's fault and they had yearned for revenge most of their life. Fuelled each time they thought about or heard of another selfish bastard like Albert. All the Alberts of the world. The Charlies. Those who threw the offer of help — the chance to redeem themselves or stop the roller-coaster of destruction before it went off the track for good — back in the faces of those offering support. Discarding chances of help like they flicked their cigarette end onto the pavement; careless, without thought or consequence.

Charlie's family had been dragged into absorbing the fallout of his behaviour for decades, just like they had been since the age of ten. They had waited years for this type of healing. No professional, medication, or substance could ever make them feel how they did after they stopped Charlie's merry-go-round of bullshit. Although a siren of fear and guilt intermittently roared in them for the people they did care about, who thought they were someone else. But the relief of closure for another family, the literal final nail in the coffin, dissolved that rapidly.

The next few days felt surreal. Like a film playing over on repeat in their head. They had to go about their daily activities without suspicion from any unusual behaviour. It was excruciatingly hard, but as Charlie was soon discovered; they could hide behind the collective shock and sadness everyone was feeling. It strengthened them to get through the times they thought their mask would crack into a million pieces and reveal the killer inside.

Arriving at the centre the morning after ending Charlie's pathetic life, they waited for news, although it was unlikely to happen that day. People didn't check on rough sleepers, well apart from the team at Homeless Helping Hands, ironically. There was a violent battle within them between anxiety and the smugness of having a secret. Emotions bouncing back and forth like a ball in a game of tennis.

No one mentioned Charlie and he hadn't been in for a few days. During his last visit, he blamed everyone else for his drinking. Sneering at staff, directing threats, and making up shit about them. How dare he? Hearing him snarl and shout, glaring at people with malice, spit falling from his vile mouth as he staggered around, sickened them.

They were repulsed, and an uncontrollable rage ignited inside as they looked at Charlie and saw Albert's face. Albert's excuses. Albert's lies. Albert's neglectful parenting and abuse. Tommy needed intervention; he needed it to stop. They did Tommy a favour. That's what they had to keep remembering, especially that first day when it was the hardest and felt like they were walking on a frozen lake. They were edgy, but no one really noticed any stark difference in them and pretending to be tired always covered a multitude of sins! It wasn't so easy outside of the centre, but the old 'I don't feel too good', could be a winner at times.

It was two days later that the news of Charlie's death broke. Everyone at the centre was shocked, but people assumed it would be alcohol related. It took another few days before the rumours about something sinister began. Overdose from drugs, or someone assaulting Charlie, was mentioned. By this time, they had composed themselves in and out of the centre. The purging of another Albert felt invigorating, and any initial doubts following the murder had been fully rationalised in their head. It was the only option, and Charlie being dead would make everyone's life better.

However, something bubbled in them; an anxiety about people finding out. The night had played over in their mind as they analysed each minute, mentally retracing what happened for any mistakes. They had avoided the CCTV camera area and disguised their appearance with an old hooded jacket. They'd worn gloves, left the cider bottle at the scene near to his empty vodka bottle, showing the bottle was always Charlie's priority, just like it was Albert's. They'd taken the blue plastic bag home with them, hidden it in their secret place. Not wanting to see it but at the same time feeling satisfaction in ending a life using that same style, cheap bit of plastic, still used years later by drunks purchasing their alcohol from the corner shop — just like Albert did for so long.

A door slamming snapped them back to the here and now. Shaking their head, they knew no one would suspect them and doubted the police would show much interest. They had never helped them when Albert was ruining lives, so why would they give a damn now? They were jumping ahead, being paranoid. There was no evidence at the scene. They'd made sure of that. The police would blame some other scumbag, or it would just all grow quiet. Then someone walked past them and said the police were coming into the centre the next day to speak to people. They nodded, mute, and felt they may be sick.

# Chapter 14: Stuart

The police visited the centre, asking the team questions a few days after Charlie's body was found. Making the place feel icy cold, they advised they were investigating. After Stuart stressed his concerns about drug use, they stated they would get the neighbourhood team to have a presence a few times a week, monitoring. As reality bulldozed into him, Stuart felt a heaviness in his stomach, his whole body like a plane in turbulence.

Sticking to their word, the police drop-ins commenced a few weeks later, providing a warning to the minority. Stuart and the team knew who was instigating the drug problem — Donald and his newest associate, Salvin Yanti — but couldn't prove it. After several weeks and no update from the police on Charlie, all assumed his death was drug related. Stuart's head was noisier than a nightclub with all the questions from staff, people using the centre, and the police. Questions that he didn't have answers to and despite trying to keep his head up and a reassuring smile on his face, he felt uncertainty gnawing at him.

On top of this, staff were fatigued and the animosity from some centre users certainly wasn't helping. Donald made no secret that he had problems with people using the service and the staff. Mo, Lorna, and Dot had all experienced his vicious tongue of late. He hoped the twice-weekly police drop-in would correlate with a reduction in using and overdoses on site. And in a way, as well as keeping people safe, Stuart wanted to prove to the police that he could manage the chaos. Evidence was almost impossible to obtain, and people would never grass each other up. In the meantime, the entire team felt like Donald was taunting them and Stuart felt there was little he could do.

A few days later, Donald strolled into the centre as if walking on the red carpet at a movie premiere. Stuart tried to remain professional; nodding and saying hello as dread back flipped in his gut. Taking a seat, Donald high-fived two associates. After a few minutes, the temperature was already getting too hot. Tightening his jaw, Stuart turned and walked back to the staff office. He knew it was the pressure that was throwing him into a pit of unprofessional thoughts, but was determined that Homeless Helping Hands would not suffer. Stuart wouldn't sit back and watch the dressing come undone.

It was soon six weeks since Charlie had died and drugs were rife in the day centre. At the team meeting that week, Stuart shared a message from the police.

'As us and the police know, the prime suspect is Donald Armstrong. But he has acquired a recent sidekick, Salvin Yanti. We haven't got enough evidence to ban them and the police suggested we keep an eye on them and share any information.' Mo tutted and shook his head. Stuart ignored him and continued. 'We need to document absolutely everything.' He emphasised the last three words, tapping his pen against his notebook.

The team meeting finished and despite staff updates on clients that were doing well, Stuart felt no chink of light dispersing the grey clouds over Homeless Helping Hands. He was feeling the pressure. First, Charlie's death, then the ongoing drugs issue at the centre. It was exhausting and Stuart was smothered by the crippling weight of responsibility, the police scrutiny, and felt he was losing the battle to prevent more crisis.

The staff also showed the impact of stress. Tired eyes, shorter fuses, and the lack of enthusiastic zest that was normally in abundance in the air had dissipated. Even Dot's chirpy persona seemed muted. Stuart couldn't remember a time as challenging. It felt like the lightbulbs around Homeless Helping Hands were dimming by the hour as he tried to stop a storm that was rattling at the front door, threatening to get in and destroy everything in its path. Stuart held his head in his hands and let out a deflated sigh.

'Alright, mate?' Mo asked, sensing Stuart's flatness and patting his boss gently on the arm.

'Yeah, I'm okay, thanks. It's difficult for us all, isn't it?' Stuart replied, looking at his colleague with watery eyes.

'Aye. It's been a hard few months, Stu. I hope we see a change soon. I wanted to ask, Boss, is it okay to have a few days off next week? Annie has mentioned a recovery conference in Leeds and we fancy going.'

Stuart saw a brief glint in Mo's eyes. 'Of course.' He forced a smile and got up from his chair to put the kettle on. 'So, you and Annie, getting on well, are you?'

'She's awesome, mate. Inspiring, kind, and beautiful.' Mo bit his lip before a grin spread across his face. 'We aren't rushing anything, but loneliness…'

'Oh aye, shagging some poor addict, are ya, Mo?' said Donald, popping his head around the open office door.

Stuart turned around quickly; Donald must have been listening out of view. The centre wasn't open for lunch yet and all the breakfast crew had left long ago.

'None of your business, you jealous idiot,' sneered Mo.

'Not very professional speaking to a client like that, Mo.' Donald laughed and tilted his head back.

'Who the...' Mo began, his face turning red with rage.

'Now now!' said Stuart in a raised voice. 'Donald, that's totally unacceptable.' Stuart walked to the front of his desk, a few metres from the doorway, where Donald stood, leaning against the frame like an entitled teenager asking for a lift. He cleared his throat. 'And you shouldn't be listening to other people's conversation,' Stuart explained, keeping a calm voice.

Donald rolled his eyes and laughed. 'Are you after shagging her as well, Stu? I hear Lance has been into her. Think I'll come along to the meetings and try my luck with the local bike.' He raised an eyebrow and looked at Mo, who jumped out of his seat, shoulders back and eyes bulging as his face turned puce. He stormed towards the doorway, where Donald stood with a smug look on his face.

Stuart, being nearer the door, knew what was going to happen and acting fast, ushered Donald away abruptly, following him, but not before turning to Mo and giving him a glare and a headshake. Stuart returned to the office ten minutes later. Swallowing anger, he shut the office door behind him as Mo looked up coyly, expecting the bollocking he was about to get.

'Mo, what the hell?' Stuart raised his hands to his head.

'I know Stu, I know. I'm under pressure, and these bastards keep pushing me. They hate it when anyone is doing well,' Mo said, brow furrowed and pleading in his eyes.

'Mo, for crying out loud, *you* are the professional. *They* are the clients!' Stuart shouted, unable to control his anger. He put a hand to his forehead and closed his eyes momentarily.

Mo rubbed his mouth. 'He's a disrespectful loser, Stu. I'm not having him and Lance speak about Annie like that.' He held his palms up, trying to justify his feelings.

'You're too involved, Mo. It's clouding your professionalism.' Stuart sighed, pacing the office. 'I can't have that. No matter how much the odd few provoke us, you can never resort to violence. I'm sorry Mo, but I'll have to suspend you pending an investigation.' Stuart looked at his colleague, who he classed as a friend. He knew he had to suspend him, not just for Mo's sake but for the sake of Homeless Helping Hands.

# Chapter 15

The last six weeks had been surreal for them, as if viewing someone else's life. The murder had been an emotional firework, and the sparks threatened to burn and expose them in those first few frantic days of trying to cover-up. However, once the funeral was over and witnessing the sense of relief they knew they saw on Tommy's face, they were certain all would be okay. Satisfied that Tommy's pain had ended provided reassurance in moments of weakening fear and guilt.

Of course, they couldn't tell anyone about what had happened, what they had done, and how they felt. People wouldn't understand, not fully anyway, and no one was 100% trustworthy — that was why people had secrets. They knew that from years of being let down. False promises and lies spouted from Albert's mouth, over and over. Years of lies from doctors, therapists, and psychologists. Everyone apart from Robyn, who they had lost in the end.

Other relatives had tried, but not hard enough. They hadn't been there all those years, attempting to lift a twelve stone man from a heap on the floor and placing bowls on a stained carpet to catch remnants of vomit. Worried their dad would choke, all the while praying that maybe it would end the nightmare of their life and free them from their psychological prison.

Even after Albert's death, it wasn't over. The flashbacks, sounds, smells that took them unwillingly, kicking and screaming back to that place. The invisible restraints their life with Albert enforced onto them. Shackles that no one could see, but to them, it was like looking in the mirror and seeing a black hole where their heart should be. Forever scarred, damaged, dark. Perhaps now that they had helped Tommy, the scab of their trauma could start to heal, and become a less prominent wound, fading into a scar.

The police had sniffed around the day centre and asked questions that no one had answers to. Then they were replaced by a regular neighbourhood team who attended and did little but eat. At least they weren't probing about Charlie. As for the media, that turned quiet after a week, the latest scandal disintegrating the importance of Charlie. After all, he was a nobody.

They had been a nervous wreck, taking a little more of their anti-depressants, Amitriptyline, in the morning rather than at night. They knew the sedative effect would calm them slightly — helping them get through the day and appear a little less edgy. The dose wasn't strong enough to make them float into sleep like it did each night, whilst also helping to keep the demons at bay.

'Karma,' they said aloud, not realising.

'What was that?' asked one of the team.

'Erm nothing, just talking to myself,' they laughed off the joke and took a sip of tea.

Resentment still lived in them, despite knowing there was one less Albert in the world.

# Chapter 16: Mo

With the drugs issues and influx of overdoses in the area, Mo knew Donald was the instigator and that he had no depth he wouldn't sink to. Sticking two fingers up to the authority, Donald was mocking staff, goading them, and the last of his patience had expelled from Mo with his morning piss.

For the first day in many, he wanted to reach for the bottle. He'd given Annie the silent treatment, knowing he wasn't in the right frame of mind to communicate with her. Everything had left an avalanche of emotions tumbling through his head, and he loathed himself and the people causing his fragmented state. Mo had felt like this before and it had led to catastrophic problems and actions.

Yesterday had been a disaster. After opening up about Annie in the office with Stuart — which was a massive deal in itself — sneaky leech Donald had been hanging around like a seagull waiting for scraps. He'd heard Mo and started insulting him and Annie. Seeing red, Mo had accelerated into fight-or-flight mode, with little control. It was something within him; a defence mechanism. His own internal armour — or perhaps a dangerous weapon — he wasn't sure. However, at times, it was the only thing that kept Mo alive.

The workplace didn't halt his internal, go-to response despite striving to be a professional. On that occasion, Mo went from zero to one hundred in a nano-second, wanting to tear Donald's jealous, vicious head off. Stuart got in the way and

Mo knew he had crossed the line. Of course he had. But in that moment, and still now as he turned over in bed and slammed his head into the soft pillow, he felt it would have been worth losing his job over; to wipe the smug look off Donald's ugly face.

Not knowing what to do with himself when Stuart ushered him off site, heat flushed through his body as he sweated anger. Mo had driven to the country park in Crosley and walked around for hours before ringing his ex and asking if he could see Mason after school. It was the only thing he could think of right then to calm him down.

Mo groaned and pulled the quilt over his head, wanting to hide from the world. Stuart had suspended him, pending investigation. Mo accepted it, but it topped up his full cup of rage a little more and he was spilling over. It was a new day, filled with old problems that Mo wasn't sure could ever be resolved.

# Chapter 17: Lorna

Lorna had started working with a new client, Eve. The young woman had an overdose in the community a few weeks ago but was reluctant to talk about it. However, Lorna saw it as an opportunity to do some more 1-2-1 support work.

'She'll do great. Her whole life can change, James,' Lorna had said, beaming during dinner the evening before.

'Sounds good. I'm pleased you have your spark back. You haven't been yourself for a while, babe. I was worried it wasn't the right career path for you.' James smiled before putting a forkful of paella in his mouth.

Lorna nodded, dropping her eyes to her plate momentarily, then returning her gaze to James. 'It's been really hard. Some people don't want help, but most do, and it's amazing to work with someone who has so much potential and is grateful.' She nodded, turning her head towards the window. 'I can see big things will happen; she won't let me down.'

Lorna hadn't been herself; she knew that. No matter how hard she tried, everything had affected her. The job was hard and James didn't always understand. Plus, she had never been one to open up fully — it didn't mean she and James loved each other any less.

The team gathered the following day, after the breakfast rush was over.

'Where's Mo? Stuart, it's not his days off, is it?' Dot asked. She handed a tray of biscuits round the office.

'Erm no. Well, let's get started.' Stuart looked at a pile of papers on his desk and began shuffling them.

Donald was temporarily barred and had been hanging around the centre, talking to some people accessing the service. Stuart warned it was likely he was dealing drugs from near or outside the premises and instructing Salvin, who was still accessing the building. Staff needed to be vigilant. They had no proof to bar Salvin, but the community police were still monitoring.

Then Dot updated all on the positive work with Beth in getting her daughter back to her care and Stuart updated the team about John, who had used the centre for a few years and after volunteering, had secured a job at Next Steps. Lorna updated her colleagues on Eve.

She clasped her hands together and leant forward. 'She's talked about going to college. There's an open day at Ashmouth College in two weeks. I said I'd go with her,' she gushed. Stuart nodded his approval as he made notes.

The meeting drew to a close and the lunch time preparations began. With a team member down in Mo, Lorna and Dot were multitasking in the kitchen whilst Stuart and Liam remained in the hall, chatting with people. Chicken casserole, crusty bread, and potato wedges were on the menu today. Followed by apple crumble and custard.

'This smells delicious, Dot. I hope there's some left for us at the end of the rush,' Lorna commented as she began the transfer to the serving trays. She carried them out to a waiting line full of hungry folk. Lorna scanned the queue and saw Eve. Thirty minutes later, all the food was served.

'I'm knackered, Dot,' Lorna said, collapsing into a seat and gratefully accepting a small bowl of casserole from Dot. She took a mouthful. 'Mmm, this is so tasty.'

Dot sighed. 'It was my son's favourite. Made with extra love.' She placed a hand on Lorna's shoulder as she passed her to sit down with her own bowl.

Lorna swallowed a lump of sadness. 'I'm sure he's watching over you and I bet you were the best mam ever.'

Dot nodded, smiled, and tapped Lorna's hand. The two sat quietly, filled with their own emotion. Lorna's thinking was interrupted with a scream, followed by a call for help, and a rushing of feet. Dot and Lorna quickly rose and pushed through the kitchen doors into the centre hall. The female toilet door was open and a centre user was shouting and screaming for help. Stuart was entering the toilet while Liam tried to calm everyone as the frantic air spread.

'Ring an ambulance!' the female shouted into the centre hall, hands to her head, eyes bulging.

Liam pulled out his mobile and dialled as he rushed towards the toilets. The hum of people talking and chairs scraping the hall floor filled the air. As Dot and Lorna made their way across the hall, she felt panic rise, her heart beating in her ears. She looked round the room, praying, hoping to find who she was looking for. She couldn't see her. She couldn't see Eve! Anxiety drumming in her throat, everything began to swirl as Lorna reached the toilet.

On the floor, Stuart was administering CPR to Eve. A shade of blue, she lay like a fragile child. Torniquet around her arm, a discarded needle lay on the floor. Lorna clasped her hands into her chest and let out a yelp. She stood staring at the young girl with so much promise as she lay like a rag doll on the cold, tiled floor.

'Lorna, please, go into the hall and calm people down!

Watch out for the ambulance coming and try to keep the path clear of people,' Liam ordered. Lorna stood frozen. 'Lorna!' Liam said louder.

Lorna looked at him, her brain slow behind. She blinked quickly, and did what had been instructed without saying a word. The ambulance arrived and paramedics took over from Stuart, who came out of the toilets, pale as snow — the colour drained from his usual ruddy complexion. The paramedics remained in the toilet for what felt an eternity as the crowds were dispersed out of the centre, asking what was happening and looking back as they were ushered away. They knew, just like all the staff knew. Twenty-five minutes later, it was all over. The paramedics' announced Eve was dead and took her lifeless corpse away in the ambulance.

That night, Lorna cried like a baby in James's arms, distraught about Eve. She knew that Eve would have been coerced into taking the drugs and that Donald and Salvin were responsible. Both charismatic drug dealers, always one step ahead. They had to be stopped or more people would suffer.

The next night, Lorna was still charged with emotion.

'There are so many people wanting help to change. These jealous, malicious bastards won't let them,' Lorna ranted.

James nodded, trying to empathise as best he could as she fluctuated from distress to anger, going through the realisation of loss.

'Baby, I know this is horrendous. But she took the drugs, no one forced her.'

Lorna glared at him across the room from their blue armchair as he lay on the sofa, propping his tired head up. Rage exploded in her like an aerosol thrown into a bonfire as Lorna picked up her almost-empty cup near her feet and hurled it across the room at James. The cup bounced off James's shoulder back to the wooden floor and shattered, remnants of tea splattering onto the skirting boards and floor. Angus barked frantically.

'Lorna, what the actual fuck!' shouted a startled James, sitting up on the sofa, rubbing his shoulder.

'Nobody forced her? Nobody *forced* her, James?' Lorna sneered, her face twisting. 'No one put the heroin in her arms, James, not literally. But they may as well have cos they would've told her that her shitty life would be wonderful and promised her the fucking earth!' she said, eyes wide, droplets of spit flying from her raging mouth as Angus continued to bark.

James pushed his back into the sofa, mouth open as he watched his girlfriend go ballistic.

'It's called fucking coercion and preying on the vulnerable,' she snarled, pointing a finger at James.

Lorna rose from her seat and marched out of the room, slamming the door. A shocked James and Angus, and her favourite broken cup remained in the lounge. She snatched her house keys off the stairs and took herself as far away from James as she could.

The following day continued in an emotional tsunami for Lorna that started at breakfast. After a weak apology and brief chat, James turned from the countertop and glanced to Lorna, as she collected the morning dishes off the table.

'Let's go out for dinner tonight, babe? My treat and a chance to take your mind off things?'

Instead of making Lorna feel cared for, she felt patronised.

Another dismissive response. She clattered their cereal bowls in the kitchen sink, her jaw tight as James remained silent, eyebrows raised. 'People cared about her. *I fucking cared about her.* She had a chance!'

James approached the sink, where Lorna stood, leaning against it. 'Babe, c'mon...' He held his arms out.

Lorna turned rapidly and smashed her fists onto the wooden countertop, sending her glass with remnants of orange juice toppling over. She screamed; a long, deep scream as she pushed her arm across where the glass was rolling. It clashed to the floor and Angus began barking. Lorna calmly walked out of the kitchen, as if a switch had turned off in her, leaving James unnerved and bewildered.

She arrived at work early, desperate to get out of the house. An axe of worry swung into her stomach. She had to take control of her emotions. She couldn't lose James; he was her world. Running her hands through her hair, Lorna felt angry with herself for blowing up in front of him for the second time in a matter of days. But he didn't *understand.* Why couldn't he just understand?

# Chapter 18: Donald

Business was slower since those pricks at the day centre had barred him. Donald shook his head and spat on the pavement where he stood outside of a greasy spoon cafe. *Who the hell did they think they were?* That stinking place was filled with hypocrites and two-faced cowards. Well, Don Armstrong would be back and he would be back stronger until he took over Crosley, then Northumberland. Sniggering to himself at the thought, he rubbed his hands together. He had handed Salvin his supplies to do the work until he could get back into the centre. In the meantime, he would cater for people outside of the dump that was Homeless Helping Hands.

No doubt even the staff would relapse and be after drugs at some point. *Bent, the lot of them.* In the meantime, Donald had to think about being cleverer, to avoid being recalled to prison. Salvin would help and if the shit hit the fan, Donald had no problem grassing Salvin to save his own skin. He owed nothing to no one.

It was cold and dusk had crept in over an hour ago. Although usually a prime dealing spot due to the poor street lighting and lack of people around once the café closed, no one had passed for forty-five minutes. Pulling his waterproof jacket close to his neck, Donald was just about to head back to the hostel when he seen someone approaching. *Maybe a bit of last-minute shopping from Armstrong's Supplies*, he thought to himself, chuckling. They got closer. Donald rolled his eyes and curled his lip, realising who it was. He could do without any grief.

'What the fuck do you want?' he asked, jerking his head back and tutting at the end of his question. It was getting colder and Donald wasn't prepared to put up with any crap. Surprisingly, Donald's visitor went on to say they were sorry about all that had happened for him. That they thought he was misunderstood and had been blamed for things. Eyes wide, he listened, nodding, a grin on his face as he lapped up the empathy and played the victim.

He was thinking ahead of what he could get from this. Inside, he felt smug, knowing the act of this person had to crumble at some point. An insider would be very handy for Donald's plans. He nodded, thanking them. A bit of boosting their ego wasn't beneath him when it came to larger gains. *It could be a trap?* Nah, he didn't think so. This seemed genuine, like they either felt sorry for him, or they wanted in. Either way, Donald was going to find out, and he was much savvier than this amateur.

'Want some?' his visitor asked, opening their backpack and pulling out two bottles of wine, a decent white at that.

*Bingo!* he thought. They weren't the professional they pretended to be after all, just another proven bullshitter, and he would exploit it for all he could. This was going to be a good night. Clapping his hands with a, 'Pleased to see you know how to relax!' he willingly accepted a bottle and commented on how he felt they were similar, maybe misunderstood and vulnerable themselves, but strong. *All the right bull*, he thought, to manipulate the situation. Negotiation skills were high on Donald's repertoire of strengths.

It felt easy talking to them, despite disliking them strongly.

Perhaps they were a little nervous. They had a lot to lose if Donald told them where to go or made threats. He knew any transaction would be of significant benefit to him — sympathy and a way into the centre as a minimum. But this could end up being a very profitable business arrangement, by threat if needed.

He sniggered at the way things change and the disguises people wear as he gulped the wine down and observed his visitor swigging from their bottle with ease. A few minutes later, Donald's visitor offered to go and get some more alcohol. *Marvellous*, he thought. They definitely wanted in on the drug dealing. He nodded, smiling at how much money he could make, especially with a 'wolf in sheep's clothing'.

Despite the warmth of the wine, the temperature had dropped, and the winter wind blew leaves and rubbish around their feet. His visitor suggested Donald going into the church grounds round the corner whilst they went to the shop — it would be more sheltered. Donald felt a flash of suspicion, but maybe his visitor wanted to talk business and sample some goods. Whatever it was, if he was getting free booze and a pack of tabs, he would play along. He nodded and they strolled off toward the nearest shop.

Swigging the wine, Donald walked into the church grounds and took shelter from the wind in the side doorway. He rubbed his mouth, considering his next moves and conversations when his visitor returned about peddling drugs in the day centre. The fancy wine tasted better as he kept drinking it and making plans in his head about the future. It was a shame that some of these young 'uns had died. Donald wasn't totally heartless. But it was survival of the fittest, and he had to make a living. He couldn't help it if they didn't know moderation.

Sniffing up, he leant against the sheltered side door of the church. The vegetation around the area shielding him from the wind, he drank more wine, its warmth coating his throat and stomach. Sliding down to sit on the concrete of the doorway, Donald supped the rest of the bottle and enjoyed the flutter of alcohol in his system. Pulling up his hood, he rested his head against the brick wall, his eyes heavy.

His visitor would be back soon, but he could have a little power nap until then, recharge his batteries for the business meeting. Laughing, he slid his chin inside his zipped-up jacket, the empty wine bottle by his feet. *Just five minutes' kip,* he thought, closing his eyes.

Donald fell into a deep slumber. He felt like he was sliding down, as if relaxing into a bed, but he could sense something around him, a movement and sound. He thought he must be dreaming, and it felt like he was in the dark, searching for the presence he could vaguely sense. Donald felt a dull, heavy sensation in his leg, as if something or someone hit him. Trying to rouse himself, he had the spaced-out sensation he got when taking drugs, but this wasn't a good high. Feeling another throb to his leg, he let out an almost inaudible groan.

Then he felt short of breath, as if he had something pressing on his face, a pillow perhaps. But this wasn't soft, it was wet and plastic-like. Anxiety crawled inside him. Donald tried to open his eyes but couldn't. They felt hefty and almost glued shut. He started trying to move, his foot kicking out gently as panic began drumming to a faster beat. He needed to wake up from his dream that was becoming a nightmare.

A weight pressed on his chest, radiating a dull ache through his torso. He could hear noises, movement, a voice, and the weight was getting heavier. He gasped, not able to fill his lungs. *Fuck! What was going on?* Panic pulsated through him, but Donald couldn't rouse himself. Telling his brain to move his head, he attempted, but his body felt weighed down as if his legs were the concrete he was lying on.

He couldn't breathe. *Where was the fucking air?* He gasped again, the pulse in his head throbbing violently, but felt something sucked into his mouth. Something plastic. It was around and inside his mouth. Donald couldn't move it or move his body. *Wake the fuck up,* he thought to himself. Willing himself, pleading to himself as anxiety engulfed him. *Was that a voice he heard?* He wanted to shout for help. It felt so real. He didn't know if he was asleep or awake.

Making a low grunt, he tried to sit up, lift his head, his hand, his foot. Anything. Knowing he needed to move, but something was on top of him. That crushing weight. *Someone* was on top of him, the weight pumping the breath out of him as every instinct in him became alert, ready to fight like a soldier in battle. But his brain wouldn't let his body move or make a sound louder than a muffle as his mouth vacuumed the plastic.

Using the last of his strength, Donald opened his eyes that felt like iron shutters. He tried to focus but could only see blue plastic. He was frantic, desperate as he attempted to draw breath. But it was an impossible obstacle to overcome and he was drowning in a blue plastic sea. Donald Armstrong realised he was being murdered as he released his last breath.

# Chapter 19

The thought of revenge had grown again in them. A tumour of anger was devouring their brain and at the centre of it was Donald Armstrong. A different breed of parasite compared to Charlie, who was selfish but not hell bent on murdering innocent people — young people at that, who had a chance to live. People like Eve. Donald was scum, he couldn't see anyone thriving; client or otherwise. Instead, he focused on exploiting and degrading people for his own financial gain, and for his need for power and control. Just like Albert and Charlie, he was another waster, never going to change.

Coming to the centre playing the 'big I am' was insulting and frustrating enough. Abusing the staff, causing trouble, and trying to sabotage the recovery of others was unacceptable. But the step of getting young people addicted to drugs, risking overdose, and exploiting them was an unforgivable move. A punishable move. It had to stop. It was going to stop.

Donald had been hanging around the centre for days, even after the death of Eve and despite almost certainly knowing the police were investigating it. He thought he was invincible and still managed to be like dog shit on everyone's shoes, despite being barred from the centre. He was almost goading them into doing something. They had been monitoring his whereabouts subtly, with no one knowing. Call it a covert operation. He had been seen sitting outside the café round the corner from Homeless Helping Hands, after the centre had closed, waiting to sell his illegal merchandise. The café owner was an unscrupulous character, known for cash in hand work. He couldn't give a toss and was probably in on it. Donald sat outside the café, even after it closed, waiting like a lion for its prey.

They knew this and went there after dinner that evening. They also knew there were no CCTV cameras, as this would only highlight the illegal practices of the café owner. They still had their hood up just to make sure and the ever-increasing winter chill and drizzle meant it didn't look strange to Donald as they approached.

'Hi Donald,' they said, trying to remain confident from the off. Donald was a dangerous man, having served time for assault. But they were strong and the contempt they had for him made them feel invincible. It had been easy with Charlie, but Donald was riskier. However, they knew what to do and had the fuel of him being a nasty killer to energise their plan.

Donald chuckled. 'What the fuck do you want? I've had enough of you lot and the grief from that shithole.' He rolled his eyes.

'To be honest, Donald, I'm worried about you,' they replied, using their best acting skills. They saw the startled look on Donald's face, taken aback by the supposed concern. 'I know what it's like at the centre and perhaps we've got it wrong. Got you wrong. I think you need help as well, just like the others. Sometimes it feels that the team can be judgemental, I know that.' They stopped for a second, focusing on their voice not wobbling, and Donald nodded. Perhaps he was buying it. 'I've done that, too. I'm sorry. We can get it wrong at times, blame the wrong people.' They shrugged, keeping their gaze on him.

Donald smirked. 'Well, you lot should sort your own fucking selves out before having a go at everyone else. You're all out of order and bent.' He spat on the ground and glanced back to them. 'You're nothing special. You're just as screwed up as the lot of us. All of you are!'

Donald's face held a smugness; as if he knew he was right. Of course, he was right. All the staff were damaged to some degree. They just didn't know each other's secrets.

'I'm a victim, too. I'm trying and people keep accusing me of things. If I was a young lass, everyone would want to help me, or sleep with me.' He laughed, clapping his hands together in delight at his insult.

They bit their tongue. Donald was of the opinion that the world owed him a favour. It was revoltingly pathetic. They had struggled all their life and vermin like Donald still played the victim.

He rubbed his mouth. 'So, you think everyone's got the wrong idea about me, eh? Well, yeah, they fucking have, actually. Maybe you can help me out with that? Maybe we are more similar than you would like to admit.' Donald winked.

They knew Donald was trying to coerce them, like he had Eve, Salvin, his probation worker, and all the young victims to his drug distribution.

'You know, I fancy a drink. It's been a hard, long day.' They opened their bag with a gloved hand and took out two bottles of wine, screw tops. One had already been carefully opened and laced with sleeping tablets. Placing the sealed bottle quickly on the ground, they pretended to open the other for the first time and held it out for Donald. 'Want some?'

Donald grinned and began laughing. 'Pleased to see you

know how to relax!'

They laughed along, wanting to crack the bottle over his skull there and then, passing it to Donald with a smile before picking up the other bottle, opening it and taking a quick gulp.

'Bloody hell, you're definitely more like me than that professional role model act,' a cocky Donald said before slugging some wine. He looked at them, laughing. 'I reckon we could be friends after all,' he said, smirking before they both took another swig of wine.

They downed a few more mouthfuls of the alcohol, trying to look convincing to Donald, who necked more, chuckling and smacking his thigh. The bottle they gave him had a high level of Amitriptyline in. They had to get Donald out of sight of any passing cars or people as soon as possible. The wintery chill and light rain were a great excuse to get him to move.

'Here Donald, why don't you shelter in the church grounds and I'll go and get some more drink from the shop up the road? I really want your side of the story and how I can help.' They held Donald's gaze and nodded, trying to sound genuine.

Donald looked at them cautiously. 'I'm not convinced you're on my side. You better not be taking the piss.'

'Do you think I'd risk drinking with you if I wasn't trying to help?' they said, holding a gloved-hand up. 'I know you've had a hard time, Donald.' They tilted their head. Their sympathy act was outstanding. They were a natural.

'Yeah, okay, I suppose. Get some tabs while you're there if you really want to help,' he ordered.

'Will do. See you in ten minutes by the church door,' they said, swallowing their disgust.

The two went in opposite directions, Donald guzzling the

wine in anticipation of more coming his way. They smiled to themselves, confident that their plan was going smoothly and knowing that when they returned in an hour, Donald would be sleeping like a bear in hibernation from the concoction of alcohol and sedatives in his bloodstream.

Returning to their car, that had been parked down a back alley, they thought about their next step. There was still the anxiety of having to kill Donald, but just like with Charlie, it was absolutely for the best. More people would be hurt if not in Donald's crusade to ruin lives. It was essential. Donald brought nothing positive to the world. Like Albert, he had not one intention of ever changing and, like a parasite; he needed exterminated.

Keeping the engine off, they unfolded a checked blanket as they sat on the back seat of their car. Lying down in the darkness, legs bent, they hugged it to their body and wondered if they had always been capable of killing? Had it been manifesting all these years? Growing in them from the day Mam became ill, through no fault of her own. A mother who had been so loving, so perfect, so everything. Turned into a terminal carcass, leaving them helpless. A child who had to watch selfish destruction poison their other care-giver whilst needing to grieve for their mother.

All these years, unable to manage the grief, even with medication. They scrunched their eyes and swallowed the lump in their throat. Despite the hatred they felt towards the ungrateful, they had been a good person. Although killing Charlie and Donald may be seen as bad, it was for the good of everyone. They knew it was — people couldn't keep suffering at the hands of others. Donald had killed several, dozens even, and needed stopped. It had to be done. They had to help. The police wouldn't be able to prove he killed Eve, and even if they could, Donald would live his life hurting people; it was in his sick DNA. It was justice for Eve and helping to prevent further harm. Plus, they had to do it for the ten-year-old in them who needed the healing of solving a problem they never could with Albert.

Taking deep breaths, they thought of all the kids like them. All the Tommys and Eves of the world. The justification pulsated through their veins. As time ticked towards another kill, they felt adrenalin surge through them. This was the right thing to do. It was social cleansing of the dangerous. A necessary evil, a protection. They laughed to themselves; it was almost safeguarding to rid society of these vermin.

Scumbags like Donald got people addicted, then made them run drugs. These dealers who got people hooked and hiked up the price, escorting addicts to the cash point each payday. Even without the abhorrent drug pushing in the equation, Donald was a nasty piece of work who wouldn't stop until people around him suffered in some way.

There was always a Donald. But after tonight, there would be one less in Crosley. The beauty of this kill was that, unlike Charlie, Donald had a lot of enemies. In the Next Steps hostel where he stayed on and off, with local dealers, with people who he had served time with. Names had been bandied about the day centre, but Donald would have more people he had hurt and who had a vendetta — a dead man walking.

They put their hand over their mouth, stifling a giggle as they got out of their car to head back to the church, placing their ski gloves on as they walked. Having parked away from the church, they returned to the area through a field and back alleys. There were some people at the top of one alley, walking along the usually quiet side street. They hid quickly behind a row of bins. There was limited street lighting, mainly only the dull glow of some windows in the houses around. They had come too far for someone walking by or a nosey neighbour to scupper their plans.

The church grounds were dark and desolate. Being near the centre and following the recent CCTV camera audit of the locality, they knew where cameras were in the surrounding area, as well as where they were needed. The church was out of sight of any buildings. They headed towards the entrance, shaded and a perfect spot for shelter. The building had no security lights and was covered with vegetation, old trees, and bushes. Donald wasn't in the main doorway, so they walked around the side. Leaves crunched and twigs snapped under their boots as they navigated the overgrown path in the dark, leading to the unused entrance.

There he was, in the sheltered doorway, slouched with the empty bottles by his side. A pathetic, repulsive sight. They kicked his thigh gently. There was no movement. They kicked a little harder, not a stir. Donald's head tilted to one side, his breathing deep. They muffled a laugh. There was something euphoric about the situation, like it was a comedy sketch and they were waiting for someone to jump out or Donald to open his eyes and say, 'Gotcha!'

They bent down, close to their prey, and looked at the poisonous man who was murdering people with substances. Donald smelt of alcohol, dirt, and stale sweat. A flashback to Albert began — lying on the sofa, sprawled out, the human in him almost disintegrating as alcoholism fought the strongest battle. They twisted their face, disgusted. 'You couldn't help yourself, could you?' They asked, glaring at him, not expecting an answer. 'Another selfish, nasty scumbag who had a chance to redeem, to change.'

They looked at him, slumped, pathetic. Closing their eyes, they pressed their lips together and puffed air out their nose, nostrils flaring. 'I fucking hate you, Dad,' they shouted, unable to contain it. The wind dispersed the noise and they slumped back, sitting on the concrete, body shaking. Everything blurred around them until they controlled their breathing and returned to the here and now.

Refocusing on a slumped Donald, they swallowed. 'The amount of people who you've fed poison to. Who you trick and manipulate. Well, here I am to make you fucking pay. You know my name, but you can call me your karma.' They sneered the last two words at an unresponsive Donald as adrenaline soared through them. Kneeling closer, they took the plastic bag from their backpack with gloved hands. The same plastic bag that was used to suffocate Charlie.

Standing over the doorway, they lifted his head. It was a cold evening, but Donald's head felt warm through their gloves as Albert's face flashed onto his and they gasped before quickly placing the bag over his head. They pulled it in at the handles, trapping the air, waiting, mesmerised by anticipation. After a few seconds, there was some grunting and gasping.

'Shit,' they said, taken aback by the noise and subsequent weak movements of Donald. They loosened their grip on the bag momentarily, unsure what to do. *What if he woke? What if he called out? Or attacked them?* This was unexpected, unplanned for. Acting fast, they grabbed the bag tightly again, around the nape of Donald's neck and leant on his chest, hoping to halt any movement. It was uncomfortable, and they knew they could only hold the position for so long. If Donald made a sudden movement, if he mustered some energy and came to, it would be over. They would be over.

Donald continued to make quiet noises as he attempted to move. His movements were weak and slow. He was struggling, coming round slightly and searching for air. They only had Charlie's dose to go off and even with more medication to account for Donald's additional weight, they didn't take into consideration drug tolerance levels. Holding their grip on the bag, they manoeuvred their weight further onto Donald's chest, hoping his last breath would expel from him soon. His hand attempted to lift off the ground as he frantically tried to rouse himself to move and shout. The grunts and gasps still coming. They were strong, but a grip with gloves was harder and Donald was younger and fitter than Charlie.

*Die you piece of shit*, they thought over and over, as they held onto the bag like it was a lifeline rather than a life terminator. A weak arm went up to grab them, the final attempt at survival as Donald squirmed like the maggot he was. One last attempt. Failed. Then it was over. Donald was dead. They got up and removed the bag with trepidation, but power surging through them. Donald's eyes were open, bulging. They looked into them and took a large intake of air.

'Game over!' they said, as they turned and rushed out of the church grounds.

# Chapter 20: Detective Sergeant Ronnie Ericson

Detective Sergeant Ronnie Ericson clicked the shutdown icon on his computer and groaned, rising from his chair. His backside felt square after a ten-hour stint at his desk, finalising the notes for the Crown Prosecution Service on his latest case. Removing his glasses, he rubbed his tired grey-blue eyes.

'Is that a wrap, Boss?' shouted a colleague across the room.

'I bloody hope so,' he laughed, running a hand through his grey hair. 'Thanks for all your help. Fingers crossed it gets passed through quickly and a trial date will be announced.'

Along with the murder of a local homeless guy, which was showing no leads, DS Ronnie Ericson had been leading an organised crime gang operation; Operation Telescope for the last eighteen months. A drugs-cultivating, trafficking, exploitation racket that had spread throughout Northumberland and beyond.

Vulnerable people, recruited to manoeuvre drugs and money on demand. Many of the victims were young kids, some care-leavers or kids from deprived backgrounds, who had been promised the world for getting on the train and dropping 'parcels' off along the east coast rail line. 'County lines' they referred to it nowadays in the force. Bunch of exploitative, greedy bastards is what DS Ericson called it.

Ronnie Ericson had joined Northumbria Police thirty-one years ago, as a young and energetic twenty-four-year-old. Over the years, he had seen it all in the force, some things that went beyond description to civilians. Offered the role of chief inspector many times, Ericson had declined, happy doing what he did. You could never be in the police for the money, and despite enjoying leading a team, getting involved with the detail of cases was where his heart lay. His role as DS provided that.

Respected in his job, he was often sought for advice from colleagues and other teams across the force-wide area of Northumbria Police. Ericson had led on several high-profile cases over the years, including Operation Shelter, a sexual exploitation and organised crime operation that had spread across the North East of England over five years ago. Ericson had been highly commended for leading the team, but as usual, he brushed it off as his job — making sure his ever-loyal colleagues were recognised for their commitment to protecting the community.

Northumbria Police was the only thing in his life. Ironically, it had destroyed much of Ronnie's life, but it was the only place he felt he had a real purpose. Kelsie, his daughter, was studying at Leeds University. She came home at Christmas and the odd weekend. Ronnie felt bittersweet about his only child growing up and their distanced relationship.

When she was home, he basked in the comfort of her presence — glowing with pride from her achievements and almost choking on regret after Kelsie returned from her mother's, talking with a spark of hope in her voice. Ronnie kept in touch with Caroline, his wife who he had separated from almost a year ago. Not as often as he wanted, but the lines of communication were kept open. It had never ended bitterly. In some ways, that made it more painful.

They'd been married for twenty-eight years. All those years of happiness and now Ronnie felt a vacuum of emptiness each time he went home to his two-bed flat; a shell with no warmth between the four walls. He had begged his wife to let him stay, as Caroline cried that they were strangers — a current of uncrossable water separating them. Ronnie knew he was the catalyst for them becoming invisible to one another. His job, the third wheel that had run Caroline off the road. Ronnie, always meaning to slow down, give Caroline more, especially since Kelsie had left home. It never happened. He neglected the love of his life, the mother to his daughter, until it became too late.

Kelsie had left for university; they should have been thinking about their retirement. Instead, Ronnie had been leading some resource heavy, intensive, high-profile case for one year too many. The midnight returns from work and early starts. The cancelled holidays as court cases were scheduled. The time in lieu that never materialised. Caroline felt lonely and unfulfilled, but swore there was no one else. Ronnie had begged, making promises he knew he couldn't keep, then compromising with a 'few more years in the force.' It wasn't enough. The locks changed on the door of their marriage as he remained married to the job.

Ronnie was still crippled by the void, feeling Caroline slipping away as each week apart passed and instead, he craved more from the relationship he had with the force; more prosecutions and prevention. And as he invested all his energy into work, gaining more outcomes and respect from most, he also gained a little concern from those closest to him.

But DS Ronnie Ericson kept it together and, more importantly, he got results.

The next morning was a dreary, cold, grey start to the day in Northumberland. Ronnie's bones had felt heavy when he woke, as if something wasn't right. That police instinct. The phone call before the kettle even boiled proved him right. A vicar had found a body on the grounds of his church.

Within forty minutes, Ericson and his partner, Detective Constable Polly McCardle, were at the scene, along with the forensics.

'The vicar said to call-handlers that he thought the deceased was another homeless guy,' McCardle said, shaking her head and glancing towards her superior.

Ericson nodded slowly. Not meeting her gaze, instead, he studied the area around where the pair stood. The forensic team mechanically sealed off the path and grassy area around the body. The rain drizzled down from a grey sky; pooling in tiny, muddy puddles by their feet. He stared at her momentarily, a blank facial expression — giving nothing away — a trick learnt from decades on the job. Ericson's grey-blue eyes returned to where the body was discovered. For a few seconds, he watched his colleagues perform their duties systematically, but always with respect to the deceased.

He swallowed and turned to leave the experts to do their job, speaking his thoughts aloud, 'Another being the key concern here, McCardle. Right, c'mon,' Ericson continued, without looking over his shoulder as he walked away from the crime scene. A second later, he stopped and turned his head.

DC McCardle remained on the spot, watching the forensics, her short blonde bobbed hair blowing slightly in the breeze. Tucking hair behind her ears, she glanced at her boss, blue eyes framed by a furrowed brow, her mind already attempting to find the pieces in the puzzle called murder. She walked towards Ericson.

'C'mon, we've got work to do,' he said, smiling at her. Ericson admired his colleague, who was relatively new to the team. She had a good balance for a copper, in his opinion — process driven, intelligent, but also with a level of empathy. It was rare in the force. The place often hardened colleagues, and made them see death as a mouldy piece of bread you throw in the bin. Of course, the coppers cared, else they wouldn't do what they did. But there was something about the process of death and the needed bureaucracy of investigations that dehumanised people. They became a number, soulless.

Solving crime was the key. Maybe detachment was pinnacle to this. But Ericson always wondered whose relative it was that had died? Whose son or daughter? What had gone wrong? Victims got forgotten in the pursuit of finding the perpetrators. A much-needed process, but it meant empathy could be negligible. DC Polly McCardle had the balance and gave a shit about the victims. He'd picked that up in the short time she had been on the team and hoped McCardle would never change.

'I'll swing by the deli for us on the way back to the office,' said Ericson, his eyes lighting up behind his blacked-framed glasses as he touched his stomach. Death was unpleasant, but it didn't put him off his grub anymore. The pair walked out of the church grounds to where their cars were parked.

'Well, McCardle, this could be a coincidence, probable given the cohort. But…' he paused.

'But if not, we could have a possible serial killer on our hands if any more bodies turn up.' McCardle completed his sentence, their minds working in sync.

Thirty minutes later, the pair were back at their desks. Ericson had done his usual of slopping tomato sauce on his shirt so tried to manoeuvre his tie slightly to cover it. Caroline used to always say he needed a bib. Maybe he just needed to eat slower and not shovel his food in like it was going to self-destruct in sixty seconds.

'DC Myers, can you get me the file on the Charlie Sinclair case, please?' Ericson called across to his colleague as he looked on the system to cross reference. He turned to McCardle, who sat on the grey office chair next to him. At six foot two and fifteen and a half stone, five foot two, petite McCardle looked even smaller sitting down by his side.

'So, here we are. Our case of Charlie Sinclair.' McCardle nodded, remembering the detail, despite it not being her case. 'Still open, but cold. Sinclair, fifty-one years old, found dead under the bridge in Churchill. Alcohol, cannabis, and Amitriptyline found in his system by toxicology. But pathology state he died of suffocation.' Glancing at her, he raised an eyebrow. 'No murder weapon, no strong suspects identified by the interviews. Like I say, it's ongoing, but not much coming in.'

DC Lola Myers dropped the paper file on the desk between Ericson and McCardle with a smile. Ericson began flicking through the documents. 'Sinclair was an entrenched rough sleeper. He had been doing this for years.'

McCardle nodded, listening intently to her superior.

'The day centre in Crosley, Homeless Helping Hands, said he wasn't a drug user. But there was a dealing issue at the time, so he may have tried drugs. There's still an issue there and the neighbourhood team is monitoring, we need to keep up to date with their findings going forward.' He tapped his top lip with his forefinger. 'There are updates on file from last week, after the fatal overdose of a female on site. Could be a murder or manslaughter charge in itself.' He raised his eyebrows to McCardle who silently nodded.

'Anyway, back to Sinclair. No known enemies. Let's see what comes back from the latest poor bastard, but I want to keep this handy.' Ericson pushed his glasses to the top of his head and tapped the Charlie Sinclair file. Taking a gulp of the now-cold coffee, something was already niggling him and Ericson always trusted his gut — even after troffing down a bacon sandwich.

'There you go, Boss, the other file,' said DC Myers, as she placed a file on Ericson's desk later that day. It hung off the edge, balancing amongst the three dirty cups, an empty crisp packet and two empty sandwich cartons. Ericson shrugged like a child being told off as DC Myers glanced at his desk, resembling a school picnic. He was a poor role model for the 'clear desk policy'. In some psychologists' world, his cluttered desk represented his mind or his fragmented personal life. Unresolved issues and denial.

He had buried his head for the last eleven months, mourning his broken marriage. His mates had done the usual blokey thing of jokingly commenting they wish their wife would leave them or they would love a chance to go dating and sleeping around again.

'Go on the pull man, Ron,' his friend Ian said. 'You're a good-looking bloke, even with your middle-aged gut.'

Ronnie chuckled, masking the loneliness that no other woman could ever replace. Desperate for one of the lads to just genuinely check that he was okay; swimming against the tide and not drowning. Work was a distraction. The crimes of Northumberland left little time for Ericson to think about his meagre existence outside of the force.

But after work, he would get into his car and travel to his lonely flat, driving the coastal route home. Late at night, Ericson would stop to watch the shadowy sea. It was like a never-ending pool of tears. The sun having retreated, only the moon illuminating its darkness; cold and vast. It had become a place of contemplation for him. But much of it felt a sombre addiction, a self-punishment of melancholy.

McCardle travelled over on her seat, the thinning carpet accustomed to the abuse as it moved with the wheels of the chair.

'Results here from toxicology and pathology on the latest case, McCardle,' he said as he pulled down his glasses from his head and opened the file so they could see the outcome. They both read it. Ericson tapped his pen on the page and turned to his colleague.

'Same cause of death as Charlie Sinclair, same cohort of people. Two bodies within a mile of each other, within two months,' McCardle said, summarising the outcome.

Ericson nodded. McCardle looked at her senior, reading the way his mind worked.

'And no prizes for guessing, but this is the guy mentioned by the neighbourhood team and the day centre as the possible drug supplier.' He puffed out air. 'It's going to be big this, McCardle. Shit has got real. Get home, be back in for 8 am,' Ericson ordered.

'Yup, Boss,' she replied, momentarily looking at him intently before rising from her chair.

Ericson's eyes remained on the two files, the case numbers and names in block capitals on the front. To his right, CHARLIE SINCLAIR. To his left, DONALD ARMSTRONG.

# Chapter 21: DS Ronnie Ericson

Ronnie left the office at 10 pm, returning the next morning at 7 am, on little sleep. Waking at 6 am, he showered, had the last of some week-old bread toasted and drank black coffee as he looked out his kitchen window into the inky darkness of winter. The only noise was his crunching and chewing on the toast — the silence both peaceful and painful.

Funny, the things you miss when someone is no longer around. Those things that you would never think of, but that punch you in the heart at unexpected times. Shoes in the hallway, two cups in the sink, the distinct lack of someone else's fragrance in the air. One set of keys, no one to say good night to, and the silence that felt so loud it screamed in his head. Ronnie's alarm on his mobile phone snapped him from his reflections. Silencing it, he gulped the rest of his coffee and prepared to leave his house.

'So, here launches a two-murder investigation.' Ericson addressed his under-resourced team at the morning briefing. The incident board was prepared, collating all the intelligence they had to date. 'Charlie Sinclair and Donald Armstrong. Both deceased. Commonalities; both middle-aged men, both homeless, and both with addiction issues. Sinclair and Armstrong used a variety of services in the county. The bodies were found within a mile of each other. The timeline, two months apart.' Ericson took a gulp of his coffee.

'Some maniac doing a social cleanse?' asked DC Claire

Boyd.

'Yeah, possibly, Boyd. But we also know serials often practice on, let's say, more disposable folk. And if any more bodies turn up, that's what we have on our hands; a serial killer,' replied Ericson, turning to the incident board. 'McCardle, give us an update from forensics and toxicology on the two victims, please?' instructed Ericson.

'Okay, thanks, Boss. So, Charlie Sinclair, ongoing case as you all know, but with no real progress to date. Found dead in November. Pathology came back with the cause of death being suffocation. Drugs: cannabis and Amitriptyline plus alcohol found in his system. No homicide weapon found, no CCTV footage from the shops in proximity to where he was discovered.'

McCardle tucked her blonde hair behind her ears as she continued. 'Colleagues spoke to the manager of the day centre he attended and some of the staff. There was talk of a possible unknown debt or mistaken identity. A guy called Lance Cole was brought up by two of the staff, but nothing of substance came back. Excuse the pun.' Colleagues gave a laugh. Her blue eyes looked at Ericson, who nodded.

'Thanks, McCardle. Lucas, can you add to that please from being on the case?'

DC Kris Lucas glanced at his notes. 'I spoke with the shop keeper near to Sinclair's rough sleeping haunt. The accounts of those spoken to indicate they suspected an overdose or suicide and nothing suspicious. Although all stressed that they believed Charlie Sinclair was not a drug user and had never been.' Lucas straightened his back in his chair and continued. 'His estranged family provided little info. He had reached out to his son, but never met him again before his death. Those on the outside assumed suicide or death caused by his old, homeless body giving up.'

Ericson turned to McCardle, tilting his head back slightly, indicating for her to continue.

McCardle pointed to the incident board. 'Now, rewind to yesterday morning. Another body found within a mile of Sinclair's. Victim: Donald Armstrong. Known in the homeless community. Found by the vicar at St Paul's Church. Again, no visible wounds or weapons found. Toxicology found substances in the bloodstream: amphetamine, methadone, and Amitriptyline, as well as alcohol.'

She took a sip of water before talking again. 'This guy was an addict on a methadone script. He had been taking his drug of choice for ten years and was a skilled user. Armstrong had been putting in clean urine tests to probation, which, of course, doesn't mean he wasn't using. His name was also associated with possible drug dealing and a recent death on site at the day centre.' McCardle looked around the room at her colleagues, some taking notes, others listening intently. She turned to Ericson, who nodded with approval before she continued. 'On top of this, you guessed it, cause of death has come back as suffocation.'

To summarise, Ericson took over. 'These are now two homicides and there's enough evidence to suggest we could be dealing with a potential serial killer on our streets, targeting the homeless and vulnerable. So, we need all boots on the case.'

Ericson set the team of DCs to work. Their task; to go over everything that was initially covered in the first month of the Sinclair case before it grew cold. To explore the Armstrong case and to identify any overlaps after liaising with the neighbourhood team. They would speak to professionals involved with the support of both victims, speak with their family, both estranged, and those who were in contact with the victims. CCTV would be analysed around the area, including house-to-house checks. All local residents would be asked about CCTV cameras, if they heard or saw anything. The forensics from the victims and scenes of death would be examined: any discarded items, fingerprints, footprints, DNA from bottles or cans, hair, anything from the deceased, along with a search of Donald Armstrong's temporary accommodation.

'There'll be a press conference tomorrow with Chief Inspector Richardson, and I'll need all the info I can get. See you all back here in the morning, dream team,' he concluded, getting up and clapping his team into action.

That evening, Ronnie called his daughter. They tended to text; apparently, young people didn't 'talk on the phone' anymore. Well, that's what Kelsie had told her father.

'Is everything okay, Dad?' she asked quickly when he said hello.

'Yeah, fine, I just wanted to speak to my little girl.' Ronnie could almost see the eye roll down the phone and chuckled. 'I know, I know, it's so unfashionable to actually talk on a mobile phone, but I thought I'd check-in before dinner. See if all is good in the hood?'

Kelsie made a spitting noise, as if her mouth were full. 'Oh my God, Dad, you did not just say that? The 2010s called and wanted their saying back!'

The pair started laughing. 'You know, at some point being un-cool will actually be cool,' Ronnie joked as he held the phone with his shoulder whilst clicking the kettle on and grabbing a cup from the cupboard.

'What you having for tea?' Kelsie asked, stifling a yawn.

Ronnie opened his fridge and saw a quarter of a takeaway pizza from the night before. 'Leftover pizza. That's quite studenty of me, isn't it?'

'Very. Just watch what you're eating and try to be healthy, Dad,' Kelsie replied, then immediately said, 'Shit, and that's very parent-like of me.'

'Who have I got to look good for?' he queried, trying to be light-hearted.

'Well, yourself Dad, if no one else!' There was a silence before Kelsie continued, her voice soft and light, 'Dad, I know you miss Mam. Maybe you should look after yourself and show her you're different? That you care?'

Her words held a sadness that Ronnie could always detect and he watched the steam blow out of the kettle, unsure how to answer his daughter. He pressed his lips together before muttering, 'Perhaps.'

They talked for a few more minutes before saying their goodbyes. Ronnie made a drink, pulled out a wooden stool from his breakfast bar and sat, eating cold pizza from the box. He was proud of his daughter, but knew it would take more than losing a few pounds in weight or a trendy pair of glasses to win Caroline back.

'Right team…' Ericson began the next morning, as they gathered in the small room, chairs squashed in and cuppas in everyone's hands. He stood, stretching his back after another poor sleep the night before. Facing the investigation board, he rubbed his chin momentarily before shifting his size eleven feet on the well-worn, itchy carpet tiles to face his team.

'Donald Armstrong and Charlie Sinclair? Where are we at? Myers, you were going to speak with the shop owner again to check any missing detail or information since Charlie Sinclair was found dead?' Ericson pushed his glasses up from his eyes to sit on his head and looked at DC Myers.

'Boss, Alan Kelly, who runs the shop, said he didn't really have anything else to add on top of what he stated in November. He just reiterated that Sinclair hadn't been in a good place for the last few weeks of his life and was drunk most of the time. He assumed suicide.'

'Boyd, you and Lucas were going to visit the accommodation where Armstrong was staying, Next Steps, and speak with staff. What's the update, please?' Ericson asked, leaning against a table.

'Yeah. The team had concerns around the drug dealing, relationships, and risks over the past few months with Armstrong. Nothing particularly alarming given their work and nothing the neighbourhood team wasn't aware of. They said it's common and Armstrong wasn't there all the time overnight, often staying out the odd night. We've taken the CCTV system away for analysis.' DC Boyd looked at her notes, then back up at Ericson. 'They mentioned some names of other residents to speak to. So, we'll try to have a word with them. Although I am certain folk will avoid the place knowing more police are around.'

'McCardle?' Ericson asked.

Nodding, McCardle spoke. 'The mobile phones of each of the deceased were found on-site. Hall, did the analysts get anything call data wise of the two victims? Any trends?'

Hall cleared her throat, 'Nothing linking the victims, call wise. No common numbers and their phones have never pinged in the same location. They had different lifestyles in the fact one was actively involved with probation, the other had a clean record. Different substances of choice.' She glanced at her notes. 'However, there is a link with recent drug use and the fact they both used the homeless day centre in Crosley. Both had been involved with altercations. Armstrong has evidence of supplying drugs from text messages on his phone,' she explained, crossing her legs at her ankles.

'McCardle and I will visit the day centre, Homeless Helping Hands today,' added Ericson, running a hand over his grey hair. 'Myers, if you can come too, please. I know you've been there before when you were on the neighbourhood team, so your input would be great. Sorry, Hall, go on.'

Hall continued. 'Regarding similar cases across local forces; nothing of concern. The only thing we found was the homicide of a homeless middle-aged man, David Toby, in Cleveland a few years ago. He had lived in temporary accommodation locally but hadn't used services. Was known to police for begging and petty offences before he became transient in Cleveland two years ago, prior to his homicide. The murderer was never found, but the cause of death was stabbing.' Hall explained, looking at her superiors.

McCardle took a gulp of tea and nodded. 'Thanks. Ericson and I spoke with the family of the two victims. Tommy Sinclair had been spoken to after his father's homicide but we visited again. He's still angry about the whole thing but was pretty shook up about the possibility of another homicide. The poor bloke is clearly struggling under the grief of someone who almost came back into his life and the anger is still there.' McCardle moved her slight frame from the spot she was standing and leant against the desk adjacent to Ericson.

'He's not a likely suspect and we know he had an alibi on the night of his father's death, as he was doing PT sessions at the local gym. He claims he's never heard of Donald Armstrong,' added Ericson. McCardle tilted her head, stretching her neck, and Ericson wondered if it had been a restless night for her as well.

Ericson swallowed and spoke again. 'Donald Armstrong had a stepdaughter, stepson, and an ex-wife. None of which were massively surprised he was dead, given his lifestyle. But when homicide was mentioned, it came as a shock. They couldn't name potential enemies. Armstrong was in and out of their lives as much as he was in and out of prison. They'd washed their hands of him. The ex and his stepdaughter have alibis that night, both at a Weight Worries group together until late. The stepson states he was at home. Although there's no obvious motive in murdering another homeless guy two months earlier.' Ericson looked around at his team; nodding and making the odd note.

He rubbed the small of his back absentmindedly and grimaced. 'As it stands, we have no tangible suspect. That may change in the next few days, with any intelligence and forensics coming in. The CCTV will continue to get viewed for any information, sightings, and vehicles whilst we interview potential witnesses and suspects. But let's keep the good work going before some other poor bugger becomes a target.'

The team rose and left the office to continue their search. The people who knew and provided support to Charlie Sinclair and Donald Armstrong had to be re-visited. It was 8:30 am and Ericson and McCardle set off for Homeless Helping Hands with Myers, who would make notes. Pulling up at the centre, people were hanging around the entrance; chatting and smoking. The three officers may have been out of uniform, but they wore the 'copper look' like a second skin. Walking towards the doorway of the centre, silence coated the air and a few people nodded. Ericson held the door open for his colleagues and as he walked in himself, he heard a snorting impression of a pig and laughing from the crowd outside. He rolled his eyes.

They wanted to speak to all the staff there and then but were asked by the manager, Stuart, to come back a few hours later to avoid disrupting breakfast service. Biting his tongue, Ericson refrained from telling Stuart that he didn't give a damn about causing disruption or for some skitzy dealer to have a sweat on because the 'bizzies' were on site. He was hunting a killer and one who was likely to strike again in Ericson's mind.

'There has been a body found, Mr Bowden; this isn't about the ongoing drug issue. We have a few visits to make, then we'll be back and will want to speak to staff and volunteers. This'll give you a few hours to round the team up,' Ericson said sternly, eyes fixed on the manager as colour drained from his face.

'Bod... body?' enquired Stuart, eyes wide, mouth gaping.

'Yes, a Mr Donald Armstrong. Please keep it to yourself until we return.' Ericson glared at Stuart, who now looked about ready to pass out as he raised a hand to his forehead.

'See you in a few hours,' added McCardle as they turned and walked towards the centre exit.

# Chapter 22: DS Ronnie Ericson

After visiting Donald Armstrong's probation worker and the local drug treatment service, McCardle, Ericson, and Myers pulled up at the Homeless Helping Hands centre for the second time that morning. Ericson, already miffed at the attitude of the manager, turned to McCardle.

'No crap from these buggers, mind. This lot will play things down, especially ones who have been there, done it, and wore every bloody T-shirt going. Do you agree, Myers?'

Myers nodded and McCardle chuckled. 'Yeah, Boss, I've got the bullshit button ready!' They walked into the centre, minus the earlier crowds, to be greeted by a tall, bald guy.

'Alright, I'm Mo. Maurice Nutman, but everyone knows me as Mo. Stu, the gaffer, he's in the office over here.'

They followed Mo into a small office as the thin manager rose from his seat and cleared his throat.

'Afternoon,' he said as he stretched his hand out. Ericson took another immediate dislike to him for the second time that day.

'DS Ericson,' he replied bluntly, repeating his introduction from earlier that day. 'These are my colleagues, DC McCardle and DC Myers, who you know from when she was part of the drug surveillance at the centre.'

Stuart nodded and gestured for them to sit on tatty chairs that made the force's look new. Ericson glanced around the office and saw a kitchenette area. No cuppas were offered by

Stuart or Mo, which added to Ericson's dislike of him.

'As I said this morning, Mr Bowden, we would like to speak to all staff to get any information on Charlie Sinclair and Donald Armstrong.'

'Of course. I've told the staff and they're available. We're all really shocked. After just getting used to Charlie not being around and now to hear about Donald.' Stuart blew out air and shook his head.

Something about his reaction Ericson didn't buy. 'Yes, of course. Well, let's start with yourself, Mr Bowden. Can we chat somewhere private, please?' Ericson asked.

'Yes, in here. Mo will go into the kitchen.' Stuart raised his eyebrows at Mo in a *you shouldn't still be in here* manner.

The officers got out their paperwork. Ericson would ask the questions, McCardle chipping in. Myers would make notes, but she was also there to see how the staff were compared to the little she knew of them from a month on the neighbourhood team before her transfer to the MIT. Ericson began gathering information, asking Stuart about the months leading up to Charlie Sinclair's death. This was harder for Stuart to recall as it was over two months ago, but the information seemed pretty consistent to what had previously been recorded by Ericson's colleagues just after the homicide.

'You mentioned a few months ago when Charlie Sinclair was found dead that there had been a period of unsettlement at the centre and amongst the homeless community. Can you talk us through that again please, Stuart?'

Stuart rubbed his neck. 'Yeah. There had been a few incidents. It isn't uncommon, Officer, but we had to temporarily ban a few people at the same time. Charlie was one of them. Behaviour mainly, and people were using drugs and possibly selling them on the premises. I suspected Donald Armstrong to be supplying the drugs.' He moved a little in his seat and took a sip from his cup. 'A month or so earlier, there'd been problems with another regular, Lance Cole, who isn't a known drug user. He had a complete change in behaviour, targeting staff, so could have been using. I don't know.' Stuart shrugged and glanced at all three officers before looking back at Ericson.

Ericson nodded, prompting Stuart to continue.

'The staff all felt a bit stressed. We had some regulars we were worried about, a few causing bother. Plus, it was getting cold again, which always adds stress to the risks for our home-less community.' He ran his tongue over his top teeth and took a breath. 'Like I said to your colleagues at the time, Char-lie had engaged better with the entire team, but mainly his support worker, Lorna. We felt he may even consider coming in, taking up an offer of accommodation this winter.' Stuart took a drink from his cup and Ericson noticed his hand trem-bling slightly.

'Lorna had been chatting to him about his estranged son and a meeting had been arranged. Charlie didn't show and was missing from the centre for a couple of days. Then came back drunk and being abusive. I went on annual leave, then he died the next day.' Stuart looked down at the palm of his hands before his gaze rose again. 'We all assumed it was alco-hol related or an overdose. He wasn't young for a homeless guy and had hammered the drink. It takes its toll; I know that too well.'

'Thanks, Stuart, that's really helpful. Did you know of any enemies Charlie Sinclair had? Anyone you may have thought about since initially speaking to the police last November?

Anyone linking Charlie and Donald Armstrong?'

Stuart rubbed his thin lips and shook his head. 'No, Charlie was a nice, likeable guy on the whole. He never really caused any bother. But then we only see a snippet of what goes on. Like I said, there was an atmosphere. When you said Donald had been found dead, it was awful to hear but wasn't a massive surprise, to be honest. Obviously, any suspicious behaviour involving his death is, but his lifestyle, well, he was different to Charlie. He would have had a lot more enemies. Charlie, not so much. The only links I know of between the two is the service and the people using it. Anything away from here, I wouldn't know,' he shrugged.

'I see, thanks, Stuart. Did Tommy, Charlie's son, ever get back in touch with the team?' Ericson enquired.

'No, not that I am aware of. Lorna was the only one who really spoke to him. She tried after Charlie died to pass on our condolences, but he never answered. Some of us saw him at the funeral but only to say a quick sorry.'

Ericson nodded. 'Let's talk about Donald Armstrong. Tell me about his use of the service? Associates? How he engaged with staff and any issues?'

Stuart swallowed. 'Donald had been using the service on and off for a few years. He spent as much time in prison as out of it. But when he was doing well, he was a great bloke. A clever man, he had a lot he could have focused on, but he took drugs from a young age and bouts of abstinence were few and far between.' Stuart took another gulp from his cup. 'Oh, sorry, I didn't offer you all a cuppa. Do you...?'

Ericson held up his hand. 'In a bit, thanks.'

Stuart half smiled and continued. 'He attended almost daily and was staying in the Next Steps hostel. But then he got embroiled in the hostile atmosphere here. I honestly can't say who instigated it. Like I said, a few people were temporarily barred and none of them had a massive association with each other. That doesn't mean much though as substances become the glue that holds people together as well as the knife that rips people apart.' Stuart stopped momentarily and tilted his head back.

Ericson knew Stuart Bowden had his own demons and a record himself from his days in services. Most of the staff and volunteers at Homeless Helping Hands seemed to have used services, and some with a criminal record. Not that Ericson thought people couldn't change. But some criminals, well, he saw the patterns, the proof in the pudding, as he would say. Ericson glanced at Myers, who was frantically making notes.

'The last four months or so, Donald declined and was at risk of being recalled to prison. And the drugs issue…' Stuart looked at his desk, then back to the detectives, with heavy brown eyes. 'He had a few incidences, altercations with people. There were multiple incidents, you'll see in his case notes. Some involved staff, but it was obviously unprovoked by my team.' Stuart grinned nervously as he shifted slightly in his ancient office chair that squeaked with every movement.

Ericson wasn't convinced. He knew other people working there who had a record for assault. One, the guy who greeted them, Maurice Nutman, also had drugs related offences. It was over a decade ago, but it was still a custodial sentence.

'Things had been deteriorating just before Charlie died, for Charlie and others. That same week, we had an overdose in the toilets. A young lad, a near miss. I'm not sure if Donald was using gear; heroin, himself. He would've been recalled as he had to do a urine sample each week for probation, although piss goes for almost the price of heroin these days.' He let out a laugh before looking back at Ericson's and McCardle's straight faces.

Stuart licked his lips and swallowed. 'Erm, but I'm certain he was dealing and I know Next Steps had a death two weeks ago from an overdose. You probably know that already, Officer.' Stuart shook his head and changed the position of his legs. 'Then we had the incident just last week with young Eve Wright. So yeah, it's been brewing. But murder, I mean that's something else, isn't it?' He breathed out, exasperated, and rubbed a hand over his dark hair.

'Okay, thanks, Stuart. Can we have a look at the computer files before we speak to the next staff member, please? And there may be some more questions in the next few days. Are you at work?' Ericson asked.

'Yeah, I'm in until Sunday.'

Ericson nodded and glanced at his colleagues before fixing his grey-blue eyes back on Stuart. 'Great. Let's crack on with these files and Stuart, any chance of a cuppa now?'

It was 4 pm and after speaking with the staff at Homeless Helping Hands, Ericson, McCardle, and Myers had returned to the station. Myers began typing up the notes as Ericson and McCardle went to make drinks.

Leaning against the grey laminate countertop of the staff kitchen as the kettle boiled, Ericson removed his glasses. 'There's something off, McCardle, and it ain't the quiche that lot gave us for lunch.' Ericson laughed at his own joke and rubbed the space between his eyebrows.

McCardle rolled her eyes affectionately. They had developed a solid working relationship since McCardle had moved from a neighbouring team. Stirring boiling water into their cups, he tapped the spoon against the side of one.

'This lot at Homeless Helping Hands; things just don't add up. Some of them seem full of hell, some holier than thou, and no one in between. But there's a sinister vibe. I could feel it.'

He picked up the battered biscuit tin from the countertop and pulled off the metal lid, looking inside to see if there were any remaining sweet gems in the treasure chest. Scooping out two half biscuits, he smiled at his bounty before holding the container out towards McCardle. She lifted her hand, gesturing she was fine.

'I know what you mean, Boss. It felt like a pressure cooker. And I get they'll be nervous, stressed, and possibly sad about what's happened, but the tension, phew!'

Ericson took a sip of his coffee, then yawned, covering his mouth with his free hand. 'One or more of them know something, are covering, or covering themselves. This is an in-the-community-job.'

McCardle clicked her neck from side to side, keeping her gaze on her boss. 'I agree. There's possible motive; drugs, old relationships, power dynamics.' She tapped her lip. 'But there feels something else, something missing around who is linked with who. The briefing after the follow-ups today should be interesting.'

'You don't get this far for so long in a career like this without trusting your instinct, McCardle.' Ericson said as he fished in the biscuit tin for some more scraps.

Soon, the morning briefing was over. Ericson had tasked the team and knew their focus was Homeless Helping Hands. Possible suspects had been identified and a police presence

was needed at the centre. People using the service and staff
had a back story and motive. Ericson had empathy for those
in need — he understood shit happened to people and wasn't
immune from bad luck himself. Life could have been different for everyone and Ericson always tried to remain humble
and understanding, well, to a degree. People made split second choices that could ruin lives. Or decisions determined
almost by the roll of the die, a postcode lottery to avoid the
problems that could lead to crime.

Ericson tried to remember that, but there was a linger of
hostility and deception floating round Homeless Helping
Hands. He felt it in the pit of his ever-reliable gut. The media
had been all over the story and the team had taken part in
press briefings. Copies of the local newspaper lay in the office
— most unread and unwanted but strangely needed, like leftover Christmas chocolates. Single homicides were quite common, even in Northumberland. But two similar killings and a
possible serial killer; that was more newsworthy.

Ericson went to the staff kitchen. Rinsing out his *World's
Best Dad* cup as the kettle boiled, he reached for the morning
newspaper from the round pale wooden table that was there
to encourage officers to eat away from their desk, but was
almost always just a place to leave things.

The image on the front page of the *Northumberland Herald*
taunted him. He shook his head and tutted, glaring at the
photo of himself and his superior, Chief Inspector Richardson — a snap from the press conference yesterday evening.
The case had made national news as well as the local.

Sighing, he reflected on how tired he looked, then berated
himself for his own fickle thoughts when two people had
been murdered. The headline a quote he had said himself,

about people society forgets. So-called 'nobodies' — people that have apparently caused their own problems and those some people call the 'undeserving', but they were still people's families; someone's father or mother, son or daughter, even if criminals themselves. He picked up the newspaper, eyes fixed on the headline, highlighting the victims were *Somebody's Nobody*.

The team had a focus but didn't get the media off their back and calls had come in already that morning. Ericson knew what would happen. He had seen it so many times before. The residents of Northumberland were aghast that there was a murderer on the loose. The only selfish, saving grace for most of them would be that the targets were 'not their kind'. Nevertheless, it would cause warranted anxiety, speculation, and chaos that would be fed into local councillors and statutory services. It had to a degree with the Sinclair case two months ago. Now it would be a torpedo of panic. The media vultures would be desperate for snippets on the *'Social Cleansing Killer'* as they had been titled by a national print media.

Back at his desk, Ericson tucked into a cream cheese and ham bagel. McCardle sat quietly, reading files, blonde hair tucked behind her ears as Ericson ate his breakfast. In between bites, crumbs falling onto his desk and gulps of coffee, he looked over at her.

'McCardle, today we go back to Homeless Helping Hands and speak to some people using the centre. Myers and maybe Boyd can talk to the service users? Myers knows them more from being a community bobby and is less intimidating.'

'Less intimidating? Speak for your bloody self,' McCardle laughed, small lines appearing around her blue eyes. The wrinkles, not yet a permanent feature of the thirty-four-year-old's face, but prominent temporarily from long hours and lack of sleep.

An hour later and the officers were pulling up at Homeless Helping Hands. DC Myers and DC Boyd had joined them, ensuring plenty of observations and questions could be conducted. It was just before 10 am and they were hoping to catch some stragglers after breakfast, speak to the staff and then chat with the lunch time crew.

The plan was to gather information on relationships, note who was associating with who. They would re-visit the list of names the manager, Stuart, had passed on and delve a little deeper. The information gathered in the case by the team so far was of no great substance. No CCTV footage, many suspects, and unclear motives. The next step was to consolidate alibis, eliminate possible suspects, and whittle down the long list. Those who remained would be formally interviewed at the station.

As they got out of the two cars that travelled to the centre, Ericson rubbed his lower back, shivering slightly in the winter wind, and glanced at his team. 'Right Myers, Boyd, if you can mooch about the centre and chat with some people using the service, please. Make it clear it's all informal. We need to build a rapport and get them on side.'

'Understood, Boss,' replied Boyd as Myers nodded, and they began walking to the centre entrance.

'Back again, eh?' was the greeting the detectives received as they entered the building. Maurice Nutman gave them a grin.

'Yes, Mr Nutman. You'll be sick of the sight of us by the end of the week,' Ericson said, looking over the top of his glasses.

'Is your boss about?' added McCardle.

'In the office. You know where it is,' Mo replied casually before heading towards someone sitting at a table.

Ericson bit his lip. 'Watch him,' he said to his colleagues as they walked across the centre hall to stares from the crowd.

'Mr Bowden?' Ericson knocked on the open office door.

Stuart glanced up from his computer screen and Ericson saw the image of a man who looked older than his probable years. His eyes were heavy, his skin sallow, and his posture displaying the impact of carrying the weight of other people's needs and anxieties. But he also saw a suspect.

'Morning, Officer. Come on in and please, it's Stuart,' he sighed.

*A crumbling man*, thought Ericson. Or perhaps a man with guilt poisoning his bloodstream.

'Thanks, Stuart. We're hoping to be here quite a bit over the next few days, gathering more information as part of the ongoing investigation of the suspected homicide of Donald Armstrong and Charlie Sinclair.'

Stuart nodded.

'You'll remember DC McCardle and DC Myers.' Ericson looked at his colleagues, then a nodding Stuart. 'And this is DC Boyd, who, with DC Myers, will be out in the centre hall, speaking informally with some of the people using the service.'

Stuart nodded again and flashed a glance at DC Boyd.

'We need to develop more of a picture of relationship dynamics of the deceased. This is as much about prevention as it is about solving the current crimes. DC McCardle and I will want to speak to staff again, cross reference our information on your database in more detail and review CCTV footage.

We'll try not to get in your way too much.' Ericson stared at the man who managed the service. He glared back; glassy eyed, as if he already knew it would not end well.

# Chapter 23

The police had been hanging around for two days, returning that morning. All of them trying to mark their scent, like dogs pissing against a lamppost. It was rather entertaining seeing the sheer panic on some faces of the people using the centre. Those of the same ilk as Albert, Charlie, and Donald; the selfish, unwilling to change despite chance after chance. Those types only turned up once, saw the police and wouldn't be seen again the next day — scurrying away, worried they would be under suspicion. After all, they were criminals.

Lance was one of them. Pathetic, sneaky, low-life Lance, who had learnt nothing from his 'self-inflicted burns accident'. They wished his life had been extinguished those months ago when they had dropped the burning cigarette onto his legs.

But they didn't quite have the courage to kill then, despite the fuel of anger and resentment multiplying at an exponential rate inside them — enough to set the whole county on fire, never mind a spiteful sack of shit like Lance. Another disgrace of a man who was on their to-do list to deal with once the police pissed off.

Scumbag Salvin was nowhere to be seen. They hoped he had snuffed it somewhere, through his own greedy drug use. It would save them a job down the line, no doubt. They chuckled to themselves. It felt like they were living two separate lives and part of it felt invigorating, like a drug itself. They were surviving with all the chaos and drama, well whilst at the centre at least; they'd been acting most of their life. It hadn't been easy at first, but they would not lie down and surrender.

They would not admit they had done something wrong, because they hadn't, really. They'd contributed to a better society by disposing of Charlie and Donald. Northumberland was a safer place now those two were gone and their families were healing; just like they had slowly started to when Albert eventually died — and their recent extermination of the rodents of Homeless Helping Hands had accelerated the process massively.

The absolute certainty of the positive impact on the county and families of Charlie and Donald made it easier for them to relax. Plus, they'd spoken to the police already, so was sure that would be it. The police wouldn't stay around for long — they had more important crimes to solve than the deaths of two losers.

Sitting on the closed toilet seat, they absorbed a brief break before the chaotic breakfast rush. Puffing out air, they looked at the cigarette burns that had melted into the plastic coating of the toilet door and thought about after Mam died. Albert nurtured the alcohol demon growing inside of him instead of his own helpless child. Acting became second nature, and they wore their mask well. It may fall now and then, true feelings seeping out, but Christ, they wore that mask.

Tipping their head back, they closed their eyes, the dull sounds of the centre audible. Standing, they took a deep breath and opened the creaking toilet door. They stared at the mottled mirror above the sink as they washed their hands. The water heating rapidly, but they didn't feel the increasing temperature as the liquid cascaded over their hands whilst their gaze fixed on their reflection. Blinking, they shook their head and looked again, not recognising themselves.

Thoughts returned to the past and their process of keeping a journal, which got them through the most difficult of days. Robyn's suggestion all those years before, gifting them that notebook, which felt like the number one most wanted toy at Christmas. Writing their thoughts and feelings had been the coping mechanism that kept them sane.

Those two words that started their own therapy; *Dear Diary* — felt like the pain could almost be locked away in its own prison once that journal was closed. A way of symbolically documenting but switching off from the hurt, anger, and fear that cannon-balled around their brain. It always worked, temporarily, at least.

The journal felt like a compulsion, something that was part of Mam, even Albert. Resentment gnawed on their organs, and writing their thoughts — that almost felt like they were possessed — helped to exorcise the demon. It wasn't daily that they wrote now, it hadn't been for a long time. But every few days, it felt essential to document their feelings and even more so of late as they started their new therapy: revenge.

It was always so much easier to manage life when they found an answer to a problem. Or, as the many psychiatrists over the years explained, 'solution-focused therapy'. They sniggered. *Not sure they would endorse my solution,* they thought as they placed their wet hands under the hand-dryer that had as much strength to dry hands as a ninety-year-old blowing through a straw. They nodded. They knew what they had done was the right thing, regardless of what anyone else would think. Killing Charlie and Donald was needed to protect people, but it was also about them processing what they had wanted to do to Albert all those years ago. It was Albert's fault Charlie and Donald were dead, not theirs.

The fear in them came from their relationships showing cracks. They couldn't let that happen. That's what Albert did, and everyone fell through the cracks with him into purgatory. They weren't like him; they were making lives better by healing the cracks permanently. Soon, the police would give up on the hunt for the killer and all would go quiet again. They would run out of information or perhaps convict a sloppy addict like Lance, who would more than likely be grateful for fifteen years inside with a bed and hot meals. That's if they didn't get to the nasty bastard first.

They smiled to themselves as they left the bathroom. This wasn't always the plan. Revenge, somehow, yes. But this wasn't necessarily the way they thought it would play out. They just knew all their life that they were there to stop people from suffering. To intervene and re-balance relationships where there was always a victim and a selfish perpetrator.

Perhaps they thought it would be more about rescuing and saving people, and it was to a degree. But there were always the deviants who didn't want to play nicely. The losers who wanted to spoil it for the others. These were the ones who needed to be taken out of the game, permanently.

Homeless Helping Hands: the divide between the good and bad, deserving and undeserving, victim and perpetrator. They received the biggest buzz from the people who wanted to change and the chance to help them transform their lives. It had been destiny for them — it was meant to be that they worked in the field. The understood, had empathy.

However, the small minority existed who would never change, draining resources from those who were screaming inside for help as they walked wounded. Yes, it was meant to be. They were needed to rebalance the scales. And the 'goodies' have to kill the 'baddies', right?

They had spent time with the police the day before. The coppers looking like some bad TV detective series, sporting ill-fitting suits and omitting the smell of too much coffee from their dank breath. They had cooperated, answered questions confidently. The police would never suspect a member of staff, someone in a role caring for vulnerable people. A person who supports and empowers people in need each day. People who are lost, homeless, hungry, and need emotional nourishment as much as the food served. They would suspect a fellow addict, a fellow criminal. They took a deep breath, content with their plan and feeling sure they could keep their mask tightly on. No, the police would never suspect someone who helps the vulnerable.

# Chapter 24: DS Ronnie Ericson

Ericson felt like the Homeless Helping Hands centre was his second home. The frosty reception from people using the service and some of the staff was compensated for by the regular servings of food. Ericson sat chewing on a cornflake cake with a milky coffee by his side. The team had spoken informally to the staff and volunteers and had ascertained some consistent information on both Donald Armstrong and Charlie Sinclair. There were several other names that were repeated in the conversations, Salvin Yanti and Lance Cole in particular. Neither of which Ericson and the team had chatted with — the place was significantly less full given the police presence.

Ericson was enjoying his work with McCardle. She had a calmness about her; often reflectively quiet, and it was nice to work with someone who wasn't always bitching about the force, its processes, and colleagues. She talked about her home life in a perfect balance of not over-sharing. The affection she held in her words and voice when talking about her wife, Lisa, their holidays, and possible plans for children took Ronnie back to the years with Caroline, before Kelsie came along.

The nights they'd go walking at midnight, even in the freezing North East winter. They would giggle and talk about the future, strolling hand in hand in the dead of the night with an energy and love that seemed to light up the darkness.

Caroline looked her best when she was just Caroline; without all the gunk on her face, and her wavy dark hair tied back to show the natural beauty of her cheekbones. She was stunning and Ronnie always knew she would be the most wonderful mother, of which she was, even now that their baby was an adult with her own life plans.

Breathing out deeply, Ericson swallowed a football of regret. He was jolted into the here and now by DC Myers entering the office McCardle and Ericson had evicted the Homeless Helping Hands staff from.

'Boss, need some backup. A client is outside calling all the staff murderers and two others are fighting.'

Ericson and McCardle stood quickly and followed Myers outside. A few of the crowd rushed off as if chasing a £50 note along the ground. One bloke had clearly drunk twice the recommended weekly units of alcohol in an hour and was mouthing off as two men rolled around on the ground, shouting and grunting — one exposing his bare backside as the other grabbed his loose jogging pants.

'For crying out loud,' Ericson said as he walked over to the drunken tousle. 'Break it up, you two,' he shouted at the rolling ball of entwined humans.

'Are you pulling those murdering bastards in, ya useless pigs?' The drunk man sneered, pointing at Ericson, McCardle, and Myers. He bent down to pick up half of a brick from the gutter.

'McCardle, nick that divvy, will you?' Ericson muttered as he walked towards the men scuffling on the road. 'I said, *break it up!*' Ericson shouted as he leant in and tried to pull the entanglement apart — legs were interlocked and arms were flying about.

'Piss off!' was slurred from one mouth.

Dragging one of the two off, the bottom flasher pulled his trousers up, red in the face, and stinking of booze.

'McCardle, cuff that one,' Ericson said, pointing to the guy groaning on the floor. 'Myers, you and McCardle take these two to the station to sober up,' he directed to his team.

They nodded, manoeuvring the men towards the car park as they slurred and swore incoherently. *Can any bugger behave?* Ericson thought to himself as he returned to the centre. It was a few hours until lunchtime and Ericson was keen to observe the people using the service. The majority of those accessing Homeless Helping Hands would be sceptical, he knew that. People had bad experiences with the police; as victims of crime and offenders. And people who no longer offended, had an understandable uncertainty of the police.

He planned to be as discreet and personable as possible. Not everyone would be wary of the police, but Ericson also knew there was always 'a grass' — someone who would want to help for their own benefit. For Ericson, it was just identifying this person and utilising his informant training; something he had years of practice with.

McCardle returned to the centre forty-five minutes later, and the pair continued to extract information from the Homeless Helping Hands database. The CCTV system had been removed from the centre and was being viewed at the station. Ericson had planned for all staff and volunteers to be interviewed at the station the next day and subsequently went to let them know.

This had set everyone's nerves off like fireworks on New Year's Eve. Half of the team had a record and were suspicious of Ericson and his team. The other half, well, perhaps naïve or maybe they had something to hide. Ericson was damn sure he was going to find out.

'Do they have to come to the station? It sounds intrusive.' Stuart clasped his hands, a frown on his bird-like face.

Ericson had to resist the urge to roll his eyes, replying, 'Stuart, we have spoken with your team here informally, which was really useful. But may I remind you that this is a homicide investigation. Now, I'd hope all your team wish to assist us in the upmost to keep vulnerable people, yourselves, and the community safe?' Ericson said abruptly, sliding his glasses from his eyes to his head.

Stuart cleared his throat. 'Of course, we all want to help. It's just an anxious time and they may feel under suspicion.'

'Let us do our job please, Mr Bowden.' And with that, Ericson walked away, thinking Stuart should really know better unless he was hiding something.

That evening, after the team briefing and returning to his flat, Ronnie sat down on his sofa and felt his body sink into the plump cushions, enveloping him like a childhood hug from his mother. He sighed and picked up his plate of toast that lay next to a bottle of beer. *Better than a takeaway,* he thought as he eyed the sad offering before biting it, sinking his teeth into the buttery stodge. After showering, he made a cup of tea. Picking up his phone, there was a missed call from Kelsie. Ringing back, she answered quickly.

'Hi love, you okay?'

'Hiya, Dad. Yeah, I'm fine. I had an idea.'

'Oh aye?' Ronnie chuckled. 'Is it going to cost me? And hey, I thought talking on the phone wasn't cool?'

'It isn't, but actually, it was nice the last time we talked.'

Ronnie put a hand to his chest. 'It was,' he mumbled.

'Yeah. So, Dad. Erm, it will cost you, but I think it will be worth it. It's Mam's birthday on Sunday and I thought the three of us could go out?'

Ronnie was silent for a few seconds.

'Dad, you forgot it was Mam's birthday, didn't you?' Kelsie said the last few words in a higher pitch.

Ronnie rubbed his forehead as he leant against the kitchen countertop. Of course, he hadn't forgotten. This time last year, he had been planning a night out for Caroline's birthday at a Michelin star restaurant in town. He had given her money to buy a new dress and get her hair done. Only for Ronnie to be stuck at work on the exploitation case, meaning the reservation time came and went.

He returned home that evening and saw the look of disappointment in the mascara-smudged eyes of the woman he loved with all his heart. In that instant where Caroline spoke no words, but shook her head and walked up the stairs, Ronnie knew it was one time too many.

'Ask your mam first how she'd feel. She might want to just do something with you, or perhaps go on a date with another bloke,' Ronnie said, biting his thumbnail.

'Mam's not seeing anyone, Dad. She was seeing a guy from the gym, only a few dates. I didn't tell you, as I knew you would worry. Turns out he had a wife he lived with. So, she's done with the dating scene.'

Ronnie gritted his teeth. 'What a low-life. Who was he?'

'Just some creep by the sounds of it. She's fine though, said it was no big deal, and he talked all about himself, although clearly not the truth!' Kelsie laughed. 'Dad, she still mentions you all the time, you know. If you could show her that work doesn't come before everything…' Kelsie left a silence.

'I know, love, I know.' And he knew, by God, did he know, and Ronnie had spent all of the last year regretting taking his wife for granted.

# Chapter 25: Stuart

'It's all turning to shit,' Stuart said down the phone to his sponsor, as he hung his head towards his knees in the locked community centre. 'The bloody police swarming around, a murderer on the loose, people using the service fighting. Then the staff dodging around.' He let out a sigh that could have whisked the leaves off the ground outside. 'I have one sneaking about and I don't know if it's guilt or because he knows he's on a warning. Another looking like she's never slept in her life or on drugs herself. Dot trying to solve everything with rock buns and pots of tea, and I just feel like running away.' Stuart rubbed his neck as he gripped the phone, desperate for some reassurance.

'Mate, you can only control what you can control. You know how to keep people as safe as you can and you're doing that. Police presence may keep some people using the service away, but it means you are safeguarding those using it,' his sponsor said as Stuart nodded to himself.

'The staff will be on edge. It's understandable. You're on edge, so they are bound to be as well. It'll get sorted. The police will catch the bastard doing this. You have to just trust them and the process.'

There was silence for a second. Stuart swallowed.

'Stu, you're not the bloke they used to lift for thieving from the supermarket anymore. You're respected.'

*Then why do I feel so bloody guilty?* Stuart thought to himself.

'Thanks mate and thanks for listening. You're right, I think it's just come after a few terrible months,' Stuart replied before taking a deep breath.

'Well, you know where I am, Stu. Be kind to yourself, pal.'

Stuart said goodbye and lifted his slumped shoulders, rising from his office chair. He walked to the sink, feeling like his shoes were weighed down with sand as he dragged them the few metres to the kitchenette. He splashed water on his face, knowing he looked like he'd been dug up. The staff had been allocated times to go to the police station today for interviewing and Stuart's stomach dropped as he thought of the prospect of being back in a police station.

However, before this, it was all hands-on to get breakfast sorted. Opening the centre, Stuart stood in the doorway for a moment, looking out into the dark winter morning. It was silent; no sounds except those in his congested head. His slim body that had become thinner the last few weeks resting against the frame. He turned, facing back to the centre hall. Stuart stared at the familiar sight that had brought him so much comfort, satisfaction, and pride over the last few years, but now covered him in a mist of terror.

After scrunching his eyes, he strolled through the centre that he had built up from nothing. The place his whole heart had gone into. His centre. His charity. Where for almost four years, he had soared against the elements, taking his flock with him to great heights. Only right now, it felt like there was an ever-constant albatross around his thin neck.

# Chapter 26: Mo

The last few weeks, months in fact, had been a clusterfuck for Mo, only made tolerable by thoughts of his son and Annie. And now the bizzies were hanging around at work. Mo would always have a grudge against the police, even as a 'reformed' character. The police had treated him like shit when he was at the peak of his offending — not giving a damn about his mental health and physical well-being.

Although not an angel and Mo would never claim to be, he had needed help and a cell had never been the answer, even his long stretch. He'd been professional at work with the coppers, reminding himself that they weren't better than him and knowing he had to play the game, as the tension in the day centre could be cut with a machete!

The main detective had instructed them all to attend the police station the next day and the truth was, Mo was scared. Frightened of saying the wrong thing, anxious his feelings would seep out of his mouth in damning words, and nervous that they had already made their mind up about the innocence and guilt of people involved with Homeless Helping Hands.

Donald Armstrong was a scumbag, no one would have said otherwise. In the police interviews, he was certain everyone from work would echo one another about Donald and Charlie. Even so, Mo had to be careful. He had a history and a current anger in him that meant it was essential he kept his composure, especially against the authority that had it in for him.

Mo was stressed and it showed. The last week had tormented him, made worse by his attendance at the Hallington recovery group two nights ago. Lance wasn't there when Mo arrived. Relief made his shoulders lighter. Then, as they all took seats, a smirking Lance strolled in. Mo felt his stomach drop and his anger flare up again. The group was painful and Mo had to switch off to avoid exploding.

'You alright, darling?' Annie asked once they returned to her house.

'Actually no, I'm not, love. That bloody Lance has to stop. He's a jealous dickhead and I feel almost harassed,' Mo had said as he paced her kitchen.

'Aren't you being a bit dramatic? He's always seemed okay to me,' Annie said nonchalantly, kissing Mo on the cheek.

'He isn't okay at all, Annie. He's been taking the piss out of me for ages. Him and others and look what happened to them! Maybe this psycho needs to do away with Lance.'

Mo squinted his eyes as he felt his temperature soaring. Annie glared at him, her green eyes wide, mouth open. Mo couldn't help himself and continued speaking.

'And you know what? I've had a belly full of people feeling sorry for these scumbags.' He shook his head and puffed out air. Pointing at Annie, he tutted. 'They are envious losers. You're a total mug to believe anything else, Annie. That bastard will be laughing his head off at your gullibility as he pulls the wool over your eyes. And you're falling for it!' He let out a sarcastic laugh.

Annie's face froze and Mo knew he had gone too far.

'An…' he began.

Annie glared at him. 'Mo, please leave. I need to be alone

now,' she said, her voice wavering with emotion.

'But, Annie, I, I didn't mean it like…' Mo held his arms out towards Annie.

'I know it's been stressful and scary for you at work, but it's your job. These people need help, just like you did. Like *I* did. Two have been murdered and you've just said…' She put her hand to her mouth.

Mo moved closer, across the tiled kitchen floor. She moved back. 'Please, Mo, respect my wishes and leave now.' Annie's voice was shaking. Her eyes shifted from his gaze and she turned, moving into the hallway, indicating she wanted Mo to do the same.

'For God's sake, Annie. This is what these arseholes want. Can you not see that?' Mo was raising his voice, desperate for Annie to understand.

The colour had drained from her always rosy cheeks. 'Leave please, Mo, you're scaring me.'

Mo grabbed his mouth, gripped with regret for what he said, but stifling the urge to say more — more of what he really felt. He wanted to punch the front door as he pulled it open and slammed it shut less than five seconds later. Shaking, he walked to his car. *I won't let them ruin me,* Mo thought. He started the engine on the dark, rainy night, feeling even the heavens were crying for him.

# Chapter 27: Lorna

'Why didn't you wake me?' Lorna barked at James. She frantically gathered her water bottle and lunch bag from the fridge as some of her long brown hair fell out of a messy bun piled on top of her head.

'Whoa, babe, I tried. You were like a zombie. Your alarm went off, and you just kept opening your eyes and shutting them again, like a sulky teenager.' He laughed, annoying Lorna even more.

'It's not funny, James. I'm stressed enough without being late. You aren't helping.' She looked up; her hazel eyes swollen.

James sat, half eaten toast in hand, shoulders slumped. He shook his head before brushing his hair from his face. 'You know what isn't helping, Lorna? I'll tell you what's not helping — those bloody sleeping tablets you've upped.' He glared at her and she inhaled deeply before looking away and retying her hair. 'That's why you're like a zombie.' Releasing a deflated breath, he pushed his chair out from the dining table, making a squeak across the tiled floor.

Mouth down-turned, he looked at Lorna, her eyes watery as she grabbed the material of her sweatshirt in her fist. His voice softened. 'I know it's hard at work and you're upset and whatever, but popping them like flamin' M&Ms isn't gonna help. See your boss for some support or go to the bloody doctors, cos it's quite clear you can't speak to me anymore.'

James rubbed his forehead as he walked away, leaving his un-eaten breakfast, and the air filled with animosity.

Lorna stood on the cold kitchen tiles, biting her bottom lip as she remained motionless. She stared at the chair where he had been sitting, feeling things were unravelling around her.

# Chapter 28: DS Ronnie Ericson

Ericson pointed at the incident board; photos plastered to it, with writing scribbled underneath. All photos were of people who worked at or used the day centre. 'So, folks, as you all know now, these are our potential suspects and this is our place of focus; Homeless Helping Hands. Today we've asked those involved with the charity to come into the station for formal questioning. So far, we can't rule any of them out as possible suspects to the two homicides.'

He held a pen up to the board and tapped a photo. 'Salvin Yanti has been asked to come in, Donald Armstrong's sidekick. He uses the service, but we have his address in local temporary accommodation if he doesn't turn up. He glanced around the room before moving his pen along the board. 'Lance Cole — another man we want to speak to — is already in the cells downstairs after kicking off at the centre yesterday.' He rolled his eyes. 'Five members of staff are coming in for questioning. One of these is our murderer, I can guarantee. So do your magic, team, and we'll meet again at 6 pm for the briefing.'

Ericson turned to McCardle, who smiled and nodded to her boss as the rest of the team left for their interview rooms, awaiting the arrival of their suspects.

McCardle stretched her neck from side to side and walked over to Ericson. 'Fancy a quick tab before the shenanigans start?' She looked at him, eyebrow raised.

'As you know, McCardle, I'm a non-smoker, but I'll come out for some fresh air from the opposite direction of your puffing,' he lectured, smiling affectionately.

'How's the missus about all the extra hours you're doing?' Ericson asked as she lit up a cigarette outside.

'Lisa's cool about it. She wouldn't be if it was all the time, but she's used the chance to study and catch up with mates,' McCardle replied before taking a draw of her cigarette and blowing in the opposite direction of Ericson.

Ericson leant against the station yard wall and looked up to the dull winter sky. 'She's lucky to have you, McCardle.' He glanced at his colleague, then back up to the clouds. 'You remind me a bit of my Caroline when she was younger. Determined, no bull attitude, but still with a heart the size of a space hopper.' He smiled to the sky.

McCardle turned to him, her blue eyes looking for a facial reaction, despite his gaze remaining fixed on the palette of swirled grey and white that decorated the Northumberland sky. 'Thanks, Boss, that's a lovely thing to say.' Her voice was quiet. 'You miss your Caroline, don't you?'

Ericson moved his head slightly, his lips pressed together. McCardle shifted her gaze to the burning tip of the cigarette that rested in between her forefinger and thumb. She cleared her throat and her cheeks turned slightly red.

'Sorry, Boss. It's none of my business. I didn't mean to pry,' she blurted.

'No. No pet, it's okay. You weren't prying.' He laughed a sad laugh. 'It's nice to be asked, to be honest. And yeah, I miss her a lot.' Ericson rubbed his mouth. 'Work is a good distraction, but she's never far away from there.' Ericson tapped his left temple.

There was a few seconds' silence as both officers realised their conversation may not have been the most professional, but had brought them closer together as humans, as friends. McCardle gently touched her superior's forearm. He flinched, not from the need to pull away, but from the unexpected and immediate feeling of missing comfort from another person. The smallest acts of reassurance and human connection that he didn't realise he needed. Ericson swallowed, then let out a deep breath. Never one to show emotions, especially at work, he felt like a kettlebell had landed in his stomach.

McCardle glanced away from him, sensing his pride was feeling like a toppling game of Jenga. She took the last draw of her cigarette as she tucked her hair behind her ear. Then leant against the yard wall, next to her boss, and looked up at the dull sky. 'I reckon she misses you, too. You're a great man. I hope it isn't the end for you and Caroline.'

Their eyes remained fixed on the ceiling of clouds. Ericson sniffed, let out a sigh, and said, 'Me too, McCardle. Me too. Now let's scrutinise these buggers.'

Two interview rooms were set up, and the team briefed. Ericson would watch the interviews from another room — monitoring for anything suspicious and could drop in as part of the interview if needed. McCardle would lead on the staff interviews. This is where Ericson felt the most useful information would be obtained. Some of the suspects were convicted criminals. Although they knew what to expect, none were masterminds, hence the string of convictions, and this was way above the intelligence of the usual burglar and shoplifter.

Even Lance Cole, who had a list of assault offences, didn't

strike Ericson as a murderer. Still, interviews would be conducted in the usual way; with plenty of scrutiny. One of these people knew more, and Ericson was certain that one of them killed Charlie Sinclair and Donald Armstrong.

First up was Maurice Nutman. He had a record, had served time, and came across as arrogant, in Ericson's opinion. Maurice Nutman arrived poker-faced and dressed like he had been in the pub all night. Alongside him, his solicitor. They had conducted their private consultation after McCardle and Myers gave the solicitor disclosure.

The interview was ready to commence. Mo slumped on the hard plastic chair in the cold interview room, face expressionless, hands on his thighs. His solicitor sat next to him in a shirt and tie, his expensive briefcase on the floor. Behind his glasses, Mo's brown eyes looked heavy; the whites tinged with yellow and dark bags surrounded his stare. DC Myers placed a glass of water in front of him. McCardle explained the circumstances behind the interview and that the conversation would be recorded.

'Maurice Nutman, you are here today as a voluntary attender. You're free to leave at any time. However, if you choose to do this, you may be arrested.'

Mo pursed his lips. He glanced around the small room; white walls, harsh spotlights, and what he knew was a one-way window. He didn't seem nervous — he knew this process all too well and McCardle saw a roll of the eyes.

McCardle began the questioning. 'Tell us about your relationship with Charlie Sinclair and Donald Armstrong, Maurice.'

'It's Mo, not Maurice,' he said like a sulky teen. 'Like I already said, both had been using the service for a while. Charlie more consistently, as Donald was often in prison. Charlie engaged on and off, kept himself to himself until a few months before he died. He had worked closer with the team, progressing, I guess.' He shrugged. 'Then it went wrong after he did a no show to meet his son. He blamed himself and started drinking heavily and taking drugs, we reckon.'

Mo paused for a second and took his gaze from McCardle to Myers. No one else spoke. Mo cleared his throat and continued. 'Charlie was an alcoholic and had PTSD from serving in the army, so his mood was never really stable. But there was a change when he let his son down again.' He took a sip from his glass and wiped his mouth.

McCardle nodded. 'Tell me again about his son. Why did he let him down, Mo?'

'Well, he was going to meet him. It had been arranged by Lorna, Lorna Andrews, who works with us. Then last minute, Charlie hit the bottle, and it all turned to shit. He chose the drink again. So, it never happened. Maybe you need to speak to Tommy?' He raised an eyebrow.

'We know how to do our jobs, thanks, Mo.'

Mo glared at McCardle and an almost inaudible tut escaped his mouth. 'Aye, whatever. Well, that's Charlie. He came in before he died. Kicking off, drunk, shouting and being a right bell… being abusive. Indirect threats and allegations, that type of thing. Calling staff and provoking Lance Cole.' He swallowed and Ericson watched his eyes flit. 'Nothing new for Homeless Helping Hands, but Charlie was vicious and out of character. He probably made enemies that week. The drugs issue started the week before Charlie kicked off and it was clear he was taking something.'

'Do you know that for a fact, Mo?'

He clicked his knuckles on one hand. 'No, but I have been around enough addicts for long enough to know when someone is using, Officer. And there was clearly dealing and possibly more starting.'

McCardle kept her eyes on Nutman. 'Who were Charlie Sinclair's enemies?'

Mo shook his head. 'None that I can think of. But like I said, when you lot came to the centre, enemies are made in minutes in the homeless community. It's the nature of the beast. He upset people that week.'

Ericson watched from the other side of the glass in the interview room. Maurice Nutman's casual response was almost carefree and disinterested, but there were telltale signs in his body language out of his control. Nutman was nervous, and that could be because he was hiding something. He observed as the questioning continued.

'Do you have any enemies, Mo? Being a former service user yourself?'

Mo straightened up in his plastic seat and crossed one foot over the other. 'I never used the centre; it didn't exist when I needed help. But yeah, I was an alcoholic and dabbled with drugs.' Puffing out air, he shook his head slightly. 'I've been in prison; you all know that. I've moved on from that lifestyle. But I'll have enemies just like Stuart will and so will Liam Mallaburn, who works there. We're all in recovery. No doubt Dot Fiddes and Lorna Andrews will have enemies too.' He made a hmph noise. 'There's always one or two pissed off folk. Those still in the chaos don't like it when people do well and sabotage people's success. I've had it. Stu's had it. Liam's had it. Christ, even staff who aren't in recovery get grief from the minority using the service — for having a house, a job, a partner. Jealousy is an all-consuming poison.' He swallowed and tapped a finger on the table separating him from McCardle.

'I see. So, can you please tell us where you were on the day and night of 8th November, Mo?'

Mo lifted his glasses to his bald head. 'I assume you've looked at the rota for Homeless Helping Hands. I was at work that day.'

McCardle nodded, keeping eye-contact with Mo. 'And in the evening? What time did you leave work and what did you do until getting to work the next morning? The morning of 9th November?'

He sighed. 'I left work and went food shopping. Then home, and was in the house all night.'

'Can anyone confirm that?'

Mo glanced at his solicitor, then back to McCardle, a slight smirk on his face. 'No. I live alone. I would have sent a few text messages earlier that night. I usually go to bed around 10 pm, cos I'm up early.'

McCardle remained still in her seat, eyes fixed on Mo, secretly scrutinising his body language. 'No phone calls that evening to anyone?'

'I only usually ring Mason, my son, and it's normally on a Thursday after his footy. The rest of the time, it's texting.'

Ericson rubbed his chin as he watched. Mo seemed like he was trying to keep his cool, but Ericson had noticed him spinning a ring on his right hand a few times and his eyes flitting.

McCardle put her interlocked hands on the table. 'Let's talk about Donald Armstrong. Tell me about him?'

Mo tilted his head up slightly and sniffed. 'Donald was a different character to Charlie. Both addicts and had the behaviours associated with active addiction, but Donald had known enemies. He was a professional at pissing people off and in the last few months, he pissed off many people.'

'Like who, Mo?'

'Well, you'll already know from the notes at the centre that we suspected he was drug dealing — as did your lot.' He pointed at McCardle. 'A couple of near misses — overdoses and a few people dying off site. Then Eve Wright overdosing and dying on site. Donald was behind it all. He had a lot of enemies.' Mo bit the inside of his lip and shook his head slightly. 'We only see the people in the centre for a few hours several times a week. They get up to all sorts outside of the centre. I'm sure he would have enemies dotted all around from over the years.'

Mo glanced at the one-way window and then back to McCardle. 'Homelessness and addiction; it's a different world, Officer.' He sniffed up and placed his hand on the back of his neck. 'We have some amazing success stories at the centre each day. Me, Stu, Liam, we are living proof, and each day people move forward and thrive.' He shrugged. 'However, I've known people to rob their own granny for a bag of heroin. People who have kneecapped someone over a £20 debt. Maybe it was something he had over someone, some info? Or perhaps it was cos he supplied Eve Wright?' He tutted and moved in his seat. 'Maybe Charlie was the same? Sometimes the quiet ones are the worst, eh? I don't know. That's your job to find out.' He took a sip of water and put his hands on his lap afterwards.

'Indeed, Mr Nutman. Do you know for certain that Donald Armstrong was dealing drugs?'

'Nah, not when it comes to actual evidence, but of course,

it was him. Don and Salvin Yanti. You don't have to be a police officer to know that!' Mo let out a chuckle.

Ericson, looking in, couldn't determine whether he was nervous or mocking the police.

McCardle remained straight-faced. 'Let's go back to enemies of Donald Armstrong. Who were they?'

'Donald caused problems with everyone; staff included. You'll know about the incidences with me.' He glanced at his solicitor again, who didn't react.

Ericson stared at Mo through the one-way glass, watching his body language. Mo was clearly uncomfortable, and rightly so, knowing the police had read an awkward and downright unprofessional account of this guy's behaviour. Ericson and McCardle had read the notes at Homeless Helping Hands and knew of the suspension and investigation against Maurice Nutman, which resulted from an almost physical altercation with Donald Armstrong a few days before his death. Maurice Nutman was a loose cannon in Ericson's mind and far from professional.

'Yes, Mo, we are aware of the incident that led to your suspension. Can you tell us about it?'

'Well, I can't see what it's got to do with this?' He jerked his head towards his solicitor, who nodded.

'At this point, Mr Nutman, we are trying to rule people out of the investigation. It's crucial we have all the information leading up to the death of the victims.'

Mo let out a sigh before continuing. 'He'd been taunting me. Me and most at the centre. Him and Lance Cole, who I hope you are speaking to. Donald was eavesdropping on a private conversation between me and Stu. Stu will confirm it. Donald was listening and commented about my girlfriend,

Annie. It was jealousy and I'll admit it got my back up, and I responded.' Mo looked across the table and held his hands up. 'Stu asked Donald to leave and then I was suspended as Stu was concerned it may have gone further. It was for my protection as well,' he said, the last few words quieter.

'Further as in physically?'

Mo nodded.

'For the tape please, Mo. She pointed to the recording device.'

'*Yes*, physically.'

Ericson shook his head from his side of the glass. Mo Nutman was an angry, volatile man.

McCardle nodded slightly. 'What did Donald Armstrong say to provoke this reaction?'

'He said my girlfriend, Annie Joyce, was sleeping with people, including Lance Cole, and that Donald might try his luck. He called her a bike. He's... he was someone who didn't like women, you know that from his offences.' Mo tapped his feet on the ground.

'And did you see Donald Armstrong again after this?'

'No, I was suspended and when I came back to Homeless Helping Hands the next week, Donald was dead.' Mo lifted his chin slightly and looked towards the window where Ericson stood, observing him.

*Come on, crack*, Ericson thought.

'Where were you on the night of 10th January, Mo? The night Donald Armstrong was killed?'

Mo rubbed the back of his neck. 'I was with my girlfriend, Annie. She came to see me at about 8 pm and stayed all night.'

'And she will confirm this?'

'Yeah.'

'Okay, thanks. And what about enemies of Donald Armstrong Mo? Anyone who may have reasons to want rid of him?'

Mo made a humph noise. 'How long have you got? Given he was dealing, exploiting and technically murdering people himself through his drug pushing…'

'That's speculation at the moment.'

Rolling his eyes, he continued. 'Aye, whatever. Enemy wise, take your pick. He was pushing, pimping, and threatening as many people as he could manipulate. Perhaps it was a parent of the kids he killed that wanted revenge? The kids he pushed drugs onto. Then there's the people he's sold to, other dealers. There are enough gangs in Northumberland for a few plastic gangsters to think they are part of the Cartel; the rural *Breaking Bad*!' Mo let out a little chuckle.

Ericson was becoming increasingly annoyed that this so-called professional was taking the fact a murderer was at large with such relaxed humour.

McCardle leant forward. 'Give me some names, Mo?'

'Kurt Harper is still a big-time dealer in Northumberland. You'll already know that,' grinned Mo.

Ericson watched the smugness in Mo, as if he was one step ahead of the law. Maybe it was nerves or diversion techniques. Maurice Nutman sure as hell couldn't stand Donald Armstrong. That was as transparent as tap water.

'He's not a centre user and won't be doing his own work. The stabbing that happened last year, in the squat in Ashmouth? The guy you lot caught. He was one of Harper's men. Crosley ain't a big place, and not when it comes to drug customers.'

'What about people using the centre, Mo?'

Mo sat forward, arms on the table. 'Salvin Yanti was Donald's partner. Yanti was relatively new to the centre, maybe sent from Harper or just a lone wolf, thinking he could be the next Escobar. Then there's Lance Cole; sneaky and likes to play the victim. Not beyond his capabilities.' Mo curled his top lip before taking a sip of water.

Ericson could tell there was no love lost between Mo and some people using the centre and wondered why Nutman was even working there, unless to commit crimes himself? It felt like Nutman carried a real insidious hatred for more than just Armstrong. Perhaps a hatred enough to want to 'dispose' of some of them. Ericson didn't trust Mo — he had an agenda and it would just take finding that weakness to expose it.

'What about your colleagues, Mo? What was their relationship like with Donald Armstrong?'

'Are you asking if I think my colleagues killed Donald Armstrong or Charlie Sinclair, Officer?'

McCardle didn't flicker, remaining composed. 'If you want to interpret it that way, Mr Nutman.'

Mo laughed and crossed his arms, looking at McCardle and glancing at Myers for only the second time during the interview. 'No one had any reason to hurt either of those men. We work hard, put up with crap and do the jobs of several professionals, including yourselves.' His top lip curled. 'So no, I don't think any of my colleagues had reason.' He sneered and let out a hmph noise.

'Mr Nutman. Do you drink alcohol, take any prescription drugs, or other people's prescription drugs, or illegal drugs?'

Mo's eyes widened. He looked at his solicitor, who nodded slightly, then looked back at McCardle and Myers. 'Seriously? No, I do not. I'm an alcoholic. So even though I want to drink and more than bloody usual right now, funnily enough, no, I'm abstinent. Why are you asking about drugs? You think I'm using drugs, or friggin' selling them?'

'No one said that, Mo. Just please answer the question.'

Mo shook his head and clenched his jaw. 'Just some anti-depressants, okay? Citalopram, a small dose.' He almost spat out.

'And your GP details, Mo?'

Again, Mo looked at his solicitor, hoping for him to inter-ject, but got a brief hand gesture indicating for Mo to give his details. 'Seriously, you lot wanna be out there catching this maniac!'

McCardle made a note of Maurice Nutman's GP before asking the further questions that she knew wouldn't go down well, they never did. 'Would you be prepared to volunteer your mobile phone for examination? And consent to a search of your home if required?'

'You want to check up my arse for any heroin while you're at it, do you?' he sneered, pushing his mobile phone across the table and tutting.

'That won't be necessary, Mr Nutman. I think that's all we need to ask for now. Interview terminated.'

DC Myers turned off the recording, and the officers stood up to see Maurice Nutman and his solicitor out.

McCardle and Myers returned to the interview room and Ericson joined them.

'Great work. Get Annie Joyce in here asap,' Ericson said to his colleagues, as he left the room to see how the interview of Lance Cole had gone. It was going to be a long day.

# Chapter 29: DS Ronnie Ericson

Ericson walked down the corridor to the other interview room where DC Boyd and DC Lucas were finishing questioning Lance Cole — who by now had sobered up and been given a fixed penalty for drunk and disorderly following the fight the previous day.

'He was shifty, Boss, but not sure if that's down to nerves or guilt. He had an alibi for the night of the Sinclair homicide. Said he was at the B&B in town, where he had a room. They have CCTV and night concierge, so we can check that out. The night of Armstrong's death, he has no alibi and said he was sleeping rough in the park until his brother took him in for a few weeks. He said the Homeless Helping Hands outreach team saw him the night after, but he claims he had a skinful on the night of Armstrong's homicide, before passing out. There's no CCTV in the park, but he would have walked past the shopping centre. Might be something there. We will check it out, Boss.'

'Great, thanks, Boyd. Did he throw up any names, any enemies?'

'He mentioned Armstrong, in particular, was dealing. A few overdoses associated with the heroin he was supplying. But he said Sinclair was a different type of bloke; no harm. He has a real issue with the staff and reckons it's one of them — that the victims had something on the staff or on the place. Corruption, fraud, cover-ups; he named them all, Boss.'

Ericson leant against the interview room door and rubbed his chest, feeling indigestion.

'Reckons Maurice Nutman has something to do with it. He seems to have it in for him in particular and mentioned he sleeps with vulnerable women. But that Stuart Bowden always knows what's going on. He even mentioned the female staff, Lorna Andrews and Dot Fiddes. Lance Cole reckons the only one not involved is Liam Mallaburn, another staff member.'

Ericson rubbed his mouth, pondering on what his colleague was telling him. Sometimes people using services saw and knew a lot more than staff realised.

'Did Cole mention a drug dealer, Harper?' Ericson asked.

Lucas shook his head. 'No Boss, he only mentioned Salvin Yanti, but thought he wouldn't have the balls to do away with Armstrong. He was too wet behind the ears, apparently,' he said, smirking as he shrugged.

'Okay, thanks both.' Ericson left the room with an idea for another plan of attack if required. It was a risky one, but something that just may be essential if they didn't get the bite they needed today.

The next interview was with Lorna Andrews, accompanied by her solicitor. McCardle and Myers had the Homeless Helping Hands worker in the interview room following consultation with her solicitor. Water in hand, Lorna's knees bounced slightly. She was the youngest staff member at twenty-nine, but looked younger as she hunched on the seat and shivered. The room was cold and clinical, designed to be a comfort repellent. Ericson watched from behind the glass as the interview got going.

McCardle began. 'Lorna, we understand you were Charlie Sinclair's support worker. Is that right?'

'Yeah, I worked with Charlie. Just brief interventions at first, but then I started key-working him.'

McCardle nodded. 'What does key-working involve?'

Lorna put her hands on her lap. 'Well, it's more 1-2-1 support. Whatever the person using the service needs.' She shrugged. 'Referrals to alcohol and drug services, mental health help, housing help, benefits, that sort of thing. Sometimes it's just a chat and emotional support.'

'Alright. So, what 1-2-1 help did Charlie need?'

'Charlie was homeless, as you know. He was a loner, really. I mean, he chatted with other veterans at the centre, but I think pride, or maybe trust, kept him a little separate. He hadn't opened up much to the staff until I started working with him.' Lorna smiled weakly and glanced at her hands in her lap before meeting McCardle's gaze again.

'Why do you think he opened up to you rather than any other staff, Lorna?'

'I dunno. Maybe cos I was new, didn't have any knowledge of him. He'd been using the centre on an off for years, chatting to Dot occasionally, but not really anyone else.'

'Do you think it could have been that he didn't want to work with staff in recovery themselves?'

Lorna put her palms up slightly. 'Erm, I dunno.' She shrugged. 'Perhaps. But he knew nothing about me. Not that there is anything to tell.' She laughed nervously and Ericson moved closer to the glass, observing her run a hand over her long brown hair.

Lorna Andrews was the only staff member they knew little about given she had no previous involvement with the police, except receiving a caution for a public order offence four years ago — an argument with a now ex-boyfriend on the streets of Newcastle after a night out. *She was right,* thought Ericson. *The people using the service wouldn't know her.* Lorna was from Wallsend, in North Tyneside, thirteen miles from the centre, and had only recently moved to Northumberland.

Lorna rubbed her thumb and forefinger together before moving her hand to her wrist. 'All the other staff and most of the volunteers are from Crosley, or Ashmouth, and Hallington. I'm not from Northumberland originally. Those staff in recovery, well, the people using the service, always know one of them.'

McCardle nodded. 'Tell us, Lorna, what work did you do with Charlie Sinclair?'

Lorna touched her mouth before speaking. 'Some benefit work, budgeting. We talked about him getting a flat. We did some work on reconnecting him with his son, Tommy.' She took a sip of water and looked at both McCardle and Myers.

'But that never happened, did it? Charlie never met up with Tommy?'

She turned her gaze to the floor momentarily. 'He, Charlie, didn't go through with it. Tommy had agreed to see him and Charlie didn't turn up.' Lorna shrugged and pulled at the cuffs of her sweatshirt as if still chilly.

'Sounds like you did a lot of work to set it up for Charlie?'

Lorna swallowed and her gaze went to her lap. 'Yeah, I did. Charlie had said he wanted to meet up with Tommy, try to be a dad. He was in a better place. But then he just stopped caring again, I guess. That's what alcohol does to some people, sadly.' She pressed her lips together.

Ericson leant forward, his head almost touching the one-way glass. He could see the emotions seep out of Lorna — on her face, in her body language, and voice. She had cared about Charlie and Tommy. But emotions can take us to the extreme.

McCardle placed her hands on the table. 'Take me back. Charlie had been drinking again and then went missing for a few days around the time he was meant to meet Tommy?'

Lorna's gaze returned to the detectives. Nodding, she cleared her throat. 'Stuart and me saw him on night outreach. He was drunk and swearing. The next day he didn't turn up and the day after we were meant to meet Tommy. When Charlie came in to the centre, a few days later, he was intoxicated and abusive. We think he started taking drugs and then he was dead.'

'How did it make you feel after all that work and Charlie didn't turn up to meet his son, Lorna?'

Lorna glanced at her solicitor, who nodded. She moved slightly in her chair, clearly uncomfortable physically and by the questions. 'Disappointed. Charlie had a chance. He chose the drink over his son. That's the bottom line. This is the way people in addiction go on though. I bet Tommy knew after being let down so much in the past.' Her nostrils flared.

'Did Charlie have any enemies?'

Lorna shook her head. 'I don't know. Probably. People in our service often do. They've lied and deceived people, caused heartache and stuff.'

She looked over to the one-way window where Ericson stood behind. He was certain Lorna Andrews wouldn't know what it was for.

'He was vicious in the days before his death and came in arguing with anyone he could. Calling staff, arguing with his friends and other people using the service. Then he was abusing staff. But we're used to that. We don't take it personally.'

'Where were you on the night of Charlie's death, Lorna? The 8th November?'

'I was at home all night, weary from work,' Lorna answered quickly.

McCardle held her gaze. 'And your partner, is it James Ord? He can vouch for that?'

'Yeah. Well, he was out until about 10:30 or 11 pm as he plays football, you see, with work.' A smile flashed across her face. 'Then he went for a few drinks — celebration drinks he calls them, even if they lose!' She let out a bizarre laugh that made Ericson squint his eyes. 'So, it was just Angus, my dog and me, until then.'

'Did you call anyone? Anyone pop by?'

Lorna paused for a second. 'No, I don't think so. I just had dinner and flicked through the TV, read a bit, had a bath. It's what I usually do when James's at footy.'

McCardle nodded. 'How did you feel when you heard the news of Charlie's death, Lorna? Sounds like you did lots of work with him, tying to help him?'

Lorna took a gulp of her water before placing her hands back on her lap. Ericson moved slightly and could see her knees were bouncing again as her eyes dropped to her lap. Lorna Andrews remained silent for a few more seconds than was comfortable. Myers coughed and Lorna glanced up, blinking rapidly. It was like she had been in a short trance, thought Ericson, as he rubbed the small of his back.

'Like everyone else, I was sad. Charlie could have turned things around. He had help and opportunity. We all assumed he'd overdosed after starting to take drugs. It was sad.'

'I understand you took it badly when the young girl in the service died, Lorna. An Eve Wright?'

Lorna touched her collarbone and swallowed. 'We all did. She was so young and Eve was different. She hadn't become entrenched and addicted like the older ones. Her death was caused by people pushing drugs onto her and exploiting her. We all know that.' Lorna looked away and bit her lip before returning her gaze to the officers in front of her.

'Who do you think was pushing the drugs?'

Lorna sighed. 'Donald Armstrong. That's probably why he ended up dead. He would have made many enemies through his life, I guess, and even more in the past few months. Lots of people have been hurt and died cos of his drugs — most of them being young people.'

'Donald Armstrong had lots of enemies, you say?'

'Yeah. Everyone knew what he was up to. Your colleagues who kept dropping into the centre knew. She knew.' Lorna pointed to DC Myers. 'But we had no evidence. Donald was clever, manipulative, and not a nice person.' Lorna took a drink of water and Ericson noticed her hand was unsteady. Placing the glass back down, she moved her watch strap that popped out from the cuff of her lilac jumper before interlocking her fingers and putting her hands back on her lap.

'Okay, Lorna. What was your relationship with Donald Armstrong?'

'I didn't keywork him, so it was more general support and interaction. I was assigned to keywork him, but he never engaged properly. I got the feeling he didn't like women, to be honest. Although, he didn't seem to like men either.' She raised her chin and sniffed.

'What about the staff? How did they feel about Donald?'

'Donald was dangerous. He was really mean and manipulative. Vindictive. He was always stirring and causing bother, especially involving the people he knew. Mo, in particular, he was vicious with him and there were a few outbursts.'

McCardle remained focused on Lorna Andrews and she leant forward slightly. 'Can you give us examples of any outbursts between Mo and Donald, Lorna?'

Lorna straightened up in her chair before speaking. 'In the weeks before he died, there was an altercation outside the centre. Another person was involved, Lance Cole. I didn't see it, but Dot did and everyone was talking about it,' she rushed, almost breathless as she said it.

Ericson pulled his hand over his mouth, leaving it on his chin momentarily as he observed.

'Donald and Mo were arguing. Lance got involved. Mo got into trouble. Then Liam from the team said another incident happened where Mo was going to physically attack Donald, but Stuart intervened. He was suspended from work for it.'

*Was that a smirk on her face?* thought Ericson as he narrowed his eyes.

McCardle nodded as Lorna put her hand up to her lips and bit on a fingernail. 'Thanks, Lorna. Sounds like Donald upset many people?'

Lorna stared almost past McCardle — just catching her gaze, but somehow, in her own world. 'He went around, causing chaos to get what he wanted. He didn't even seem bothered when Eve died, when he killed Eve. She died in our toilets from the heroin he pushed onto her. He was a murderer and she was…' Wringing her hands together, she took a second before continuing. 'A scared, abused young woman who he preyed on. He was a bast… a horrible man, to be honest, and he would never change.'

Ericson studied Lorna. Emotion was carved into her face when she talked about Eve. She held her sweatshirt to her arms, as if to provide herself comfort. He made a note for any further interviews to bring Eve up again.

'What about Lance Cole? What are your thoughts on him, Lorna?'

'Lance is a troublemaker and nasty with it. He's abused staff and sticks his nose into everything. It wouldn't surprise me if he was involved. He hated Charlie and Donald and hates most people, including staff. He's a liar.' She pushed her bottom lip out and frowned.

'Okay, Lorna. I want to ask your whereabouts now on the night of 10th January?'

Lorna replied quickly, 'I was at home all night.'

'Can anyone corroborate that? James Ord perhaps?'

Lorna nodded. 'Yeah, James can.'

'Were you together all night?'

'Yes, all night I was in with James.' Lorna's eyes remained on McCardle.

'Do you drink alcohol, take any prescription drugs, or other people's prescription drugs, or illegal drugs?'

Lorna hesitated. *Was it the shock of the personal question or something more?* Ericson wondered.

'Erm, no, I don't. I drink rarely, not a massive fan of the stuff, to be honest.'

'And any medication or drugs, Lorna?'

'No, none,' she replied.

'We will need to get your GP details. And Miss Andrews, would you be prepared to volunteer your mobile phone for examination and consent to a search of your home if required?'

Lorna's eyes widened.

'This is procedural, Lorna.'

'Alright. I guess. I haven't got my phone with me, but yes.'

'Great thanks Lorna, you've been really helpful.'

Lorna nodded as Myers got up to see her out. Ericson, still on the other side of the one-way glass, wondered why people went into this field of work. It seemed there was such a divide between people who wanted to change and those who had no intention. Lorna sounded exasperated, as had her colleague, Maurice Nutman. Ericson knew people in the field cared and wanted to help, but the burn-out and realisation that you can't force people to change must be demotivating.

Lorna had only worked in the field a short time and volunteered a brief period before that. But she was young and perhaps a little naïve. Or the opposite. Maybe she had more experience than she was letting on.

# Chapter 30: DS Ronnie Ericson

Ericson listened in on the interview with Salvin Yanti, who answered questions with a mixture of one-word answers and 'no comment.' A few snippets of possible useful information were obtained and at least the shitters had been put up Yanti for a while. There were still three more Homeless Helping Hands staff members to interview. Boyd and Lucas were interviewing Liam Mallaburn and Dot Fiddes.

Stuart Bowden was next to see McCardle and Myers. Then there was Kurt Harper, who Ericson knew from other operations. It would be interesting to hear Harper's take on Donald Armstrong as a drugs lord. Annie Joyce and James Ord, the partners of Maurice Nutman and Lorna Andrews, also needed speaking to ASAP. Then there was the family of the victims to speak to again.

Ericson walked past the vending machine on his return to interview room one. He glanced at the treats and, almost immediately, his tummy rumbled. Ignoring it, his thoughts bounced to Caroline's birthday celebration and meeting up with her and Kelsie. The last eleven months had made him reflect. Perhaps not the first six when he was in denial and threw himself into work and wine each night, but there was fuel in his belly for more than solving crimes and in Caroline, he had lost someone that was irreplaceable.

It could be different. It would be different if Caroline gave him another chance. Ericson snapped out of his daydream as he returned to watching the interviews. Stuart Bowden had just arrived and McCardle was waiting for Myers to come back from a call before starting the interview. She was outside the room as Ericson approached.

'Third time lucky, perhaps, Boss,' she said, nodding towards Stuart Bowden, who sat in the interview room with his solicitor.

Ericson looked at Stuart Bowden, who appeared pale and tired, with his jumper hanging off his narrow shoulders.

'There're a few leads from Boyd and Lucas. We'll know more at the briefing.'

Myers returned, chewing on a half sandwich. Two things the job always prevented; going to the toilet when you first feel the urge and eating at normal times.

'Let's get this show on the road,' Ericson said sarcastically, rubbing his hands together as his colleagues walked the few steps to the interview room to speak with Stuart Bowden.

After introductions, McCardle explained the interview process, reiterating that although questions had already been asked at the day centre more informally, Stuart needed to give as much detail as possible — even if that meant repeating what he had previously stated. Stuart nodded quickly, acknowledging understanding as his clasped hands bounced slightly on the table between him and the detectives.

McCardle got started with the questions. 'Stuart, tell us about Charlie Sinclair and your relationship with him.'

Stuart nodded. 'Charlie had been using the service sporadically for several years, engaging now and then with support. He was a quiet man, had a few friends, mainly the veterans. He'd been sleeping rough for a while. I think he suffered more with his mental health than he ever let on.'

Stuart looked down at his hands that rested on the table. 'Charlie was of that age, where, well, asking for help is harder. He was a nice guy, respectful to me and the team, until the end. Lorna did most of the recent work with him until his death.' Stuart took a sip of water and leant back in his seat, running a hand over his dark hair.

Ericson could see he was twitchy and he looked like he needed a decent meal and a good wash.

'How had he been the last few months before his death, Stuart?'

'Up and down, to be honest. It felt like he may be at the point where he might accept accommodation. We also thought he might engage with treatment services better as he was reducing his drinking and had arranged to meet up with his son, reconnect with his family.'

Ericson noticed Stuart Bowden's legs twitching about under the table. Not quite a full-on Irish dance, but there was definitely some restlessness and Stuart was losing his cool by the second.

'What about the days leading up to his homicide? His behaviour changed. Do you think it was to do with not meeting his son, Tommy?'

Stuart nodded. 'He began drinking heavily again, taking drugs that we know of now. We think it was the build-up to seeing Tommy. Nerves perhaps, regret, reality. Alcohol and PTSD don't make for a sound mind.' He chuckled, but seeing no response from the police officers, he coughed and continued. 'Charlie started drinking, not engaging and then he missed seeing his Tommy on the arranged visit and it turned more intense. We saw him on outreach and he was less than pleased to see us. Then he came to the centre shouting and swearing, abusing the staff.'

Stuart shook his head. 'He was threatening and squared up to other service users. It was a shock, to be honest, and it felt like a kick in the teeth for the team. Lorna in particular, who as a newer member of staff, wasn't used to the let-down that comes with the chaos and complexities of some people using the service. Us older, time-served workers have a thicker skin. We've been there, know it can be hard, and know we don't give up on helping people.' He moved in his seat and Ericson saw him wipe his sweating brow, despite the room being cold.

'Who were Charlie Sinclair's enemies, Stuart?'

Stuart took a deep breath. 'I don't think he had any. Well, none that we were aware of. He was a likeable bloke, not a threat. But that last week, he annoyed people, so who knows?'

McCardle kept her eyes on him as she continued. 'There were suspicions about drug use leading up to his death. Could he have made enemies in the drugs circuit?'

Stuart shrugged. 'I doubt it. I can't see Charlie going from years of alcohol misuse and no drug taking to being the biggest drug user or dealer in Northumberland in a matter of weeks. I suspect it was just the green, cannabis, and that's hardly top of the money chain. But you never know what goes on outside and even inside the centre.' He took a sip of water and readjusted his position in the hard chair. 'Obviously, someone was angry enough to kill him! Maybe something that went way back or someone from the past. I honestly don't know.' He shrugged again and looked at Myers before back to McCardle.

McCardle nodded. 'What about your staff's relationship with Charlie Sinclair?'

'The team liked Charlie. I can't recall any major issues.

Only a few outbursts in the week leading up to his death, which you know about. A bit of name calling from Charlie to the staff, me included. But we all knew he didn't mean it.'

'Do you have any enemies, Stuart, being a former service user yourself?'

Ericson stood closer to the one-way glass, eyeing the man he hadn't liked from the moment they met. Stuart Bowden laughed slightly at this comment. Perhaps nerves, perhaps because it was true. It was a small world, and even smaller in the recovery community. He straightened his shoulders and didn't respond to the query, as if it was a joke question. McCardle raised her eyebrows, and he cleared his throat.

'I'm sure I have many, Officer. I bar people from the centre. I submit safeguarding referrals people don't want me to make. I ring the police regularly. It's my job and part of that makes me unpopular as much as we also help.'

'I understand. So, can you tell us where you were on the day and night of 8th November, Stuart?'

Stuart swallowed and itched his nose. 'I was at my brother Johnny's that night. I go most weeks when he has his daughter, my niece. She normally goes to bed about 9 pm, then Johnny and me have a catch up. I would have gone home about 11 pm. I drive past the shopping centre, so I'm sure one of the many CCTV cameras would have picked up my car. Then when I got in, I was on social media for a bit until I went to sleep just after midnight. I was at work by 7 am the next morning, as usual.'

Stuart seemed confident in his answer, despite the nervous body language he displayed, and Ericson knew it was rehearsed.

'Okay. Let's talk about Donald Armstrong. Tell me about

him.'

Stuart sighed. 'Donald was a troubled soul. He had been around the circuit for a long time and was in and out of prison, as you'll know. Some people are more challenging to work with.' He rubbed his slightly pointed chin. 'But we never give up on folk. It's our job to keep supporting, keep believing. It's just what we do and for so many, it works.' He paused and sighed, shifting in the hard seat. 'At first, we thought Donald might make a go of it this time. But then the usual behaviours, the cracks started to show. Donald didn't care; he had that invincible attitude.'

Ericson wasn't sure if that was a sneer that scurried across Stuart Bowden's face.

McCardle leant forward. 'You suspected he was drug dealing in and around the premises of the day centre. Is that right Stuart?'

'Yeah, it was obvious, but we had no evidence and your colleagues were monitoring. Even with the overdose and subsequent death of Eve Wright and others in the community, nothing was found on the premises. But we knew it was Donald; he was just clever with it.'

'What do you think Salvin Yanti's role was?'

'Salvin was running and pushing drugs, no doubt about it. He was Donald's second in command. But he's gone quiet these last few weeks, strangely!' Stuart Bowden let out a sarcastic laugh.

It felt inappropriate to Ericson, from someone who managed a service and had built it from scratch. But he was saying the same things as his colleagues. Stuart was the manager, but really, he was a man who had lost it all and then got a little back and based a charity on it. Didn't make him professional and certainly didn't make him squeaky clean when it came to adhering to the law.

'What about enemies of Donald Armstrong? Who were they?'

'He probably had quite a few, to be honest. Families of the people his drugs had killed, allegedly, of course. People from prison, other dealers.'

'Any names, Stuart?'

Stuart shook his head. 'None that I know for sure, but you know the names of the people who possibly deal drugs in Northumberland, Officer.' He raised his eyebrow as he took a gulp of water.

'Kurt Harper? Does he ring a bell, Stuart?'

Stuart nodded.

McCardle pointed to the recorder. 'For the tape, Stuart?'

'Yes, Kurt Harper does ring a bell,' Stuart said slightly abruptly.

'What about anyone else using the centre? Perhaps Lance Cole?'

'Lance Cole is harmless in general. A drinker and trouble maker in some ways, but more of a gossip than anything else. I doubt he would be in at that level.'

'What about the link between Charlie Sinclair and Donald Armstrong? Can you think of a possible relationship, Stuart?'

Stuart crossed his arms over his chest and leant back. 'Both in and out of homelessness. Both in addiction. Both are estranged from their families and both use Homeless Helping Hands services. That's all I can think of.'

Ericson made a quick note. He needed to find similarities in all the interview notes once they were done; indicators, trends, things that made no sense. But ultimately, he needed to find the one thing that linked the two victims. Stuart Bowden had the most information, the greatest knowledge of people using his service and of his staff team. He knew everyone the most — it was his job.

'I want to ask you about your team's relationship with Donald Armstrong. What was that like, Stuart?'

Stuart opened his mouth and hesitated, then glanced at the glass where Ericson stood behind, unseen. 'Donald was someone we all tried to help at some point. Dot tried, using her son as comparison to encourage Donald off the drugs before he went into prison last time. Liam had done a little work with him as well. I tried years ago and he would still often come to me if he needed something minor, like a support letter or information on a service. I think he trusted me as I'd been around the longest and had never been addicted to drugs or been in prison with him, you know?'

McCardle nodded. 'What about Maurice Nutman? I understand they had a little more of a history?'

Stuart took a long drink of water and rubbed the back of his neck. 'Mo was in prison with Donald a good few years ago. They didn't get on and they never gelled in the centre. Mo will tell you that himself. They made no bones about it, but Mo was always professional and did his job.'

'Always professional?' McCardle glared at Stuart.

He coughed and his cheeks flushed. 'Yeah, well, on the whole. You'll know about the few incidents recently, from the system notes. Donald was getting unmanageable, and it was linked to the suspicion of the drug dealing. He was being abusive, flinging accusations, and being deflective. There were a few run-ins with staff. Mainly shouting and name calling from Donald, but also some vague allegations, saying Mo was bent.'

Stuart wiped the back of a hand across his mouth. 'Donald went for Mo outside one day and then another time, he was winding Mo up, after listening in on a conversation between Mo and me. Mo got upset, and I dealt with it.' He took a deep breath. 'Mo is a good worker. A good person and a role model to many. It can just be hard. Conflicts of interest...' He stopped mid-sentence and shook his head.

'Why was Mo upset, Stuart?'

'Well, like documented in the notes, Officer, Donald heard Mo and me talking about his new girlfriend, Annie. Donald then started talking disrespectfully about her, saying she was having sex with multiple men, including Lance Cole, and that he might try it on with her. You can understand why Mo would have been upset. Nothing went further. It got dealt with, like the notes say.' His brown eyes widened.

Stuart Bowden sounded defensive. *Who was he defending?* wondered Ericson; himself or Maurice Nutman?

McCardle continued. 'What happened outside with the altercation, Mr Bowden?'

'Lance Cole was there. No staff were, but Dot Fiddes caught the end. By Donald's account at the time, Mo was looking down on him. Calling him a loser, saying people were after him. Mo said Donald was talking about his private life and indicating he was a liar. It was clear Donald was jealous Mo was in recovery and had kept sober and clean. It happens in the community; jealousy and sabotage. They become obsessions. It got heated, then Dot intervened.'

McCardle nodded. 'And how did you deal with it, Stuart?'

'I gave Mo a bollocking, told him it was unacceptable, and he had to walk away from confrontation. And told Donald he couldn't be shouting at staff and he was on a warning. I wasn't there, so it was a case of trying to piece it together. Lance has it in for Mo, so I couldn't be convinced his account was the truth.' Stuart shrugged.

McCardle paused momentarily, and Ericson knew she was trying to get Stuart Bowden to reveal something through his body language. He kept her gaze for a few seconds before shrugging again and McCardle spoke.

'Why does Lance Cole have it in for Maurice Nutman?'

Ericson watched Stuart Bowden fidget in his chair. A nerve had been touched. That was what McCardle had wanted.

He ran his tongue across his bottom lip. 'Jealousy and sabotage, again. Lance has taken a fancy for Mo's new girlfriend, by all accounts. He's been turning up to Mo's regular recovery group in Hallington, far out of Lance's way, and flirting with Annie. I'm sure Mo can update you. Lance likes to gossip, so he was stirring it and trying to provoke a reaction. The staff team have all seen him do it on some level.' Stuart Bowden smiled nervously.

He was protecting his colleague, his friend. McCardle and Ericson had already read about the incident in the Homeless Helping Hands system notes that they had been analysing the last week. But hearing Stuart talk about it was important for more context and, most importantly, emotion.

McCardle nodded, giving nothing away. 'What about Donald's relationship with another member of staff, Lorna Andrews? I understand she was meant to be key-working Eve Wright? If Donald was the suspect, that must have been difficult for you all, but especially Lorna?'

Stuart swallowed. 'Eve's death was hard for us all, but we support one another as a team and we supported Lorna.

Lorna had little interaction with Donald. He didn't engage. We all just provided brief interventions with him, despite trying.' He shook his head.

'And where were you Stuart, on the night of 10th January?'

'I was home alone all night. I was exhausted from recent events, as you can imagine. So, for the last few weeks, I've had as many calm and early nights as I can get.'

'Can you remember ringing anyone? Any social media?'

'No calls. But I would have been on Facebook until I went to sleep, which would have been around 10:30 pm.'

'Thanks, Mr Bowden. Would you be prepared to volunteer your mobile phone for examination and consent to a search of your home if required?'

Stuart looked at his solicitor, who nodded it was okay. 'Yes, I suppose so, if needed. I've got nothing to hide.'

'Thanks Stuart. And can I ask, do you drink alcohol or take any prescribed, non-prescribed, or illegal drugs?'

Stuart let out a sarcastic chuckle. 'I've had enough substances to last me five lifetimes.'

'Is that a no?'

'Yes, Officer, it's a no.'

'We will require your GP details if that's okay, Mr Bowden. Then there's nothing else we need to ask at this stage.'

Ericson looked down at his notebook with scribbles of observations from the interviews that he would cross reference with the recordings and notes. He yawned and shook his head. It was going to be a long evening and Ericson was determined to have something of substance for the briefing in the morning.

# Chapter 31

Sitting in their car, they stared at their shaking hands as uncertainty threatened to suffocate them. Surely the police wouldn't ring their partner straight away to make a statement verifying they were an alibi on the night of the incident? Licking their dry lips, they closed their eyes and attempted to steady their breathing.

*I answered the questions. It'll be fine*, they thought to themselves, hoping that when they opened their eyes, they would be in a different world — in a different life, where Mam had never died. Where the domino effect of their trauma wouldn't have placed them there, in the car park of the local police station, having endured a grilling, and now engulfed in doubt.

That smug detective and her nodding dog colleague had people to interview all day from Homeless Helping Hands as well as people using the service and hopefully others. Perhaps the police would blame someone else. Maybe there was some questionable evidence that was enough to suspect another. Then it hit them, like a speeding train. The severity. It was murder; times two.

Yelping, they felt a jolt of panic earthquake through them. Blood pulsating to a deafening beat in their temples as their heart fought with their tongue for space in their mouth. They looked straight ahead to the misty day outside but their eyes almost wouldn't function as anxiety encased them and an internal voice screamed that time was perhaps running out.

'Fuck,' they cried, banging their hands off the steering wheel. They knew this would happen possibly at some point; the formal questioning of the team and people using the day centre. But somewhere, in their mind, they felt certain some dead beat, like Lance Cole or some scumbag criminal or drug dealer, like Salvin Yanti, would get the blame.

There were a few people dossing around the day centre, existing rather than living, who would jump at the chance for a prison stretch and for some folk to think they were capable of disposing of people. Hands gripping an unmoving steering wheel, they bit back the anger and fear. The police had no evidence. Nothing. They had to remember that.

They thought about the blue carrier bag, hidden in its secret place. Perhaps they could plant it somewhere in the centre, or on someone. Would it have any fingerprints on? They'd used gloves but weren't convinced. It could get them off the hook or implicate them. Putting their head on the steering wheel, they dug their fingernails into their scalp. Life had always been painfully hard. *Why had it always been so hard?*

'It's not fucking fair!' they shouted before biting hard on their inner lip until they tasted the metallic flavour of blood. They couldn't bring themselves to acknowledge they were a murderer — it felt sinister and, in their head, murder hadn't been what it was about. It was about saving others, ending mental torture for loved ones.

They had done the world and, more importantly, Tommy, Donald's family, and all the young people Donald would continue to murder, a favour. What they wished someone would have done for them all those years ago. What they had done was a positive thing — they believed that, even after the awful interrogation from the police.

That detective; McCardle, didn't like them. Looking at them with a sneer and trying to trip them up. Funny how the police were never any help all those years ago. When Albert would be drunk driving. No one helped the way they should have; their 'duty of care'. All those professionals let it get worse, or couldn't read between the lines of a child too scared to be honest. Then, as an adult, no one wanted to know.

They rubbed their wrist and looked at the dull sky; the white clouds merging into murky grey. Their own sunshine was fading. Life was getting colder, harder, uncaring. The snippet of happiness that they'd had, beginning to freeze. No doubt, there would be more questions from the police. They needed a plan, but their brain felt like it was melting inside. Squeezing their head, they pushed their teeth together, closing their eyes for a few seconds to think.

Perhaps they could instigate conversations at the centre, drip feed false information that could implicate someone who was already offending. It would give the police and the courts more evidence to get these leeches off the streets and away from people trying to recover. They nodded slowly, a finger to their dry mouth.

Kurt Harper, he deserved it and he didn't attend the centre, so a string of rumours could seep out into the wider community. Harper, another scumbag dealer who murders young people and feeds the habits of selfish old men like Albert. Men who prefer substances to their children and have done for decades. Nodding quicker, they swallowed. They could spread the rumour subtly or implicate nosey bastard Lance. Perhaps they could get him drunk, goad him to say something incriminating, record him.

Clasping their hands together, they felt a surge of hope.

Maybe they were looking too much into it, being paranoid. No one would suspect them. They helped so many at Homeless Helping Hands, after all. They felt a spark of positivity, of potential. Then it hit them hard in the stomach again. The fact they would have to tell their partner to lie and somehow make it out like it was all a big misunderstanding.

# Chapter 32: Stuart

Stuart came out of the police station feeling annihilated. The police definitely suspected someone using or working at the centre; him for all he knew, and it made Stuart feel his world was being starved of oxygen. He placed a hand on his bony chest as he tried to gulp in air, pushing his shoulders back. He only had an alibi for Charlie Sinclair's death, not Donald's. A sweaty panic landed on him as he tilted his head back and let the mist in the air hit his face for ten seconds.

*Surely social media could be tracked to his home on the night Donald Armstrong was killed?* he thought as he rubbed his tired brown eyes. *Surely a member of staff wouldn't, couldn't, do something so abhorrent? Murder? No Way,* thought Stuart, shaking his head to almost push the thought out of his mind. It had to be someone like Harper, or Yanti, or even Charlie's Tommy? Although what he had to do with Donald, Stuart couldn't fathom.

He interlocked his hands and held them to the back of his head as he walked to his car, mind saturated. Stuart knew that his dedicated team worked tirelessly to support homeless people. To empower, nurture, and be their advocate. They would never harm anyone. Mo, Dot, Lorna, and Liam. They were earth angels, selflessly helping other people, even with their own shit going on at times. Okay, Mo had his moments, but he was a decent bloke, a good worker who was grateful for his recovery, and with a new relationship.

No doubt the police would want to speak to them all again, ask more questions. Stuart understood. He also understood the importance of keeping everyone else safe. Perhaps the murderer knew now they had nothing else to lose? They may strike again. Right now, in Stuart's mind, it felt like no one was safe from the murderer or the police probing.

# Chapter 33

They returned home and fifteen minutes later, their partner arrived.

'Hi, nice day?' their partner asked, kissing them on the cheek as they stood in the lounge, before collapsing on the sofa.

'Erm, it was okay.' They bit the skin around their thumb nail. 'I was at the police station most of the day. We all were.'

'How did it go?'

They sat down on the sofa where their partner was tapping the seat. 'The police were bloody awful. Really scrutinising and patronising. I understand, it's their job, but still — they were arseholes.' They took a breath, trying to mask the concern in their voice.

Their partner squeezed their hand. 'Well, hopefully they don't ask you again. You lot need to just get on with your jobs supporting people. Have you spoken to the team?'

They shook their head. 'No, we didn't get a chance to talk about it. I imagine it will be top of the agenda at the meeting tomorrow. Everyone's been interviewed throughout the day.' They placed their hands on their knees to steady them. 'They were interviewing some centre users as well. People who know everyone so hopefully, that gave the police some leads.' They stared into space. 'I'm done in from it.'

Their partner knew to be gentle, witnessing the stress they had been under the last few months. It had become more than a job at that centre and if truth were told, their partner wished they would pack the place in — it was unhealthy and was altering their behaviour to someone who was sometimes unrecognisable. Now it also felt dangerous. Who was to say this maniac wouldn't turn on staff? It was clearly someone known to them.

'Maybe you should take some time off, rest, and keep safe until all this gets sorted? I know the murderer has killed homeless people, but you don't know how far people go. It just doesn't sit right. I'm worried about you.' The partner spoke gently and touched the shoulder of the person they loved.

They glanced back; the colour washed out of them like an artist cleaning a paint palette in the sink. They shook their head, brow furrowed. 'I know you mean well. But I can't leave everyone in the lurch. The team needs us all and so do the people using the centre.' They looked at their partner, their perfect match, who they had been searching for all those years. Closing their eyes, they swallowed down a lump of guilt — not for those losers they had killed, but for their partner, who was getting dragged into this, like a passenger on a plane that was crashing.

'I'm not scared and the people who still need help and want help, who want to change — well, they need me.' They bit their lip as they looked at the floor, then back to their partner. With an attempted blasé tone, they said, 'The police will want to speak to you, cos you were my alibi one night. It was the night of 10th January.' They smiled and grabbed their partner's hand whilst watching their partner's mind working overtime for a split second before shrugging slightly.

'Okay, no bother. What day was that?'

Inhaling, they tilted their head from side to side. 'Last Wednesday.'

Their partner rubbed their mouth. 'I wasn't here. Well, not until late. It was the night I was out with work for Sam's leaving meal, remember?' They looked at them.

'Are you sure?' they replied, scratching their head and knowing the truth.

'Yeah, cos if you recall, I wasn't going to go with it being a school night. But Sam has his kids on weekends, so we all had to make it a Wednesday and everyone was moaning. You said you were in all night and had a chilled one.' They moved slightly on the sofa, stiffening.

'Oh yeah. Well, you can just tell the police you were with me. It's no bother. They probably won't even ask you.' The panic was rising, so they stood, trying to end the conversation.

Their partner looked at them, eyes wide, and nervously laughed. 'I can't lie to the police. It's against the law. Just tell them you made a mistake. You forgot I was out, no big deal.' They shrugged. 'I arrived back about 11:30 pm and you were asleep. Then we were together all night until work the next day.'

Their partner waited for a response. 'I'm only asking you to tell a little lie so that they stop asking bloody questions. It was really fucking intimidating.' Their fists formed balls and they dropped them to their sides, standing a few metres away from where their partner sat on the sofa. 'They need to concentrate on getting this scumbag and not asking me and the team questions. The detective doesn't like me, I can tell.' Panic reverberated in their voice.

Their partner tilted their head. 'Maybe you're being paranoid. They can't be all nicey nice. I bet the team will say the same at work tomorrow. The coppers will know it's some revenge killing, someone owing money or turf wars,' their partner said gently, trying to reassure them.

They nodded, frightened to speak.

'So, I can just tell them. You made a mistake; I was out that night. Or you tell them you were in alone. They'll probably not even ask to speak to me.'

They moved closer to the sofa, desperation and anger soaring from their feet up their body. 'Can you not do one fucking thing for me?' They asked, their voice getting louder as they leant forward almost over their partner as they sat.

Their partner pushed their body back into the soft cushions of the sofa. 'Now come on, that's not fair. Just tell them the truth. You made a mistake!'

They bent forward, even closer, and pointed a finger. 'One fucking thing. One little, insignificant thing…' They could feel the panic dissolving into rage as they jerked their head.

'It's hardly insignificant, lying to the police. What's wrong with you? Just tell them the truth, for crying out loud!' their partner said, shaking their head, mouth grimacing.

'One fucking thing! One small lie to help reduce my stress! You're selfish — I should've known you'd be like the rest of them!' they screamed as they turned and stormed out of the lounge.

'Woah, woah, woah. What the fuck? Hang on a second, that's right out of order…' their partner said, jumping up from the sofa and following.

In the hallway, they were shaking their head quickly, mouth contorted. 'You don't care about me. It's all been a lie. One little thing to help and you won't!' They travelled up the first few stairs, getting hotter by the second, as adrenaline and anger pumped through them. Their skin felt almost itchy with the nerve endings charged.

'This is insane. What the hell…' their partner shouted; hands interlocked on the back of their head as their gaze travelled up the stairs.

'Get out of my sight right now! Go! fucking go!' they said, turning as they made their way up the stairs, sneering and shaking with rage. Their partner looked, eyes wide, before holding their hands up, puffing out air, and turning to leave. Less than thirty seconds later, they heard a car engine start, and they were left alone again. Abandoned, rejected, let down. They dropped to the top stair; heart pumping, mind throbbing, and wondered what the hell they were going to do next.

# Chapter 34: DS Ronnie Ericson

Ericson had been awake most of the night, going over the recorded interviews, notes, and trying to piece the investigation together. Motive? He needed a solid motive, and right now he couldn't pinpoint it. Mistaken identity? Drugs? A relationship connection? A secret or threat? Nothing jumped out, and it was tedious. He almost always connected the dots. This time, the dots seemed to be all over the place.

Ronnie had fallen asleep around 3 am, only to dream about the investigation and to wake at 6:15 am, feeling like he'd been in the ring with Tyson Fury. He had a text message from Kelsie, checking how he was — quickly replying, he typed that he was looking forward to seeing her and to wrap up today as it was forecast snow. She would always be his baby.

Ronnie peeled back his quilt, exposing the cold air; his central heating yet to click on. His feet met the laminate flooring as they searched, without help from his eyes, for his slippers. Locating them, Ronnie stood, groaning as he shifted his achy body. He had joined the local gym to get back into shape, but right now, it felt like the library card that he never used.

It was mornings like this that he really missed a cup of coffee made for him by Caroline — served with a smile that felt like his suit of armour for the day. He clicked his neck and shuffled to the kitchen. After two coffees and some porridge, he showered, dressed, and left for the team briefing.

Ericson and McCardle stood on either side of the incident

board. McCardle looked at the team and began to summarise yesterday's interviews.

'What have these two men got in common that could make them a target? We can rule out relationships and money. They could almost be the victims of two different offenders, had the homicide technique been dissimilar. Both had problematic addictions and were homeless in their own way. Both had broken relationships and both used the day centre.'

Ericson put his hands on the desk in front of him and glanced at his team, then focused on McCardle, who moved her slight frame on the spot as she spoke.

'Sinclair wasn't a known offender. Armstrong was. They didn't have an obvious relationship between them in the form of exploitation on any noticeable level or co-dependency. Charlie Sinclair was not the next Crosley drugs lord.' McCardle turned to Ericson, who chipped in.

'The two had little in common regarding past and current problems. They had no strong links associate wise, except for the staff at Homeless Helping Hands. Drugs aren't the issue. Charlie was a nobody in the drugs or criminal circles. Blackmail, possible, as Charlie in particular, had nothing to lose and little in the way of collateral.'

McCardle ran a hand through her blonde hair and continued, pointing to photos on the incident board. 'Salvin Yanti. He was new on the scene just before Charlie Sinclair was murdered. Sinclair, of course, could have been a practice run or a case of mistaken identity by someone on the drugs circuit.' She pointed to a picture of Kurt Harper. 'This guy is a person of interest and will be interviewed today. He has a history and a current pending case. A nasty wannabee Pablo Escobar.' Colleagues grinned at the reference, with some making notes.

'He's involved with the modern slavery and county lines drugs supply — Operation Telescope that's now been submitted to the CPS.' McCardle glanced at Ericson and smiled. It had been his case and as soon as it was sent to the CPS, this had landed on him, like a seagull shit explosion covering a freshly washed car.

'There wasn't enough damming evidence for remand. But he and his cronies are due in court in the next few months when the trial starts and hopefully more witnesses will come forward in that time.'

Ericson nodded, gulping his coffee and moving on the spot slightly. 'That's right, McCardle, and there may be links with Op Telescope and this; with Donald Armstrong in particular. Maybe he knew too much, or it was becoming a turf war. Sinclair had nothing to do with drugs, except a little cannabis found in his system. But they were both causing trouble at the centre; verbal outbursts and threats. Maybe they both knew something, knew too much,' Ericson said, looking around the room at his concentrating colleagues.

'A sedative, Amitriptyline, was found in both the deceased and neither victim was prescribed it. It isn't a common drug used for its highs, so it was most definitely used by the murderer for sedation.' He paused, lifting up his cup and drinking the dregs of his coffee.

'The likes of Harper and other drug barons are unlikely to use this. More likely something that the victims may have taken themselves, such as street Valium or Gabapentin, to appear more self-inflicted. Plus, it's something the known peddlers can get as easy as you lot can get a decent cuppa, well outside of this building!' He glanced at his cup, then back to the room and winked as colleagues laughed.

'What about the staff then, Boss?' asked Boyd, keen to get his thoughts from the update and interview notes with Dot Fiddes and Liam Mallaburn the day before.

'I don't want anyone ruled out at the moment. On paper, some have more of a possible motive than others but this bunch, well, let's just say there's a question mark above each of their heads.' He glanced at the board where photos of the suspects were displayed. 'We have some cross-referencing to do: check their NHS records, social services background checks, some alibis to confirm today, then we can re-evaluate. The main thing we need to find team, is *the motive* and all the staff at Homeless Helping Hands could have one.'

Ericson pulled out a seat, sat, and pointed to the photo of Dot Fiddes on the incident board. 'Take this one, Fiddes. Her son died of a drugs overdose. Possible link back to Armstrong before his last stint at His Majesty's pleasure. Recent overdoses, drug dealing. Perhaps she wanted him dead to prevent further drugs related deaths.' Colleagues nodded.

'Then we've got Stuart Bowden, the manager. Possible reputation and shutdown of the service, of his livelihood if drugs and drug-related deaths continued on his patch. Maybe he's relapsed himself and receiving threats. Perhaps Armstrong and Sinclair had something on him.' Ericson rubbed his head and got up from his chair, moving closer to the incident board.

He tapped a pen onto a photo. 'Lorna Andrews, a newer member of the team. We know little about Lorna, except for she doesn't appear to be in recovery herself. But what's her background? What motivated her to work in the field? All the other members of staff have an obvious personal reason. What's hers?'

Turning away from the board back to his team, Ericson put his hand to his chin and took a second in thought before continuing. 'Maurice Nutman. A known offender who states he's in substance recovery. Violent past and long history of addiction. Altercations with Armstrong and Lance Cole,' Ericson pointed to the photo of Lance Cole on the incident board. 'Has Nutman relapsed? Ghosts haunting him? Did Sinclair and Armstrong have something on him? He's definitely of great interest.

Next, Liam Mallaburn, also in recovery. Liam's worked at Homeless Helping Hands for years. But he's quiet, blends into the background, a bit vanilla overall. Could he be hiding something?' Ericson crossed his arms whilst looking at his team. 'So, today's about speaking to Harper and confirming the alibis of the five members of staff. Some of you will go to the centre. Lucas and Boyd will look at the NHS and social services records, so need help. Let's find that motive, okay?'

There was a unison of yes before all the team got up to get to work. Ericson faced the investigation board, scanning the faces of the people of interest; all the Homeless Helping Hands staff, Salvin Yanti, Kurt Harper, and Lance Cole. *What was the bloody motive?* He thought to himself, tapping his lips with his forefinger. What was he missing? He looked at the pictures, willing something to land in his brain. He was hoping the interviews today would help the jigsaw start to come firmly together.

# Chapter 35: Stuart

Stuart questioned whether to close the centre for a few days, but there were so many people in need — it was a lifeline. Perhaps the only communication they had in their day. Their only hot meal, their only safety. Although the latter was up for debate at the moment. Stuart didn't know who he was protecting who from and somewhere, in the pit of his stomach, he also feared for his own safety. Dragging his hand over his prominent jaw, he closed his weary eyes.

This felt bigger than two dead people, which was bloody big enough. Then there was Eve Wright and possible foul play. The more he thought about it, the more Stuart felt the sickness of dread inside him, growing like a weed threatening to strangle his organs. Anyone could be at risk. The victims, so far, were middle-aged men in active addiction. Stuart hit two of those himself and would always skirt on the edge of addiction by virtue of his recovery.

Something linked Charlie and Donald together, which made him feel it wasn't the work of the usual suspects — drug dealers playing with high stakes. For the first time in a long time, Stuart wasn't sure who to trust and decided the team meeting that morning would be brief, with the agenda of business as usual but with more staff presence.

The staff came in, the normal colourful energy they carried, slightly duller. Dot held a tray of biscuits. Stuart took a few ginger nuts, having not been able to face breakfast.

Everyone was sombre, stressed, and uncertainty infused the air over the smell of casserole cooking for lunch.

Stuart swallowed and put his best smile on, followed by an upbeat, 'Right, troops, I just wanted to check in on everyone and talk about a bit of a plan going forward.' He sighed and looked down at the worn carpet for a few seconds. 'Were you all okay after yesterday?' Stuart knew it was a stupid question to ask. Everyone was far from flamin' okay.

'To be honest, Stu, nah I wasn't,' said Mo. 'It was shit. I felt like they had it in for me cos of my past.' He ran his tongue over his teeth and bounced his knees.

'Me too, mate,' Liam said, shaking his head.

'They didn't give me an easy time either and I've got no record,' Lorna commented, pulling at the sleeves of her cardigan.

'Alright Lorn, no need to be a smug cow about it,' Mo snapped, rubbing his bald head.

'What the hell?' Lorna said, standing up. 'You think you're the only one fucking worried and scared, Mo?' Lorna shouted.

Startled, Stuart looked over at Lorna, taken aback by her behaviour.

'Piss off, Lorn, what do you know?' Mo retaliated, sneering.

Lorna went to speak and Stuart interrupted. 'C'mon, man, this isn't helping. We all feel the bloody same and it was awful. But bickering won't help, will it?' He rubbed his forehead. Stuart was exhausted; his boat threatening to capsize, and he could do without the staff falling out.

'That's right love, we're still a team,' said Dot, looking around and trying to muster some solidarity between her colleagues.

'Yes, indeed, Dot. So, the board wants us to carry on as a *team*. It's business as usual for everyone needing the service.' Stuart's eyes dropped to the notebook in his hands, open to an empty page.

'What about our needs, Stuart, and making sure we're okay?' Liam asked.

Stuart was trying to hold it together. He felt he was going to scream or cry. Placing the notebook on his desk, he interlocked his hands, hoping it would stop them from shaking.

'Good point, Liam. So, we're going to get some extra staff in from the agency. I know they aren't all trained directly in supporting homeless people, but they'll be bodies…'

Mo burst out laughing. 'Really, Boss, that's not the best term to use right now, is it?'

Dot looked across to Mo. 'Son, this isn't the time to make jokes.'

Mo rolled his eyes as Stuart continued, a nervous laugh at realising his faux pas. 'We're keeping open and just have to be vigilant. The police seem to be on the case. However, I don't know about you lot, but I left the cop shop feeling more unnerved yesterday about possible further victims.' Stuart omitted his feelings about suspects.

The team nodded and muttered their agreement. Stuart leant forward in his chair. 'We're getting some more cameras fitted and can set up counselling for anyone who needs it, given the events and ongoing stress.' Stuart noticed everyone seemed despondent; looking at the floor, their hands, or looking at him with heavy eyes and weak smiles.

'We're all going to take a few days off after each other for the next week. Everyone's worn out and getting away from it, even for a few days, will do us all good.' He sighed and Dot passed around the biscuits that nobody wanted.

'And please make sure you are all logging any incidents. Anything, even if it's minor. The police are going to be here every day, scrutinising. It's important to keep everyone safe until they catch the murderer.' Stuart put his hand over his mouth. He felt he would crack open at any point, like an egg falling on the ground. The team sat silently. A strange tension in the air. Stuart didn't know what to do. A few seconds later, there was a knock on the office door. The police had arrived.

# Chapter 36

Consumed by anxiety, they wavered between staying and running away. But they couldn't leave their home, their life, the little family they had. *Could everyone not see that they had done it for the right reasons? For Tommy? For the people trying to get clean from drugs? The people who were vulnerable and easily exploited? They were keeping them safe from the monster that was Donald.*

The police were looking for a link between the two. The questioning, the interviews, and now the police were constantly sniffing around the day centre again. It was too much, too close, and they worried they would overflow — like water running into a plugged bath for hours. Their mind and body felt ready to drown. Perched on the closed toilet seat in the centre toilets, they tried to regulate their breathing as they picked at the skin on their wrist. The team meeting had been weird. Stuart was teetering on the edge of a cliff, and everyone else was deflated, paranoid, or frightened.

Their mind had been swirling like a spinning top, but they had played their role; concerned around safety of everyone using the centre and staff. Offering to do inductions with any agency staff coming in to help. The lack of usual personality, not overly noticed given they'd all been grilled by the police. However, sitting in the toilets, their stomach spasmed in protest at their absence of appetite and a churn of emotions was eating their insides like acid.

'Shit,' they whispered to themselves as they rubbed their

fingers over the flesh on their legs, wounds covered by jeans. Old scars that had become the map of sadness their story told. Scars that were hidden out of sight from anyone but their partner. The years of self-harm that felt the only release from the grief of losing their mother and the nightmare that they endured for almost two decades after. The cutting had started again when Robyn left. When they could no longer have their weekly visits at school with the only person they wanted to see. The only person they thought cared.

Albert mocked them, saying they had invested too much emotionally. That Robyn was only, 'A wannabee counsellor' and that they would be okay and had to just get on with it and grow up. Albert, failing to see that they grew up the day Mam died when they were dragged into an adult's world, no longer allowed to be a carefree child.

Their resentment towards Albert had poisoned their life. Burnt their happiness and charred opportunity. And he continued to be the infection, turning their world septic. They sniffed up and pressed their lips together tightly, trapping a scream. *You don't give a damn about people and they hurt you and leave you. You give a damn about people and they still hurt you and leave you,* they thought, as they closed their eyes.

People they cared about in their younger years had left in one way or another. Died, abandoned them, or distanced themselves. Then they had to wait for Albert to go. Even after he died, they still had to pick up the pieces — feeling even more fragile with a head full of unanswered questions and no apologies.

The cutting helped when it all got too much. When they felt sure they would explode into a million pieces or scream so loudly that they would crack the earth in two. Cutting and writing. Writing and cutting. Their thighs were the worst affected area. Like Artex on the human body; lumpy, raised, unattractive. But they didn't care. They were the only things that kept them alive; they were sure. Their partner had understood, knowing they'd lost loved ones and had a hard time. Detail left out; the past was the past. No one could help. It was too late now.

It had been such a long time since they cut or even had the urge. But there had been times over the years when they picked at one of the deeper scars on their legs or the more recent ones hidden under their watch strap. Sometimes it would be just to press into the scar, feel a pressure. Sometimes a light itch with an item such as a pin, or a paperclip, sometimes with their nail. It never went deep, but the release was there.

Until the last few months, when the paperclip on the surface hadn't been enough and blood was needed. They had hidden it mostly, especially at work. They were the master of disguise, after all. They hid the scars on their wrist with their stretchy watch strap. It was soft and concealed the truth, like a pillow that had been sobbed into night after night. Something they could control. Their own secret. Just like the murders were, for now, anyway.

# Chapter 37: The Partner

The phone call had come, like they knew it would — dreaded it would — that morning before work.

'Can you come into the station so we can ask a few questions?' the police officer had requested.

'Of course, not a problem,' they had replied calmly, despite their mouth feeling as if it were filled with sand.

The outburst last night from the person they loved was a side they didn't sign up for. Everyone had emotional baggage, they acknowledged this. A past; previous painful relationships, family deaths. No one was immune and people weren't unharmed, perfect, and always in control. The partner knew this about them and their past, snippets anyway.

The traumatic loss of their mother at a young age. The lack of support, preparation, and explanation of her death. That overnight, they became an adult in a child's body. Having to be brave, organised, and support their father as alcohol became a daily staple. Their own brief misuse of alcohol, struggles with their mental health, relationships, and seeking help.

But they always said it was the past and that they had dealt with it as if not relevant anymore. They seemed so strong and everything was fine, stable; the partner had thought. Their relationship showing no signs of concern until recently. No major flashing light on the dashboard of their happiness until last night, when it became an illumination of warning lights and the engine of their blissful life abruptly cut out.

A build-up of the last several weeks where mood swings were becoming as frequent as breakfast, and they felt anything they said would be interpreted differently on any given day. They put their head in their hands and thought back. The odd snipe here, the smallest of outburst there, extreme emotions, fluctuating. All accumulating like soot up a chimney, blocking the flue and threatening to choke the room.

They had tried to help their partner; wanting them to be happy and appreciating their work could be emotional, challenging, and frightening. Yet still, they remained closed, not explaining what was going on in their head, just talking about that bloody job all the time — as they listened, knowing at any time it could lead to an eruption.

They rubbed their eyes and let out a sigh. There was something about these murders, the first in particular that left an unpleasant taste in their mouth the more they thought about it. They'd read about people on the news, in online articles. These folk who enter the caring profession and turn insane, or maybe they always were insane.

People who abuse, harm, and murder vulnerable people in hospitals, care homes, boarding schools, even the police. Those with a vendetta, who train or seek opportunities to join a discipline enabling them to harm others. Nurses who kill children. Doctors who murder old people. Police officers who are sexual predators. Professionals, perpetrators disguised as caring people who would never be suspects.

The partner sat on the sofa, taking a few deep breaths as tears dampened their cheeks. They got up and opened the lounge window, gulping in air as the thoughts ricocheted around their mind. Inhaling the almost freezing air, they prayed some common sense would clear their foggy head.

*This is madness,* they thought to themselves. They had fallen in love with a kind, funny, resilient person. *They couldn't be a killer, no way.*

But as they drove to the police station ten minutes later, doubt filled their stomach with every second, to the point they were certain they would vomit. As they pulled up outside of the police station, they held their mouth and got out their car with legs weaker than a tree branch in a hurricane.

# Chapter 38: DS Ronnie Ericson

Ericson and McCardle were speaking to the potential alibis and Kurt Harper that day. The other members of the investigation team were visiting the families of Charlie Sinclair and Donald Armstrong and gathering information from the day centre. The team had been instructed to shadow the staff as much as possible and to look out for any slipping of their act.

Someone in that building was responsible, and Ericson was sure their disguise would soon become transparent, as pressure forced the truth out or his diligent team discovered evidence. Even after all the years in the force, the thousands he had arrested and interviewed, the abhorrent crimes that he and his teams had investigated and solved; Ericson still felt sickened by each case. It helped him to never become complacent and to never stop caring about victims, and even sometimes offenders.

At home, before work that morning, Ronnie absentmindedly stirred his coffee. Watching the winter sun slowly push through thick clouds, he knew the net was closing in. The predator was now the hunted, with fewer and fewer places to hide.

That day, there were five alibis to interview: Stuart Bowden's brother, Dot Fiddes's husband, Liam Mallaburn's partner, Lorna Andrews's partner, and Maurice Nutman's partner. Phone data was due back, and some of the alibis were of more interest than others, but Ericson wanted to keep on top of the investigation. No minute to waste and his superior, as well as the media, were pestering him like chuggers on a busy high street.

He arrived at the office, stifling a yawn as he sauntered to his desk. McCardle sat at the desk to the right of his. She looked up, eyes tired but with a warm smile on her round face, greeting him before saying a hello. She nodded to the freshly made cup of coffee on the edge of her desk for him — brown liquid, welcoming him in his *World's Best Dad* mug. Ericson smiled and reached into his backpack, taking two Kit Kats out and placing one on McCardle's desk before picking up his cup. McCardle put her hand over the chocolate biscuit and chuckled, sliding it towards her — team work went further than the actual job.

Neither Ericson nor McCardle had taken a day off in the last eight working days. It was showing and both looked like they had been on a three-day bender at a music festival without the beaded bracelet and suntan. Instead, the pair sported puffy eyes and matching sallow complexions from the relentless, all-consuming twelve-hour shifts. They did, however, still have smiles for one another and a fuel in their stomachs to solve the case.

Ericson was off in two days, by order from his superior, Richardson. He would keep his phone on, but his day off was Caroline's birthday meal out. Kelsie had arranged it — to a new Thai place in town. It was the thing keeping his spirits up at the moment, and he was hopeful they would have someone arrested and charged by that point. Catching the murderer was keeping his exhausted body and mind going; his jackpot.

He gulped his coffee, unwrapped his biscuit and shoved it

in his mouth. 'Right, McCardle, let's go,' he said, through crumbs. She rose from her desk and the pair walked towards interview room number one.

# Chapter 39

Sitting in the cemetery, they stared at their mother's grave. It was soothing yet a punishment as Albert was now also in the ground alongside their precious mam. The purity and solace they previously had from visiting their mother's resting place and taking care of it was now polluted — like sewage cascading down a waterfall. Albert's body contaminated the grave and despite them trying to stop it from happening, it was in both their wills.

Mam had loved Dad; he hadn't been the selfish alcoholic that they had to tolerate until he died. Christ, even they had loved Dad until he began to love whisky more than them. Memories were sour, tarnished with the alcohol, neglect, and Albert's selfishness — childhood manoeuvring into the lane of adulthood before the age of ten.

Sitting on the checked blanket from the car, their journal on the ground next to them, they stared at the headstone. It felt so long ago that Mam was around, yet they could see images of her in their mind so vividly, as if watching life through a window.

The wound of loss never healed, and they were covered in the scars that showed an attempt to cope with childhood, adolescence, and adulthood. The crippling mask they had worn for so many years. Nodding when asked if they were okay. Smiling to hide the burden of grief and responsibility. The mask was cracking, sliding, falling, and taking them with it.

Dissolving their façade like snow in the rain. Exposing them to the element of truth. It felt imminent, and they felt out in the wild with no places to hide — a sniper waiting to strike them down. Maybe they were going insane. Hell, maybe they were already insane. They let out a tired sigh as a tear trickled down their cheek.

The police would speak to their partner today, leading to more suspicion and need for excuses, playing dumb, pretending to remember something forgotten. The police needed more evidence, they knew that. But they were becoming surer that no one would ever understand the reasons they killed Charlie and Donald. The desperate need to protect their families and other vulnerable people, and to heal the child inside them whose screams haunted their sleep.

To protect a damaged son from further harm. Shielding him from having to continue to know his father chose alcohol and he would die slowly, like a starving rat in a cage. Just like Albert. And they were protecting Donald's family, as well as safeguarding all the young, damaged, and vulnerable people he was pushing drugs onto and exploiting. They dug their fingers into their scalp and winced.

No, the police wouldn't understand. Their partner wouldn't understand. Murder is murder even when it feels like it's for the best; for the right reasons. The staff team wouldn't understand either. They would lose what they spent so long trying to find; love that wasn't poisonous. They closed their journal, snapped the metal clip from their pen off and dug it into the fresh wound on their wrist as they let out a sob.

# Chapter 40: James

James left the police headquarters after vomiting into the station toilets. His eyes bloodshot from retching and crying, he sat in the car and ran his hands through his floppy brown hair. Staring into space, he wondered what the hell had just happened. The two detectives had asked him his whereabouts on the nights the two homeless men were murdered. He knew they would ask everyone else that. Then the officers questioned him about his relationship with Lorna. What her demeanour had been like the last few months. What he knew about her, her routines — really intimate questions.

He'd stuttered; shocked and frightened. It was like a surreal scene from a soap opera. They asked about the medication she took. Not knowing details, he knew she took something to help her sleep that was also a pain killer. He had taken one a few months ago after a football injury and slept amazingly. Laughing nervously, the police had written it down, not returning the laughter. James realised none of this was funny. It was anything but as the questioning continued. Some of which he understood. Some felt strange to ask; invasive and unnecessary.

They scrutinised him about those two nights. He wasn't bloody home. What could he say? That night in November, he knew he wasn't as it was a footy night. His heart was pounding so much, it threatened to mute out their voices with its drumming. The officers had gone on to ask about last

Wednesday, when he was out with work for Sam's leaving party — querying if Lorna had text or called that night.

That frightened him on many levels. He didn't know if it was usual and if the police were trying to eliminate or incriminate. Not sure if he wanted to know, he was unclear what to say for the best as he gulped down the water they gave him, hoping it would wash away this nightmare.

But James knew he had to be honest. Lorna hadn't been herself lately. But she wasn't capable of this; of murder, the way the police explained to him. Not his Lorna, surely? She had problems, a past. But don't we all? His girlfriend was a good person, even after her difficult childhood. She had overcome, building her knocked-down house back up, brick by brick.

He shook his head, as if to shake away all of this nonsense. The police must have it wrong. A complete misunderstanding or a trick, a set-up. Some ridiculous practical joke. James had answered the questions bombarded at him by the two intimidating detectives — each question making him feel like he was hallucinating; not really there, in that clinical room. Feeling like a suspect himself from their cold, relentless questioning.

Lorna had exploded last night and after being interviewed by those two officers; James could see why. Eventually, the police finished asking questions in monotone, thanked him for his time, and told him he could leave. He'd rushed to the toilets and vomited, then sat there for five minutes, frozen yet desperate to go home as he silently sobbed, wondering *could his beloved Lorna be a monster?*

Now in the car, his mind a thunderstorm of the unexplainable, the unwanted houseguest of doubt had crept in. *If she hadn't done these unspeakable things, why had she lied to the police? It was only last Wednesday, not months ago. She couldn't have mixed that up, surely? What was she hiding?* James didn't know what to do.

He couldn't call his mother, or his best mate — not about something as possibly catastrophic as this. Anything playing on his mind, James would always talk to Lorna, ironically. She was a good listener, a good person. *Capable of this? Of murder? Drugging and suffocating two vulnerable men?* Not his Lorna. James rocked his head, then clasped his hands together and put them towards his mouth, biting hard on his forefinger to stifle a scream.

He closed his eyes, trying to regulate his breathing, which was bordering on a panic attack, and he thought of Lorna's behaviour of late. She had been erratic. He'd been honest with the police about that. But she was stressed. That place, Homeless Helping Hands, sounded like a complete nightmare and he took his hat off to people working there. James attempted to rationalise. Recently, with all the carry on, it had been stressful. Lorna had been working extra hours to help. Weekends, night times. He told the police that, then instantly regretted it. *Would him saying she had been working nights incriminate her further?*

'Fuck!' he shouted, running his hands through his hair as he sat trembling in the driver's seat. He had been sitting in his car for over twenty minutes and still nothing made any sense. He had to talk to Lorna. The police would want to talk to her again, as their stories were conflicting. James had told the truth, he had to. They may even arrest her. He let out a gasp. Opening the car window, he breathed in the winter air slowly and deeply, attempting to placate the nausea crawling like a tarantula inside him.

He needed to think straight, in amongst this screwed up soap opera. He had to get Lorna to tell her story right, honestly — whatever it was. *Why had she wanted James to lie if she had just made a mistake and mixed up where he was that night?* She had to tell the police the truth that they weren't together. But then what did she do last Wednesday night when he was out? And what did she do on the 8th November last year, when Charlie Sinclair was murdered? James scrunched his eyes and yelped.

Lorna was off work today; her boss had insisted. They had all been working so hard. James had to get home, talk to her, and get some sense of all this. They could sort it out, he was certain. Maybe she was seeing someone else? Yes, that could be it. Her mood, secrecy, lack of intimacy between them. James would be heartbroken, but would take that any day over the woman he loved being a murderer.

# Chapter 41: DS Ronnie Ericson

Ericson and McCardle sat opposite each other in the staff canteen, a cup of coffee each and a plate of chips in front of them.

'Well, that was interesting,' Ericson said as he dipped a chip into tomato sauce. 'Looks like angry Mo Nutman is off the hook given what his misses said.'

McCardle nodded. 'You thinking the same as me, Boss?'

'Almost certainly the same thing as you,' Ericson replied, smiling. 'We still need more.' Ericson tapped the table. 'Some detail on the motive, a direction to look for evidence. The alibi doesn't stack up, so we need to get the suspect back in and ask more questions. The others could be lying, but the phone records can be analysed. Let's get the suspect in, ask the questions. See if she cracks under more pressure. I'm thinking it's more likely to be a house search after arrest, but just to make sure.'

McCardle nodded, and they both stood up. Ericson grabbed a few cold chips and shoved them in his mouth. He was hungry, tired, and smelt of coffee and sweat. It wasn't a good look, but as fatigued as he was, Ericson felt the team was an extra step closer to nailing the murderer. They walked in sync along the corridor for the briefing.

'You look knackered, Boss, if you don't mind me saying. You need your day off on Sunday.' McCardle gently tapped Ericson's forearm.

'And you need yours off on Monday.' He smiled at her and sighed. 'I am cream-crackered. Seeing my Kelsie and Caroline and the anticipation of an eight-course Thai meal is keeping me going. Just need this arrest off our to-do list.' Ericson laughed as he pushed open the office door. 'Right, you lot, briefing time,' he said as everyone got up from their seats, a chorus of groans from staff sitting hunched over computers for way too long.

Taking a seat in the briefing room, McCardle and Ericson went to the incident board. 'So, we've been interviewing all day. Boyd and Lucas, you've been with the families. Any update to share?'

'Tommy Sinclair's alibi stacked up. He had no further info that he hadn't already given about his father and services he used,' Boyd said.

Lucas added, 'Armstrong's family had little else to say and are all accounted for at the time of his death.' He tapped his pen on his notebook and Ericson nodded. 'We interviewed Kurt Harper. He was about as helpful as a barber fixing your car. A lot of no comments and dirty looks. Reckoned he had an alibi at the B&B he's been staying at for both nights. We've rung, and they have checked records and confirmed. We can look at the CCTV footage first thing tomorrow.'

'Thanks, great work. Any update from the lot at the day centre, Myers?' Ericson enquired.

Myers nodded. 'They were all super quiet, Boss. There's a bunch of agency staff in and not all the staff were around. No sign of Yanti either at the centre, but he's still in his supported accommodation. We are continuing to look through the notes for anything else, the archived ones now.'

'Good work. Just keep the presence up.' Ericson turned to

McCardle, who began sharing their finds from the interview and referenced the incident board showing photos of the Homeless Helping Hands staff team.

'We interviewed several people today. Alibis, partners of the five people who work at Homeless Helping Hands. Liam Mallaburn's partner, Dylan Allen, verified his story that they were together both nights. He said the neighbour also knocked on the door around 9:30 pm on the night Donald Armstrong died, to ask if he could use their bin and saw them both. Phone records for Mallaburn have come in and rule him out.'

She tapped her pen on the next photo. 'Dot Fiddes's husband, Kevin, confirmed her presence and said the phone records should show that one of the nights they called their grandson from their landline. Dot had also mentioned this. The records are still trickling through.' She glanced at her notes then back at her colleagues.

'Stuart Bowden's brother, Johnny, confirmed he was at his home until around 10:30-11 pm on the night of 8th November. The other night in question, the 10th January, phone data will verify.' She turned to Ericson, who took over.

'That leaves two suspects. Two very different suspects, but one with an alibi who didn't corroborate their story. Annie Joyce confirmed she was with Maurice Nutman on the night of the 10th January.' Ericson paused and took a gulp of tea. 'Lorna Andrews's partner, James Ord, said he was out on a work leaving do the night of 10th January. The night of 8th November, he was also out, playing football with his work colleagues, which is what the suspect said. However, the suspect has lied about the 10th January. This night, Donald Armstrong was murdered. And we've spoken to James Ord, who confirmed Lorna Andrews takes sleeping medication.'

Ericson looked at his team, then at the incident board. He lifted his pen and pointed at the prime suspect. 'Team, this is our prime suspect.' He circled the picture on the board with a thick red marker. 'Our murderer could very well be Miss Lorna Andrews.' The photo of Lorna Andrews stared back at Ericson. When he looked at it now, he could almost see the coldness behind her eyes.

Ericson got the green light from Chief Inspector Richardson before the end of the team briefing and actions were disseminated. It was 4:15 pm, and they needed to track down Lorna Andrews and make an arrest. Reasonable suspicion from the interview with James Ord was enough to arrest. Despite trying to keep James Ord at the station, away from Lorna Andrews, they had no grounds and with no power to detain, they had little choice but to let him go. Ericson knew this meant time was critical.

They had to get to Lorna Andrews and make an arrest. Once they arrested her, a search of her property and the day centre could happen. Ericson knew James Ord would have talked to his partner. She would know some of their thinking and be aware of her probable arrest. Ericson and McCardle had been careful not to frighten him. They were the Olympic medal standard for keeping it cool.

Boyd and Lucas had been part of a small team conducting the background checks on Lorna Andrews; accessing GP records, family checks, previous employers. Information was trickling in at the station. Some officers would have to speak with Stuart Bowden again, as her manager and possibly the other staff members.

Ericson rounded up colleagues to travel to Lorna

Andrews's address, fifteen minutes' drive away, and hopefully arrested her there. The pair and Lucas headed towards the station car park. Boyd and Myers would be back-up in another car. Ericson doubted Andrews would have gone on the run. But then again, psychopaths wear many disguises and two are never the same, despite some familiar traits. Ericson had met many in his time. They were clever, manipulative, and eclectic. The profile always had something in common; a childhood experience, an ignorance, an emotional façade to take away from a narcissistic, sociopathic underlayer.

Ericson relied on his gut; his second brain. He'd felt it over the years so many times; intuition, a sixth sense. It always indicated there was more. He had it with Lorna Andrews when he watched her interviewed by McCardle and Myers. However, there was something else, and it wasn't psychopathic. There wasn't a visible evil he had encountered countless times over the years. An evil from child killers, perpetrators of domestic abuse, sex offenders, and murderers. Lorna Andrews didn't have that, but there was something bubbling away. Ericson knew only too well that soul sickness came in multiple forms and the devil wears many disguises — including masquerading as a saint.

# Chapter 42: Lorna

James had called Lorna's mobile half an hour after she arrived home from the cemetery. She had sat for a long time on the kitchen floor, writing in her journal, and reading the entries from the last few months. Some of the words and emotions documented felt like it was her, written from the heart, and others felt like they were scrawled by another person — an alien who had landed in her life and taken over her brain. Lorna knew things were closing in on her, that feeling of being stuck in traffic in a tunnel. Only this time, the traffic wasn't going to move, and the tunnel was going to collapse. She felt ten years old again, helpless.

'I'm not going to work, Lorn. I'm coming home. Are you there? We need to talk,' James said breathlessly, voice shaking.

Lorna sensed the urgency and knew it hadn't gone well at the police station. She just didn't know if he had covered for her or if James had given the police more fuel to look at her as a suspect. They'd argued about it the night before. She'd told the police she was at home with James all night on the 10th January, but he'd been out for Sam's leaving party. On the night she killed Charlie, James was at football. He wouldn't have had to lie about that, at least. But it meant she had no alibi and therefore, created suspicion.

She remained sitting on the light grey ceramic tiles of the kitchen floor. Angus approached for the second time, tail wagging. She ignored him and after a head nudge, a paw to her leg, and a few whimpers, he admitted defeat, retreating to his dog bed. Lorna closed her eyes, willing to open them to another life — her former life, just a few months ago, before getting involved with Homeless Helping Hands. She would take that again, even with her Albert-induced trauma. She squeezed her temples and yelped.

*If the police came, what would she say? She killed because she couldn't cut herself. They would think she was insane.* Lorna laughed, a defeated, exhausted laugh before gouging her wrist with her fingernails and screaming. *It's all Albert's fault,* she thought to herself as she sat on the hard, cold tiles, letting the blood from her re-opened wound on her wrist drip onto her jeans.

She stuffed her journals back into their hiding place. It was her secret. No one else's business, and every relationship had secrets. Her journals had her most inner thoughts from all those years, right back to her time with Robyn. They were as precious to her as James and Angus. But they were still just hers and hers alone. She would never let James read them, or even know her past in any great detail.

All those years ago, inspired by Robyn with the beautiful, green shiny notebook she gifted Lorna. Robyn was the catalyst in Lorna's self-soothing through her written mind. Documenting her thoughts and issues, progress and secrets. The journals had become part of Lorna, a substitute mother who you would pour your heart out to without judgement.

Cutting provided the rest and Lorna felt, even with a few missing jigsaw pieces, she could function. She could cope most of the time. But over the years, she had drifted too far out to sea, where she had no life jacket and no rescue boat. Where no lighthouse shone its beacon of direction and hope. No one came to find her, to save her. She was alone.

Even during the last year and a half with James, she still needed her coping mechanisms, despite him providing another piece of her jigsaw: love. Unconditional love, Lorna was sure of it. His love had been equal, gentle, and kind. He had helped her to stop binge drinking on alcohol and to love herself more.

James helped her believe happiness existed and that she could find it, grab it, and keep it — until now. However, cutting never went from Lorna's mind completely and she always kept her journals, pouring her emotions into them, relishing them — almost like a secret lover.

Their relationship had to be with secrets. But her journal and cutting were simply no longer enough to soothe the pain and hatred she harboured for Albert. Being reminded of him by selfish men like Charlie and Donald had kicked down the front door of her control, and ignited her need for revenge.

Her tumour of secrets, encased in resentment, anger, hatred, and revenge had grown, maiming Lorna. Making it impossible to function with as Albert began haunting her once again, becoming the faces of people at Homeless Helping Hands. People became duplicates of Albert. Clones of the selfish bastard, walking around threatening and abusing others. Placing people at risk, hurting people, not taking responsibility, and never wanting to change.

She remained on the floor, blood on her fingers, staring at the ghosts of her past. Less than ten minutes later, Lorna heard a car speed onto the drive and the front door open then slam. There were no calls of hello like usual.

'Lorn?' he bellowed as she sat quietly like a startled rabbit in the headlights; big, glassy eyes fixed on the cold kitchen floor. James dashed into the kitchen and looked down at

Lorna sitting on the floor.

'There you are. What the hell you doing down there? What's happened to your wrist?' James asked frantically, his brow furrowed, glancing at Lorna's wrist smeared in blood and the small patches spread on her jeans. He bent to help her up, eyes wide, shaking his head. The colour was drained from his usual bright complexion.

Instead, Lorna sobbed and curled into a foetal position on the kitchen floor, clutching her knees into her chest. James said nothing, his bottom lip quivering. He slowly sat on the tiled floor. She sensed his trepidation. *Was he frightened of her or just of knowing the truth?*

Angus approached again tentatively, only the sound of his claws clacking off the floor. He tilted his head, mouth open, and let out a low woof, sensing something was wrong. He went to James, who patted his head.

James was such a wonderful man. He had always made her feel adored, cherished, protected. Lorna thought in that instant how much she didn't deserve him. She had lied to him, put him at risk, never really been her true self. James had done nothing but love her. She had ruined it, destroyed it — knocking down the house of cards that had been their chance for happy-ever-after. She had set it on fire and watched it burn.

'Lorn, what the hell is going on? Tell me, baby,' James said with pleading urgency in his voice as he glared at her, squeezing her hand in his. 'They know we weren't together on that night. Where were you?' His voice cracked. 'Is it another bloke?' His eyes bulged as he leant in towards her and she saw sweat coating the hair dangling against his forehead.

'Are you seeing someone else? Is this why you've lied?' James raised his voice; it was coated with emotion as his eyes became watery.

She straightened her posture and took her hand away from his, placing it on her mouth. James chewed on his lip, frowning, waiting for an explanation to divert away from the unthinkable.

'I, I...' Lorna stared at James. He momentarily covered his face with his hands, shoulder slumped in emotional defeat.

'Where were you, Lorna?' James shouted, spittle forming around his mouth as tears fell from his eyes.

Angus darted away.

'Start fucking talking, Lorna! Please, this is serious,' James sobbed. 'Did... did you hurt those men?' He grabbed his mouth as if saying the words themselves was criminal — and it was, to his future, which would never be the same again.

Lorna knew James couldn't bring himself to ask if the person he loved had murdered two people. She grimaced and began crying, shifting her gaze away from him.

'Lorna, Lorna, look at me! Where were you?' He shook her gently. 'The police are going to ask you again. You said you were home, alone. Did you have someone here with you? Is that it?' He pleaded, grasping her upper arms. 'Look, it's okay, we can work through any cheating, Lorn. I love you.' James was begging, anything but the truth.

He took his hands from her upper arms and grabbed his scalp as Lorna remained mute, shocked, as if a pride of lions were walking through their kitchen.

'Baby, you need to tell me. What happened? Where were you?' James spoke gently, but with a face full of frantic sadness.

Lorna knew James wanted the truth before the police came seeking it. He looked into her eyes and Lorna's heart felt like it would stop beating through the pain that was inevitable. She began to sob and James leant in, putting his arms around her. Lorna sobbed uncontrollably — a tsunami of tears she had been holding in for many years. A build-up of grief, trauma, rejection, fear, and anger cascading out. The dam had burst.

Pushing her face into James's chest, Lorna wanted to melt into his being and become him, leaving the soul and shell of a broken woman behind. She willed it to happen as he held her tightly, kissing her head, rocking her gently, and saying it was okay. But it was far from okay, and Lorna had needed this moment twenty years ago. She had needed James's reassurance from Albert.

All those years ago when her skeleton felt like it would collapse into a pile of dust almost daily from the burden of grief, anger, and pitch-black sadness she had to walk blindly in each day — limping whilst Albert got his comfort from a bottle named Jack. She wanted to stay in James's arms. A minute of silence passed. Lorna had sobbed so hard she had to try and regulate her breathing, like a child after a meltdown.

James pulled away slightly, holding her at arm's length. 'Baby, we *have* to talk,' he whispered, looking into her eyes and cupping her face. 'I'm not sure how much time we have.' His bottom lip trembled.

Lorna knew what it meant. The police were going to come and take her away. Snatch her from the happiness she had waited so long for. Rip her away from her safety, her love, her recovery. James was her everything. He was so handsome, so caring, so perfect. She had screwed it all up, threw a lit match on their happiness and burnt it down.

Nodding at James, he stood and held a hand out to help

her up. They silently went into the lounge, James leading as Lorna felt a helpless complacency, her legs unsteady and her head pounding. They sat on their sofa that they had excitedly picked out together even before they had the offer accepted on their first home as a couple.

'Tell me, Lorna, what's going on? You know I love you. I'll do my best to help, but you have to tell me.' His voice was gentle, his eyes saturated with sadness.

Lorna looked at James, then her hands, back at James, and began crying again.

'Please, for fuck's sake Lorn, we can sort it,' James said with desperate pleading as he gripped her hand, frowning.

Lorna shook her head, feeling defeated. She needed to know what he had said to the police. 'Wha-what did you tell them?' she mumbled, not really wanting to know something that would change their lives forever.

James sighed and Lorna almost saw the feelings of betrayal he held behind his eyes. She knew the answer. She knew *her* James. He just didn't know her.

'The truth, baby, I had to.' He looked away, wiping his bloodshot eyes as Angus came and sat by his feet, head stooped slightly.

Lorna nodded slowly.

'But there must be some explanation, Lorna. I know you. Where were you those nights?'

Lorna sat silent, as the reality that she had spent her whole life lying sank in. From a child, watching her mother die. The years after, lying for Albert, pretending it was fine at home. Lying to counsellors, to social workers, her grandparents, even Robyn. Lying to her best friend Chantelle, lying to James, to her colleagues, and lying to the police. A mask, an act, a conveyor belt of lies that became second nature. Secrets and lies. Pretence and distraction. She had done it all these years; to everyone, including her darling James. Lie after lie after lie.

'Lorna?' James prompted, getting angry again.

But Lorna sat, staring at her hands, twisting them around as the welt on her wrist glistened with blood. 'I, I, can't…'

Angus let out a bark and within a second, there was a knock at Lorna and James's door, followed quickly by two more knocks.

'Shit,' said James. A yelp escaped his mouth before he grabbed it.

They glared at each other, both knowing who it was at the door. Lorna shook her head as James looked pleadingly at his precious love.

'Lorn?' he said, tears falling from his eyes.

The knocks came again, louder and more forcefully. Their cars were outside. It would have been obvious that Lorna and James were likely in the house. Whoever was at the door only had to move ten or so steps to the left and could see into the lounge where the couple sat like frightened children, hiding from a monster. They scurried into the hallway, trying to get away from the monster, but she was part of them. It was too late. They knew they couldn't escape and their fate was sealed.

# Chapter 43: DS Ronnie Ericson

Ericson drove the car to Lorna Andrews's address. McCardle sat in the front and turned around to Lucas in the back, who came off a call with Lorna Andrews's doctor.

'They're going to get full records emailed over in the next few hours,' he said. 'Doctor Burden has been Andrews's GP for most of her life. Andrews kept her GP in North Tyneside, even though she recently moved to Northumberland. Doctor Burden talked about the death of Andrews's mother, Lillian from cancer, when Lorna was around the age of ten. Various interventions and support were offered to the family. Not taken up by dad, Albert Andrews. We've asked for both records. Albert Andrews is now dead, cirrhosis of the liver.'

McCardle looked at Ericson, who nodded, knowing this could be critical information.

'Does she take any meds according to records, Lucas?' Ericson asked, his eyebrow raised, his eyes remaining on the road.

'Yeah, Boss. You can probably guess, Amitriptyline. It was prescribed three years ago as an anti-depressant. Reduced around a year ago for helping more with insomnia.'

'Bingo. Great work, Lucas,' Ericson said, slapping the steering wheel in victory. 'Get one of the team out for a written statement from the doctor.'

Lucas nodded and immediately tapped his phone.

They were five minutes away from Lorna Andrews's

address. Myers and Boyd followed in the car behind. Ericson knew Lorna's partner, James Ord, would have talked to her. Ericson also knew James Ord had no record and his nerves were like shattered glass during the interview. It was quite clear to Ericson that he was in the dark about what his partner had been doing. Either that, or he had attended the best acting school money can buy.

The plan was to arrest Andrews, take her to the station to question, while more evidence came through from her doctor and the team conducted a house search. They soon pulled up into the street where Lorna Andrews lived — a quiet, aesthetically pleasing new-build cul-de-sac.

'Number 34, Boss,' McCardle offered as Ericson slowed down and scanned the house numbers. Two cars were on the driveway at 34, making it likely that they were in unless out for a walk. James Ord should have been at work. He had made a right performance about it in the interview, claiming his supervisor wasn't happy. Ericson thought he was just saying it out of nerves as he changed his tune when Ericson commented that his supervisor could be seen as obstructing an investigation.

They parked outside Lorna Andrews and James Ord's house. A regular semi-detached house with a tidy garden. It could be anywhere in the country, but this house was home to what had become a notorious predator, and Ericson was certain of that. Getting out of the car, McCardle double checked her covert holster, ensuring she had handcuffs. The holster was like putting on your underwear, albeit not as comfortable. You went nowhere without it. Even so, the officers always double and sometimes triple checked.

Myers and Boyd got out of their car further down the

street, nodding to their colleagues and remaining silent. They would go around the back of the house, securing the rear exit. Lucas stayed at the top of the drive, monitoring the upstairs windows. Ericson and McCardle walked down the driveway in silence, listening for anything from within the house. It was a police officer instinct — another sense that understood what their colleague was thinking, how to get the best out of a situation, and how to keep each other safe.

Ericson knocked on the composite door three times, with moderate strength and rhythm. He glanced at the pots of miniature conifers on either side of the grey door. Forty seconds later, there was still no answer. McCardle turned back to Lucas, who gave an encouraging smile as he stood sentinel at the top of the driveway.

To the left of where McCardle and Ericson stood was a large window. Likely a lounge, with vertical blinds. A garage was attached to the right. The gardens backed onto other gardens in this cul-de-sac, but it was an option that Lorna Andrews could escape through the back door. First time criminals were harder to predict in so many ways, although of course being caught for the first time wasn't always indicative of the number of crimes committed.

Ericson's hand went up to the door knocker and he lifted and dropped it a further three times, with a little more force. McCardle shook her head, both of them thinking next steps. The winter air was cutting and Ericson didn't appreciate the cold and the possibility of a suspected criminal absconding. His grey-blue eyes looked at McCardle and he nodded to the large window to their left. Stepping to the side, McCardle leant forward, cupped her hands to her temples and stared into the house, before turning back to Ericson and shaking her head.

He wasn't prepared to wait any longer. 'Police. Open the door or it's coming in,' he shouted through the letter box. He didn't have a 'bosher' with him, as they called the enforcers, so any battering rams would be in human form — his, specifically. He glanced at McCardle, who rolled her eyes. Still no answer.

After ten seconds, Ericson gestured for McCardle to move back. He raised an eyebrow, walked backwards five steps and went charging to the front door, pressing the weight of his body sideways on to the door of Lorna Andrews's property. The sound of splintering plastic could be heard, as if hundreds of lolly sticks were all being snapped at once. Ericson kicked the bottom of the door and it creaked open, revealing James Ord on his knees on a striped hallway rug, looking like a terrified child.

Ericson and McCardle saw Lorna Andrews on the stairs, hunched over and sobbing as she leant against the banister. She appeared tiny, doll-like and not like the tall, broad woman of almost thirty years old that she was. A dog peeped its head around what must have been the lounge door, nervously whimpering and sensing something wasn't right from the chaos and emotions in the hallway.

James Ord stood without speaking a word. He knew why Ericson and McCardle were there. The police officers stepped further into the hallway and stood at the bottom of the grey carpeted stairs, less than a metre away from Lorna Andrews, who was glaring at her shaking hands. A streak of blood glistened on the back of one. She looked up, blotchy-faced with mascara smudged down her cheeks.

Ericson stared at her, and saw a flash of terror, as if the

child in her just realised that this had gone way beyond naughty. Her body trembled, shoulders slumped, as mucus dripped from her nose.

Ericson's gaze remained on her as he spoke. 'Lorna Andrews, I am arresting you on suspicion of the murder of Charlie Sinclair and Donald Armstrong. You do not have to say anything, but it may harm your defence if you do not mention when questioned something which you later rely on in court. Anything you do say may be given in evidence. Do you understand?'

Lorna Andrews kept looking at Ericson. Eyes wide, a child-like desperation for pain to stop etched on her face. Her chin trembled as a tear fell onto her top lip. She nodded and whispered yes. McCardle gently pulled Lorna Andrews up from the stairs and cuffed her. There were no words and no struggle. The three walked out the house as James Ord stood startled, frozen to the spot.

Ericson nodded to Lucas, who had radioed Myers and Boyd. They would stay with James and secure the property until the search team arrived. He looked back as they began walking up the drive. His gaze on James Ord, who stared back, arm across his chest as if holding his broken heart. Ericson turned away as he saw James's hands go to his face and his shoulders heave.

They drove to police headquarters, McCardle in the back with a cuffed Lorna Andrews, who shook like she had been walking the streets all night in the winter temperatures. McCardle began talking about the dog in the house. After any arrest and the drive to the police station, there was always chit-chat, whether the suspects liked it or not. Officers were trained to instigate conversation, to put the suspect at ease.

It could be a real challenge for an officer, but rapport was essential to get the truth and, ultimately, justice, and the process started immediately. The weather, TV, family, in this case, a dog — anything was discussed, or attempted to be discussed, so suspects saw the officers as humans. Negotiation skills, persuasion skills, safeguarding, even empathy. You could call it numerous things, but many times, it helped. Most of the time, people arrested are emotional. Ericson understood this, and McCardle's approach was perfect.

Over the years, he felt part psycho-analyst alongside being a copper. People committing petty crimes and repeat offenders such as shoplifters, drug dealers, D&Ds, and assaults were often vocal. They would slur words and insults at officers. Knowing they were busted, they would swear, be offensive, use racism, sexism, or general disrespect and would often try to implicate others or make excuses, ranting about their own needs. Ericson had heard and seen it all; the bullshit and the bizarre.

This bunch, the serious offenders, they were often silent. The sex offenders, OCG leads, murderers, they would act differently. These monsters would often sit in the police car silent, calm, collected, with little or no response to the attempts from the officers to communicate — their psychology not like ours. Over the years, Ericson had learnt some people are wired differently, in a way that their circuit board is just waiting to short fuse.

Ericson always thought we all had capabilities to commit crimes; by mistake, by revenge, by circumstance. Someone killing someone in a fight that escalated, stealing to feed a starving family, crimes committed by someone being exploited or in a situation that led to such desperation.

He had never forgotten a case he had worked on where a middle-aged professional woman stabbed her husband. Years of domestic abuse perpetrated against her by the controlling, violent husband who pretended to neighbours, friends, and family that he was the model husband. Physical and sexual abuse, psychological torment, and financial control by the bastard, that she had never told anyone about. Until one day, she snapped, unable to take anymore and put a knife in him.

The scumbag survived the stabbing, unfortunately, and sold his story to a magazine; *'Stabbed as I ate my muesli'* was the sensationalised title of the article, whilst his long-suffering wife was sent down for wounding with intent.

Ericson empathised how a person's mind and a shit serving in life could lead to the often unthinkable. Without doubt, people had to conform to the law. There was no deviating from that. The law and upholding it was why Ericson went into the force all those years ago and why he maintained pride in his work. But as the years went on, he understood more about psychology and need.

People's true colours often came out in interview but even from arrest and that journey to the station, the thinking and mechanics of someone's mind started. The perverts and planners of crimes beyond human conception were always quiet. Often speaking with their body language — a look, a sneer, a smile. The amount of times Ericson had seen colleagues during his career on the brink of losing their composure; a flash of what they wanted to do to the sex offender or mutilator in the car next to them.

We are all human. But they never did. Justice was enough. Although it took Ericson himself many years and countless sessions in the gym to digest this. Ericson had become the king of chit-chat over time. There were topics most offenders wanted to talk about; football, someone in their family they loved, how shit the world was. He was good at getting a single spark of rapport with people and even better at hiding the disgust he often felt about the scumbag sitting cuffed in the back.

As they drove to the station, McCardle tried to talk to Lorna Andrews about her dog and then her career. She had gone into social care for the wrong reasons; all three of them in the car knew that. It may have been for good purposes on paper, in principle at some point, but now it was a twisted, sick, criminal reason and Ericson hoped they would get the truth at the station.

The police search team was on their way to Lorna Andrews and James Ord's property as Lucas, Boyd, and Myers waited. They had been on standby to minimise the timeframe of any evidence being destroyed. Ericson still felt Ord was in the dark and seemed shell-shocked; a victim of Andrews's deceit himself. But love makes us do things beyond comprehension and the team needed evidence. Instinct, intuition, gut feelings — they weren't enough. Beyond reasonable doubt. That's what Ericson needed, which required evidence or a confession. And by God, he was going to get it!

# Chapter 44: James

An army of more police arrived at the property. Invaders, taking over their home, their sanctuary. The neighbours twitched their blinds and put rubbish in their bins; anything to satisfy their curiosity. James sat on the stairs, looking at the broken front door blankly as a detective showed his badge and a football team of police traipsed into his home as if it was entry to the newest nightclub. No consideration for him and Angus, or for Lorna and the home they had created.

James felt numb to the reality of what was happening and the possible future. His world had cracked and was shattering like a window pane targeted with a stone. He would need to ring his parents, speak to his mother and explain. This might be in the news. *Shit, would reporters turn up at the house next?* He dropped his head into his hands. *What the hell was happening?* Angus was barking, clearly traumatised and confused by the chaos going on around him.

'Come here, son,' said James, tapping his calf. Angus trotted over.

'James Ord?' an officer said.

James nodded.

The officer introduced himself and the search team. 'We have the authority to search your premises for any evidence. Do you understand?'

James nodded again, feeling the cold sweat of sickness wash over him.

'We'll try to be as least disruptive as possible, but this is going to take some time and the search will be invasive. You may need to join us at the station for questioning.' His tone was serious, even with a slight softness behind his eyes.

*It wasn't his fault*, thought James. *Not this copper's fault that his girlfriend appears to be some unhinged murderer of homeless people.* Even thinking about it made him want to vomit. James gently pushed the detective out of the way and ran into the downstairs cloakroom toilet. He threw up small particles of breakfast — the last thing he ate, hours ago.

Crouching on the floor of the bathroom, elbow resting on the toilet seat, he placed a hand to his mouth. James wondered how was he going to explain it all? To his parents, his family, and friends? Where would he even start? His mam would be hysterical. Everyone would find out, though.

The whole bloody world would know if the police have something on Lorna. Even if they don't, the neighbours will ask questions. It felt like an elephant on James's chest. He leant back, away from the toilet bowl, and took a few deep breaths. Maybe he could just switch his phone off and run away. Take off and have some space until it was over. Although, how could something like this ever be over?

Angus pushed his head in the door and squeezed beside James. Lifting his hand, James stroked Angus's head and his tail wagged. Sitting on the tiled floor of the tiny bathroom, with Angus squashed up against him, he sobbed. His world would never be the same. He would lose Lorna. If she hadn't done those horrific crimes, there was clearly something wrong with her, something that required immediate intervention. He put his fist to his mouth. If she had done those crimes... shit, it wasn't worth thinking about.

James felt his head was going to explode — his brain pulsating, like toothache, inside his muddy skull. Was this some sick nightmare? Was he going to wake up cosy in his bed, spooning Lorna as Angus lay in his deluxe bed across the room? Would he wake up and over breakfast tell his love what a bizarre nightmare he had, laughing, recounting the story?

Slowly standing, he leant over the sink. Cupping some water, he swilled it around his rancid mouth, spitting out the taste of vomit. He splashed water on his face, grabbed the nearby towel and looked in the mosaic-framed mirror hanging on the wall. All colour from his usual bright complexion had gone, leaving the murky grey of a winter day looking back at him.

He had to see what was going on in the house, what happy memories these strangers were tearing apart with gloves and evidence bags. In the frightened part of his mind, James was terrified they may find something that proves the woman he fell in love with was capable of such abhorrent crimes.

# Chapter 45: Lorna

'I'll be back in ten minutes,' the solicitor said to Lorna, in a pleasant but professional manner.

Kindness was gone now for Lorna; she felt sure of that. It was over. The world was going to be cruel to her again, like it had been for most of her life. The few years of relief, of what others would class as 'normal', would now be gone and replaced with the torment, sadness, and despair she had from the age of ten. She sat, her head a hurricane of pressure, fear, and panic as the solicitor talked to the two police officers that arrested her.

Maybe they sussed her from day one, she wasn't sure. Recently, she hadn't been sure of much, only that she loved James and now she could lose him as well. She instinctively touched the damp skin where her cuts were. The police had removed her watch and other personal items when they arrived at the station as the stripping of her personality began.

Rubbing her nails into the fresh wounds, she felt no pain, no relief. Instead, she felt waves of despair and confusion about what would happen next. Thoughts going over and over in her head with a buoy every so often that perhaps she could lie and get away with it? Or perhaps they will take pity on her and give her some help in the community?

'You stupid, fucking little girl,' she whispered to herself, clenching her fists as she sobbed. She wiped her hand across her eyes, diluting a small amount of blood from her wrist that had dried on the front of her hand. She looked at it, smudged. Smudged like her shit-stained life. Smudged like the love from Albert that faded as he chose the alcohol. Smudged like the love James had for her. Smudged and ruined. She heard the door open and saw her solicitor.

With a strained smile, she stood close to Lorna and began speaking. 'Lorna, I've chatted with DS Ericson and DC McCardle. Do you understand what's going on?'

Lorna nodded weakly. 'I, I don't trust them. They don't understand. I want James.' She began sobbing again and pulled the sleeves of her jumper.

The solicitor nodded, a flicker of empathy across her face. 'I appreciate that, Lorna, but this isn't a choice. They are going to interview you now. Until we have the full information on this situation, my advice to you is to answer no reply.'

Lorna stared at the solicitor, not responding, not blinking. The door opened again and DS Ericson informed Lorna it was time to be interviewed. Yes, kindness was gone and things were going to get a lot more unpleasant for Lorna Andrews.

# Chapter 46: DS Ronnie Ericson

Ericson and McCardle entered the interview room and took a seat. Lorna Andrews and her solicitor sat opposite, a desk separating them. Ericson spoke on the recording, confirming the date, time, and who was present before he repeated the caution given.

'Lorna, can you tell me where you were the night Charlie Sinclair was murdered, the 8th November?'

'I already said where I was. I was at home.' Lorna Andrews sounded like a child, protesting to their teacher that they had lost their homework.

Ericson continued. 'When last interviewed, you said the following Lorna: "I was at home all night, knackered from work". You then stated that your partner, James Ord, "Was out until about 10:30 or 11 pm as he plays football, you see, with work. Then he went for a few drinks, celebration drinks he calls them, even if they lose! So, it was just Angus, my dog and me, until then". You said you didn't call anyone and, "Just had dinner and flicked through the TV, read a bit, had a bath. It's what I usually do when James's at footy". Is that right, Lorna?'

Lorna Andrews nodded and looked at her lap.

Ericson kept his gaze on Lorna. 'For the purposes of the recording, the suspect is nodding. You have nobody to corroborate placing you at your house on that evening. We are currently asking neighbours if they have CCTV footage that covers any of the street.'

Lorna glanced up to Ericson's eyeline without blinking. There was no expression for him to read.

'Lorna, do you maintain you were home, alone on the night of 10th November when your partner, James Ord, was playing football, returning home at 10:30 or 11 pm?'

The solicitor chipped in. 'Miss Andrews, I have advised you to reply with no comment.'

Lorna turned at her solicitor, her brow furrowed and looked back at Ericson. 'Yes.'

Ericson nodded. 'Tell us again, Lorna. What was your relationship like with Charlie Sinclair?'

Sighing as if being told the dishes need put away, Lorna spoke. 'I've already said. It was fine. I supported him like everyone else did. There were no issues.'

Ericson could see nothing in her eyes. He saw a vulnerability on the stairs before the arrest, a child scared. Now she showed nothing, gave nothing away in her face. 'What about when he didn't meet Tommy? You were pissed off, weren't you?'

Lorna ran her tongue over her teeth and swallowed. 'No more than anyone else. It was his choice.'

'But you were angry, weren't you, Lorna? All that work for nothing and what about poor Tommy? More rejection from his dad?'

'It didn't bother me. He was letting himself down, not me. I'm paid to do a job. I did what I could.' She shrugged, almost robotic in her monotone answers.

Ericson remained expressionless. 'Did you feel sorry for Tommy? Another rejection from his drunk of a father?'

Lorna looked across the room to the blank wall, her

mouth down turned. She flared her nostrils. 'I was used to it'. She jerked her head back. 'He was used to it. It wasn't a surprise to him, or me.'

Ericson side-eyed McCardle, acknowledging Andrews's slip up and nodded. 'But you wanted this to happen so much. You invested time and energy in a reunion. A chance for Charlie to turn his behaviour around, make amends. Didn't you?'

Lorna shook her head and remained silent. There was silence for twenty seconds. Ericson's and Lorna Andrews's gaze remained fixed, staring at each other, both trying to work out one another's next move; a game of chess with the highest stakes. The solicitor shuffled in her chair, the legs scraping against the hard floor and the stare off ended.

'I think you were pissed off, Lorna, that Charlie let Tommy down again. That Charlie let you down after all your hard work and effort. I think you wanted to teach Charlie a lesson. So, you hurt him Lorna, you punished him?'

The solicitor cleared her throat. 'You can think what you want, DS Ericson. Miss Andrews, I advise you not to answer that question.'

Lorna swallowed. She turned at her solicitor and rubbed her cheek before speaking. 'No, no I didn't.'

Ericson studied Lorna; her teeth pressed together and the colour drained from her face. He knew she was using all her strength to keep the act up. He had seen it thousands of times; the guilty trying to control their emotions. Refusing to accept the inevitable. Thinking they can get away with it.

'I think you did, Lorna, and I would recommend you tell the truth.'

Lorna said nothing and looked blankly at Ericson through

tired, blood-shot eyes.

'Donald Armstrong, he didn't sound like a very likeable chap, Lorna?'

She shrugged.

'It was thought he was drug dealing and targeting young people in particular. Is that right, Lorna?'

Lorna cleared her throat. 'That's what we all thought at Homeless Helping Hands, yes. We've all told you this.' She let out a sigh, her shoulders slumping.

'It's believed he may have given drugs to someone you worked closely with, Eve Wright. Is that what you think, Lorna?'

Lorna shrugged again.

'You really liked Eve. The file notes said you were doing some great work with her. Really trying to change her life and support her. Such a young lass with loads of potential, wasn't she?'

Lorna nodded.

'Then she died. Drugs overdose, on site at the day centre. You must have been devastated?' Ericson saw a slight expression change. He knew Lorna was upset by the mention of Eve Wright. Or perhaps it was anger bubbling away. The same anger that over-flowed and led her to kill Donald Armstrong.

'Did you want Donald Armstrong to be punished for him giving drugs to young people, Lorna? Young people who died because of him pushing drugs onto them?'

'No,' Lorna shouted, looking past the detectives, towards the interview room door.

'I think you did, Lorna. You were angry, understandably. All that work and potential in Eve and other young people. It was getting destroyed by Armstrong poisoning them with heroin. Isn't that what was happening?' Ericson's tone remained the same, with little body movement.

'No, I mean yes, he was. You should have stopped him, stopped it.' Her voice crackled on the last few words and she scrunched her eyes shut before opening them again. 'I want a break. I, I don't feel well.' Lorna turned to her solicitor and Ericson saw a glimpse of those child's eyes again, pleading, needed rescuing.

'I'm sure we can have a ten-minute break. My client is complying with your questioning,' the solicitor said firmly.

He nodded. 'Very well, ten minutes.'

Lorna rubbed a finger across her wrist, where the fresh cut glistened. She pressed her lips together, the pressure of the situation building in her by the second. Ericson knew her brain was ticking as to what to do next. Lorna Andrews wasn't a criminal mastermind and Ericson was sure until recently, she probably hadn't done more than speeding in the last year. However, there was something sociopathic in her and it had been bubbling under the surface for years, waiting to splash out like hot oil from a frying pan — and this had led to murder. Of that, Ericson was certain.

# Chapter 47: Lorna

As she sat in the interview room, Lorna felt a delirious wave of surrealism. For the last few months, she had lived a double life. But she was a victim, and she didn't know how to make people see that. The victim of a horrific childhood, where no one had the courage and skills to rescue her. A desperate, grieving child in need who had to fend for themselves and tolerate a drunk of a father. She was *the* victim and what she had done these past few months had been punishment to Albert and all those who didn't give a damn about her for so long. A way to stop other people's suffering, to prevent more victims. Victims like her.

Lorna wanted to scream, to explain that she did what she did to help. And until the conversation with James — right until they sat in their lounge and Lorna saw terror in the face of the man she loved more than life itself — she still felt she had done the right thing killing Charlie and Donald. It had been pain-free for them, a blessing.

Their lives were just a lame existence. They were seen as the shit on the shoe of society. People pretending to feel sorry for them, feigning compassion, but really, they did nothing to help. Or simply pretended to help for their own ego. Charlie and Donald were of a population that people crossed the road to avoid, pretended to be on their mobile phone as they passed them, and didn't want it on their doorstep.

They were the 'nobodies', the 'scroungers', the 'undeserving'.

Lorna had heard it countless times throughout her life. Society was selfish and always looked for something, or someone to blame.

The solicitor went to get some tea from a machine that charged for piss-warm liquid, tasting of nothing. An officer sat in the corner of the cold, depressing interview room — drafted in to supervise and baby-sit whilst the two bastards who arrested her went to gloat. Lorna closed her eyes and sat back in the hard seat. She stretched her legs under the table and let her arms flop down from the chair. If she tried really hard, she could picture being in another place, another time, where she wasn't in pain. A place she never knew. Tears burst the dam of her eyelids. She let them fall, not wanting to move or make a sound.

She returned to her thought process. Charlie and Donald would never have changed. That boat had sailed long ago into the sea of addiction and selfishness. They could have been offered all the chances in the world, but their selfish needs and skin-crawling greed would always make them prioritise themselves, just like Albert had. Charlie had said himself that his life was meaningless and he was a drain. He had told Lorna right at the start. The spark of Tommy wasn't enough to light a fire of recovery and determination. Charlie got what he wanted and what he needed.

Donald was a leech, a parasite. A scumbag who would have killed and killed. He took innocence and chance and made it rotten, filling its heartbeat with drugs. He was coercive, exploitative, and couldn't care less that it was someone's child he was pushing drugs onto and murdering. He thought he was above the law; above the systems devised to make scumbags like him conform. The world was a better place without Donald. He deserved everything he got and more. Lorna couldn't feel remorse. She did the world a favour. She could see Albert in Charlie — pathetic and attention seeking, playing the woe is me card. But in Donald, she also saw destruction and suffering of innocent people, something she had been on the end of as a child.

Lorna didn't expect James to fully understand. He never truly knew her. Well, not the version that she hid. But when he looked at her a few hours ago, she saw a fear in his eyes that reminded her of her childhood self. For the first time in many years of being self-sufficient and independent, Lorna didn't know what to do next.

# Chapter 48: DS Ronnie Ericson

Ericson stood outside in the station yard, watching McCardle smoke. He hated smoking, and the illnesses it contributed to, but there was something about observing people do it that Ericson enjoyed. It was almost hypnotic seeing the inhalation, the cigarette burning and the smoke filling the air. Filthy, no doubt, but mesmerising all the same.

'She's gonna crack,' said McCardle, tapping some ash from her burning bad habit.

'Yup, I keep seeing that flash, then blankness behind the eyes. It's like she is almost two people, a child in an adult's world. I think she's a monster and a mouse all in one.'

McCardle nodded. 'Absolutely. I remember working on a case a few years back, over in Newcastle. You'll remember it, the Scott Sansom case?' McCardle looked at Ericson, the concentration of trying to recollect on his furrowed brow. 'The guy who was going around terrorising pensioners? He would break into their homes and make them eat food with him, cuddle them, then beat them up.'

'Ah yes, I remember. Warped bastard.'

McCardle laughed. 'That's definitely one name he was called. Well, when we got into it, turns out he had been raised by his grandparents. Grandma was really strict and Grandad was soft as clarts. They had died within eight months of each other and he was left, a loner, distraught. Grandma died first, and he blamed her for Grandad dying a few months later of a broken heart. He had some perverse way of trying to get comfort from pensioners but punishing them.'

Ericson shook his head. 'Nowt as strange as folk, McCardle, and in this job, there's always a new psycho in evolution. A catwalk of insanity and depravity that fresh faces continue to walk down.'

The pair stood in silence for a few seconds, reflecting on the depths some people fall to or intentionally go to. Ericson turned to McCardle, a serious look on his aged face.

'Now this bonkers bugger in there, we can keep her in custody for now. The press is going to want an update. They'll be all over this — pretty young lass turns to murdering vulnerable men.'

McCardle raised an eyebrow as she inhaled her cigarette. Blowing out air, she then spoke. 'I'm not sure anyone would call Donald Armstrong vulnerable. Well, perhaps the pope, at a stretch!' She shrugged and they both let out a light laugh.

Ericson went on. 'We need to check in with James Ord, question him again, then perhaps offer some support. I'm certain he isn't involved, but we need to rule it out completely.' He tapped his thumbnail against his lips. 'Also, we need to keep this under wraps until we can do the press conference and not have anything announced to the world via bloody Facebook.'

McCardle made a pffttt noise. Social media had a lot to answer for. It could be the lottery ticket or the gutter, and rarely anything in between.

'In the meantime, Boyd and Lucas can work on information about her past. We'll get more about her medical record, any professional intervention over the years and any further detail on her parents and their deaths. We could easily be

looking at some childhood trauma or neglect that's mani-
fested. Myers will go back to the centre, and also check any
CCTV footage of Andrews's neighbours. The search team
may find something. We've got her McCardle. I feel it in here.'
Ericson put his hand to his stomach.

'Is that not just you wanting a bacon sarnie?' McCardle
asked, tapping his forearm with her elbow.

'You're not wrong there. Come on, we've still got five
minutes. Let's see what they've got in the canteen.'

McCardle laughed, stubbed her cigarette and the two went
for some much-needed fuel, knowing it was going to be a very
long shift.


Ericson and McCardle spent a further hour questioning
Lorna Andrews, with no success. She had been placed in a
cell at the station, given some food, and could speak to her
solicitor at any point. In the meantime, it gave Ericson and
the team the chance to collate potential evidence before the
team briefing that was due in an hour. This would then get
reported to Chief Inspector Richardson, ready for a press release the next working day.

The team had been on shift for over twelve hours already.
They were used to it and when there was a major incident; the
team were solid like a skein of geese migrating — supporting
and navigating together. But they also had to get some rest,
so Ericson hoped the briefing came up with the goods and
the team could get a few hours' sleep before returning in the
morning. An hour later, the investigation team gathered in the
room, eager to share their findings.

DC Lucas started. 'There is nothing much on Albert Andrews, Lorna Andrews's father. A few public orders and

several D&Ds from around fifteen years ago. Nothing of major concern,' Lucas said as he glanced between Ericson and Boyd. 'He died six years ago of alcohol related illness, cirrhosis in the main. Before that, he had been to his GP sporadically with illnesses from alcohol misuse; gastro problems, bowel, passing blood, etc.'

Ericson nodded to Lucas, who scratched his head and glanced at his notebook briefly.

'He never engaged with services and no record of family support. He lived in the marital home until a few years before his death. It was repossessed, and he stayed in temporary accommodation in North Tyneside. A B&B called Beside the Seaside, which houses homeless people. We'll check out the B&B tomorrow and speak with the landlord around any family visiting Albert — to get a picture of his final years.'

'Great work. What about professional involvement for Lorna Andrews?'

Lucas turned to Boyd to update.

'The medical records refer to children's services involvement. She was assigned a social worker when she was eleven-years-old, about a year after her mother died. It was the school raising a concern that she was attending unkempt and smelly. Turns out Albert had already replaced his wife with the bottle at this point. Sounds like the social worker, a Karen Dunn, was involved for around eight months. Albert must've cleaned his act up temporarily or lied. There was a mentor at the school appointed for Lorna Andrews; Robyn Wilson,' Boyd explained to a nodding Ericson before she took a sip of water.

'The duty social worker gave us the information, but we can go in tomorrow morning and have a look at the archived files. Doctor Burden has said we can have copies of the more in-depth medical records tomorrow, showing referral dates for services and medications for Andrews. The team got no answer from the neighbours, but saw two CCTV cameras that may show a good image of the road leading out of the cul-de-sac Andrews lives in. We'll go back first thing to prioritise.'

'The team are working on the city centre CCTV for images around Crosley of Lorna Andrews's vehicle, a blue Vauxhall Corsa, at the time of the murders,' Myers said, crossing one foot over the other.

Ericson clasped his hands together as he walked across the front of the room. 'Excellent. We've established Lorna Andrews's father; Albert Andrews was an alcoholic for most of her childhood and he was in temporary accommodation until he died six years ago. This was before Lorna Andrews met James Ord, so he's likely to not know the truth of her family. Lorna Andrews had a live prescription of Amitriptyline, which we know was found in the bloodstream of the two victims, Sinclair and Armstrong. She has no alibi on the night of the murders. The team are still searching the property and we could have possible neighbour CCTV footage,' Ericson summarised as his team listened intently.

He leant against a desk, back throbbing from the long shift and hard interview room chair. 'Lorna Andrews is in the cells. If the magistrates' court agrees, we can keep her for ninety-six hours, while we build the evidence. But I think we've already come close to the threshold. Thanks all. Get yourselves home, you brilliant buggers, and get some rest. We'll see you all in the morning, bright as a button,' Ericson ordered, giving the team a round of applause as colleagues rose from their chairs, groans of tiredness travelling around the room.

'You too, McCardle.' Ericson looked at McCardle. She was pale, with dark circles under her eyes. 'Get home and get some kip, some hot food, and I'll see you in the morning.' He gave her a smile.

'And you, Boss. Need your sharp brain so we can nail this one and you can then enjoy the birthday meal with your Caroline and Kelsie.' McCardle returned his smile.

'Thanks, pet.'

They left the station together, passing a message onto the search team to call Ericson if there was an update on any evidence. Ronnie drove the coastal route home with Nathaniel Rateliff and the Night Sweats playing quietly. It was a longer journey, but he enjoyed the peace of the sea, dancing with melodic charm, holding its own mysteries and secrets. There was little light illuminating the coast, just the odd lamppost and the lighthouse in the distance. The air was icy-cold, but Ronnie still had the windows down. He could almost feel the gravitational pull of the moon against the tide soothing him after a long, brain-dissolving day.

After passing the coastline, he let thoughts fill his head again. He felt so ready for the birthday meal with Caroline and Kelsie the following night. It was something his soul needed. Even though it was nothing spectacular, it kind of was for Ronnie. An opportunity, possibly a first step. Just a nice hot meal would feel like luxury right now! After this case, if there was a chance to make amends, to repair the missing floorboards of his marriage, Ronnie knew he would grab it and not let go. He just had to get a charge through for Lorna Andrews, else the meal would be another missed opportunity.

# Chapter 49: Lorna

Lorna sat in the cell on a piss-proof mattress, with a serving of food on her lap. She was expecting pig swill, like what they get fed on the TV, but maybe that happens in a proper prison and not in a cell in police headquarters. The thought made her silently cry again. She had only stopped sobbing five minutes earlier and her eyes stung like wasps had attacked them.

She ate some of the vegetable curry in its microwaveable container, pushing around the rice that she would normally devour. A polystyrene cup of weak, luke-warm tea accompanied her meal. Lorna felt out of reality, like she was watching someone else's story unfold — out of control and not knowing how it was going to end.

She cycled between the strength of denial and the worry that the police would gather the evidence for her demise. Lorna wavered between confidence that she did the right thing to terror that she couldn't survive in prison. Letting out a weak wail of distress, she ran a hand through her long brown hair. It felt contaminated from the dank cell, that despite the smell of disinfectant, still held the scent of urine. She didn't know what to do, and her solicitor was as useful as a bikini in the Arctic.

Pushing the tray of food across the tiny, soulless cell, Lorna lay down on the squeaky plastic mattress. Looking to her left, she saw the autographs of detainees past carved into the dirty, sad, white walls; 'Piss off pigs', 'Danny loves Emma', 'Don't let the filth beat you down'. She sighed. If only this room could speak. She curled up on her side. A scratchy blanket, her single comfort, although God only knew when that had last been cleaned.

Lorna lay, feeling hollow as she thought of James. Her James. Her dream man, Mr Perfect. It was all ruined. She couldn't expect him to stay with her if she was sent to prison. He was young, successful, gorgeous, and had a heart to match his handsome face. Lorna sobbed, curling into the foetal position, knowing this could be the end of her dream come true. Her first proper experience of stability and happiness was likely to have expired; melted faster than ice cream in the summer sun.

If the truth came out, he might think she was a monster. He wouldn't understand, no one would. Grandma, Grandad, her best friend Chantelle, the staff at Homeless Helping Hands. She would be seen as evil, a predator. They wouldn't see that she had done it to protect people. They wouldn't understand that it wasn't her fault. It was Albert's fault. Everything was Albert's fucking fault. As Lorna closed her eyes out of sheer exhaustion, she felt herself drifting off with the realisation in her mind that it was the beginning of the end.

# Chapter 50: DS Ronnie Ericson

Ronnie was awoken by his alarm blaring at 6:30 am. His head thumped from dehydration and lack of sleep and it felt like the Salvation Army band had used his skull as a practice room. He groaned and touched his head, his body telling him, more often of late, to slow down. Walking to the bathroom, Ronnie thought about the process of the day. He was surprised the search team hadn't rung him. They would have been finished hours ago. Then again, Andrews was in custody. CCTV would be prioritised today and speaking with all neighbours, social services would be visited, and the GP practice for the in-depth records.

Ronnie heard his stomach rumble as he got out of the shower. He hadn't eaten a decent meal for a few days. Although staff at the canteen looked after them, trying to enjoy a plate of homemade pie, chips, and mushy peas was not something he had afforded time for during his last shifts. Ronnie decided he would have a takeaway breakfast. It was likely he wouldn't eat again until the hopeful meal that evening with Caroline and Kelsie. *Bloody please let me get to the meal,* he thought to himself.

Twenty minutes later, he was on the road to work via the independent café at the end of his estate for a cappuccino and a sausage and egg sandwich. Arriving at work, he was almost salivating as he rushed into headquarters to get to his desk so he could scoff his breakfast. Ericson bit into his bun, the crispy bacon coated in a squirting of soft yolk as he punctured it with his teeth. He closed his eyes, savouring one of his favourite breakfasts. A streak of egg yolk dribbled down his chin as the response inspector seemed to appear out of nowhere at his desk. Ericson snapped out of his breakfast euphoria, dabbed his chin with a serviette, and looked to his colleague who handed him bagged evidence.

'Morning, pal. This is from the search team. Looks nice.' He pointed to the breakfast sandwich. Ericson nodded, chewing on the mouthful of food and putting an enthusiastic thumb up. The response inspector continued.

'Forensics has a possible murder weapon, a blue plastic bag. It'll all be in your email. Some evidence came in last night. We didn't ring as the suspect is in the cell and you looked wrecked, pal.' He smiled at Ericson. 'But search officers found a large quantity of notebooks in the early hours, diary type things at Andrews's property. In the kitchen, behind the kickboards. Twelve all bagged up. But basically, looks like as near to a confession as you could get in the notebook they've tagged separately.'

'Bloody get in! Thanks, mate.' Ericson clapped his hands together.

Picking up his mobile, he walked over to the window. It was the start of a gloomy, cold, North East England day outside. Mid-January and it felt like it had been dark and cold for months. As he clicked to redial on his mobile to call McCardle, he saw her car pull up in the staff car park. Ericson returned to his desk to eat the last of his breakfast sandwich whilst his partner got into the building. Then they could go to the CSI manager and look at the journals together. *Looks like I may get to the birthday meal after all,* Ericson thought to himself as he gulped his coffee.

McCardle came into the office, carrying her own takeout breakfast bag and cup. 'Morning, happy campers,' she called, walking across the office to her desk.

'It's happy campers alright, McCardle. Looks like we have diaries of potential evidence from Andrews's home!'

She placed her takeaway on his desk as she put her bag down, taking her long black coat off quickly, eager to get started. Placing a hand on Ericson's shoulder, McCardle saw the satisfaction on his face. It was a respectful, supportive gesture, and Ericson was grateful. McCardle had become more than a colleague, she was now a friend and although Ericson always maintained boundaries and professionalism; they had connected in a way that could only make their working partnership more effective.

'It came in during the early hours. Are you ready for some morning reading?' Ericson said with the enthusiasm of a goal keeper saving a shot.

'Too bloody right,' she replied, rubbing her hands together.

Ericson gathered up the diaries, and they took the books down to the CSI manager so they could be examined in a sterile environment, preserving the evidence. When they arrived, CSI Manager Malcolm was there. They got to work on the long but essential process, with Malcolm taking photos of each page to email to Ericson. McCardle and Ericson looked on at the array of diaries, some aged but had asked Malcolm to photograph the individually bagged notebook first. She did and the pair returned to their desks.

The photos soon began coming over to Ericson's email, and he and McCardle studied them in silent concentration.

The pair flicked through the first few images, nothing of any great detail, and the bulk of images were historical entries.

'Find the week of Charlie Sinclair's murder in November,' McCardle said, leaning closing to the computer screen with a hand to her round face.

Scrolling through the photos, Ericson saw an entry on the 6th November first.

*6th November*

*Dear Diary,*

*Why are people so ungrateful? It's something I ask myself all the time. All the years of wanting help and I never got any, except from Robyn. Then there's these lot. Offers crawling all over them to help change their lives, make everything easier and they decline them or say yes and do nothing about it, which is probably worse.*

*Everyone at work says the same. It's not just me. Ungrateful, the word is used a lot. Stuart, in particular, tries to be a bit more understanding and says people aren't ready just yet. Bullshit! I think some of these lot would never be ready and in the meantime, they continue to pollute the lives of others, hurting their families. That's Charlie right now. He doesn't care that I spent ages sorting for him to see Tommy. He doesn't care that he's hurt Tommy. That he's hurt me. No, Charlie doesn't care at all and has come to the centre shouting at us and calling everyone. He needs stopped. He's an ungrateful, poisonous bastard, and he needs stopped. I'm so angry right now. So disappointed and angry. He will be stopped. He's just another selfish Albert Andrews.*

'Flamin' heck, that's one angry woman,' Ericson said, shaking his head. 'See if there's an entry for the next day.' Ericson rubbed his hands together like an excited child.

There was no entry on 7th November, but one on 8th

November; the day Charlie was murdered. The pair looked at each other before returning their gaze to the computer and the diary entry.

<u>8th November</u>
*Dear Diary,*

*It happened! Charlie died, and I honestly don't know how I feel about it. It felt like Albert was lying there, pathetic, dirty, and still blaming the world for his own behaviour. There's never any acknowledgement from these lot about their responsibility for things. That might be the thing that disgusts me the most. He used to do that, say he was grieving, too. Why did he used to do that to me? Push it onto me? He was an adult, and I was 10, but it was still about him and not me. What type of dad does that? Well, I know what type of dad and Charlie Sinclair is the same breed.*

*They shouldn't be allowed to have kids. Well, he's not anymore. Thinking about it and doing it were very different. I kinda knew it would be. It wasn't easy. I'm a good person. I know that. James, Chantelle, my grandparents, the people at work — they all know I'm a good person.*

*I never wanted to do this, but it felt like I had been chosen to protect others, and it was the best and kindest thing to do. It's harm prevention, as Stuart would say! But it still wasn't easy. I know I'm a good person and that's why it's hard to do, but it's essential. It had to be done.*

*Charlie took the alcohol cos he's a greedy bastard, like Albert was. He was even ungrateful that it wasn't vodka! But he guzzled it like a greedy pig. When I went back, he was out cold, so it was easier to finish it. He struggled a little, but it didn't take long. Strength comes from unexpected places at times. I almost stopped until I remembered it was a gift to the world. It was crucial. So, I kept going until I knew it was over. He had to pay the price. Albert had to pay the price.*

*It'll come out soon. People will just think he overdosed or his tired, abused, self-inflicted illnesses had eventually taken over. They'll be pleased, fewer people to take from those who want help. No one will waste resources looking too deeply into the death of a waster like Charlie and it will help me heal, knowing I've stopped another family suffering for a minute longer. Another Albert gone. I'm a good person.*

Ericson blew out air, lifted his glasses to his head, and pushed his chair back slightly from the desk. Interlocking his hands, he placed them at the back of his neck.

McCardle put a hand on her forehead. 'Crikey, she's unhinged, Boss. She thinks she's doing the world a favour. A mercy killing!'

'Too right, but this is our bloody golden ticket. Our confession — and that's without possible DNA from the blue plastic bag used to suffocate the victims.'

Tapping her finger to her mouth, McCardle continued. 'She's only a young lass, and look what she's done. Her whole life now ruined, along with the lives of these men and their families.'

Ericson nodded. 'Go to the date of Armstrong's murder, the 10th January.'

McCardle flicked through the screen to the relevant date. There wasn't an entry but there was on 11th January.

*11th January*

*Dear Diary,*

*I think this must be what it's like to take heroin. That absolute high with a crashing low after, but on repeat. I know the lows are fear and anger and sadness about Eve still, but the highs of getting rid of the biggest bastard of all is amazing. Donald had to have been the smuggest, nastiest man I've ever come across. He didn't care that young people have died cos of him. He murdered them. Loads more that have almost died, just brought back from overdose, and lots more still hooked on drugs cos of him.*

*Young people having to do all sorts to pay for drugs that he's got them addicted to. I bet he's forced them to have sex with him. He hates women, HATED women. The bastard is gone now and the world will be a safer place. I'm so angry writing this but so pleased he's fucking gone.*

*His family, who he leeched from and upset, free from the burden of his decaying life. But more importantly, all those young people are free and safe and now they can get help, cos they want to. Eve wanted to. She had so much promise. I saw me in her. I knew she could be helped, saved. Donald was her Albert — young, relying on him to look out for her. But he would have only ever hurt her, and he caused the ultimate hurt: her death. I would have done anything to help her. I did. I helped her, even after her death. The ultimate help, saving others.*

*Donald was sleazing over me last night. I bet he thought I would have sex with him or something. Well, women are safe from the predator now. Young people are safe and his suffering family is safe and free now. I wanted to hurt Donald, really hurt him, but when it came down to it, it's not the type of person I am. I'm not violent. I'm a good person. It was harder than with Charlie, physically. But I did it and hopefully, like Charlie, it will blow over. In fact, I'm sure people will celebrate the death of Donald Armstrong. He never deserved to live.*

Ericson looked at McCardle and shook his head, lips pressed together, before a grin appeared on his face. He took a swig of cold coffee and pushed himself back into his chair.

'Flippin' hell,' McCardle said. 'This is some Netflix crime documentary right here!' She tapped the desk with her pen.

'Indeed. God knows what the rest have in them,' he replied, scratching his head.

There were fifteen seconds of silence as the pair absorbed what they had read. They knew there wouldn't be time to read the rest before the CPS received them, but what they had read seemed more than enough.

Ericson ran a hand through his grey hair. 'There we have it, McCardle. It's a confession. She can't pin this on anyone else. This is what we've needed and anything extra, well it's just a bonus for the CPS.'

She nodded at her superior as she rubbed the back of her neck.

'These will hopefully have her DNA all over them. They've been found in her house. We have copies of her handwriting from Homeless Helping Hands.' He clapped his hands together as he stood up. 'We'll definitely get two charges of homicide.' He winked at McCardle. 'Even without that carrier bag, which I would bet my flat on has DNA from both Sinclair and Armstrong on it.'

# Chapter 51: Lorna

Lorna had the worst sleep of her life. She woke, feeling like she had been winded from lying on the paper-thin mattress that had squeaked every time she moved through the night. Her eyes still stung like sunburn. Her whole face felt swollen and sore from crying and lack of rest. The minute periods of sleep she fell into had been plagued by nightmares that had woken her, skin coated in sweat in the cold cell. Images ran through her mind of Albert, Charlie, and Donald, taunting her. Then watching James walk away as she screamed his name to no response. Her throat was dry and raw.

*Was this what it would be like?* she wondered. Night after night filled with ghosts of bad people haunting her and losing the only thing she cared about over and over in her broken, troubled sleep? She couldn't do it — she wasn't strong enough. She had to get out of this place, back to her James, back to Angus, and their forever home. Lorna tasted blood, then realised she was chewing on the inside of her mouth. She needed to speak with James to explain and get him to help. He loved her; she loved him.

Then she thought of the diaries and the blue plastic bag. *Would the police have discovered them?* She'd only ever seen this type of thing on TV. *Maybe they hadn't, maybe they didn't look under the kickboards in the kitchen.* She smiled for a split second, trying to convince herself that all would be okay and she would be home by dinnertime to walk Angus and prepare their evening meal. As quick as her smile came, it cracked and feelings of hopelessness seeped out again. She was desperate to speak with James. It could be her last chance to tell him she loved him. The custody sergeant opened the cell door ten minutes later. Lorna looked at him like a child in a shop, begging for some sweets, and asked if she could call James.

He replied with, 'No, you are incommunicado,' and began walking away after handing her some porridge.

Lorna recalled her solicitor mentioning this and that it meant she wasn't allowed to communicate with anyone. She let out a scream as she used the spork utensil given to her by the custody sergeant, to scoop some of the porridge that could paste wallpaper to a wall, and flung it across the room in rage before instantly sobbing. She curled back up on the punishing bed, foetal position and willed for a miracle.

# Chapter 52: DS Ronnie Ericson

Ericson and McCardle went downstairs to the cells to see how Lorna Andrews had been overnight. The custody sergeant gave them a handover. Andrews's solicitor was due at 9:30 am when Ericson and McCardle would question her. Before that, it was the investigation team briefing, and Ericson was eager to update everyone on the overnight developments around the diary and possible murder weapon discoveries.

McCardle and Ericson sat in the briefing room, talking about the agenda for the day whilst they waited for the team to arrive. The information and evidence around Andrews's medical records and professional referrals was still crucial for after the charge was made — as much evidence as possible was needed in case Andrews pleaded not guilty at a later date. They also had to be on the mark for Chief Inspector Richardson and an imminent press release.

Soon the troops arrived, looking weary from a long day yesterday and little sleep. Staff from the canteen had brought some sausage and egg sandwiches up, along with cups of tea and coffee. The force wasn't perfect, and they had their fair share of issues, like any team. But there was kindness in abundance and much of it was around the likes of the canteen crew and the domestics, who always seemed to make an effort in a world outside of their own.

'Right, you motley crew,' began Ericson, as they all clambered over the trolley full of breakfast. 'There's been developments from the search. Bloody big developments,' he said, rubbing his hands together in excitement, before scooping up a breakfast bun.

'Get in, I need a short day, Boss,' said Myers.

'Well, it mightn't be that good, Myers. But the good news is here.' Ericson pointed to McCardle, who held up the evidence bags like trophies.

'These, my fine team, are diaries taken from Lorna Andrews's home. The sickening journals contain confessions from Andrews to the murder of Charlie Sinclair and Donald Armstrong.' There was an eruption of applause and lots of smiling faces between mouthfuls of food.

'So, this morning, we will question Lorna Andrews and build the file for the CPS of two counts of homicide. We still need to keep on track with the evidence gathering, though. Boyd, Lucas, we need medical records and social services information.' They nodded at their superior as they chewed their food.

'There's been a possible murder weapon; a blue plastic bag. It's been sent to forensics. Likely to be the murder weapon given both victims were suffocated.' He took a bite from his sandwich, chewing and swallowing it at a record-breaking speed as his eyes moved to DC Myers.

'Myers, if you can lead the door to doors with anyone else available for CCTV footage and continue to look at city centre footage.' Myers nodded. 'We can leave the day centre for now and Andrews's old employment. They're back-up if we need more info or depending on any admission and CPS requirements. Can you update us please, Boyd?'

Boyd placed her cup on the carpeted floor.

'There's evidence from a neighbour's CCTV system that Lorna Andrews's car was seen leaving her house close to the time of Armstrong's murder. The file is getting typed up for the CPS,' said Boyd, a big smile on her face.

'Bloody marvellous!' Ericson punched the air. 'You've all worked so hard. Right, finish these breakfast buns. McCardle and I will get our confession!' He winked at his team as he and McCardle left the room, a bounce of achievement in their step, and got prepared to interview their suspect.

It was 9:40 am and a pale and tired looking Lorna Andrews came into the interview room with her solicitor. Ericson set the recorder away, and they got straight into it, with Ericson putting the diaries on the table.

'Lorna, do you recognise these diaries?'

Lorna swallowed and wrung her hands together. 'No.'

'Are you sure, Lorna? They were found in your house. In your kitchen, hidden behind the kickboards, along with a blue plastic bag that's being tested for DNA as we speak.'

Lorna shrugged and looked down at her wrist, where the wound of her self-harm was visible.

Ericson continued. 'We've established they aren't your partner, James Ord's diaries, Lorna. They go way back in date, to over fifteen years ago. Right up to a few days ago.' He paused, waiting to see if she would look up, but her gaze remained on her wrist. 'You see, Lorna, we believe they are your diaries, as they are so detailed with things about you that no one else is likely to know. As well as feelings and people in your past and present.'

Ericson saw a tear fall onto her lap. 'Now is the time to tell us, Lorna.'

Lorna's solicitor spoke. 'Can I have ten minutes with my client, please?'

'Of course.' Ericson nodded and rose from his chair. 'DC McCardle and I will leave the room.' He leant over the table and stopped the recording and they left the interview room.

'Let's have a quick tab, eh?' McCardle asked

'You make that sound like a team sport. I will accompany you though, yes,' Ericson said, grinning.

They stood outside, McCardle inhaling her cigarette like it was her last breath. 'Bet that solicitor is thinking what the hell?' she commented, blowing out.

'Andrews is in some warped denial that it's all going to be okay. She's still that ten-year-old who's waiting to be rescued by a professional.' Ericson rested his head against the wall and looked up into the gloomy sky. 'Someone who'll cuddle her, soothe her, tell her everything's gonna be okay. That she'll heal and go on to be fine. She's still that kid.'

He rubbed the back of his neck and turned his head to McCardle. 'The fluctuating behaviour from a child unable to make eye-contact and the look of a practiced sociopath, dead behind the eyes, is two of the three people she's been for decades,' Ericson said.

'Who's the third person, Boss?'

'The third is the person who wears the mask. The granddaughter, friend, partner, professional. The mask that slips now and then and either of the other two Lorna Andrews oozes out. Unfortunately, for poor Charlie Sinclair and Donald Armstrong, it wasn't the kid, Lorna, it was the killer, Lorna.'

# Chapter 53: Lorna

Glassy eyed, Lorna looked at her solicitor.

'Are they your diaries, Lorna?' the solicitor asked like a firm mother.

Lorna nodded and began crying.

'Okay. What's in them, Lorna? Are there details of the men who have been murdered?'

Again, Lorna nodded, and rubbed her hands together in anxious stress before reaching for her raw wrist that she had refused a bandage for.

The solicitor's voice softened slightly. 'Are there details implicating you as the killer, Lorna?'

Lorna nodded a third time and put her head in her hands, sobbing. Neither spoke for a minute as Lorna cried like a distraught baby. Almost gasping for air, she took her hands away from her face, revealing blotches of distress.

'Wha... what will I do?' she whispered, like a kid who had smashed a greenhouse window.

Her solicitor took a breath. 'You have two options, Lorna. One is to say nothing and let them present the information to the CPS, who will then process and decide if there is a case for court. There will be in this instance, and you can enter a plea when this happens. Or you can confess, if you have something to confess now. As your solicitor, I would advise the former option. It will give you time to think and consult with me as well as formulate a defence if required,' the solicitor said calmly and methodically.

Lorna rubbed her lips together as she picked at the raw wound on her wrist. The solicitor glanced at the wound, shining red from its desperate attempts to scab over that was being interrupted by Lorna's fingernail. Lorna stared at the wall for a minute, trying to concentrate on her breathing and feeling like she could be sick at any time.

'I'm going to say nothing, and then I can deal with things as they go along. I, I can't think straight and I need some time.' She started sobbing again. Everything was such a catastrophic mess.

The solicitor nodded. 'Understood. You need to reply with, "No comment", Lorna. It's likely, because of this information they've presented, that you will be charged today.'

Lorna dropped her head into her hands again and let out a wail. 'What will they charge me with?'

'Murder,' replied the solicitor in her monotone voice. 'And they will remand you in custody.'

Before it could even sink in, Ericson and McCardle returned to the room and began firing questions at Lorna. It went on for what felt like forever and she just wanted to dissolve there on that hard, cold seat and trickle out under the door.

As the questions were shot out at her like bullets from a gun, she replied each time with, 'No comment.' Her mind felt like the waltzer at the funfair, spinning faster and faster, raising the feeling of nausea from the pit of her stomach. With each 'no comment,' her throat seemed like it would close up as they tried to trip her up. Still, she persisted in the same reply, seeing the police officers exasperated after asking the same questions paraphrased.

Ericson kept his eyes on her. 'Lorna, one last time. You've said earlier in the interview that these diaries aren't yours. Are you sure of that?'

'No comment.'

'Did you kill Charlie Sinclair?'

'No comment.'

'Did you kill Donald Armstrong?'

'No comment.' Lorna wanted to say, 'You've already asked that ten times, you bastard.' But she didn't, understanding the solicitor had given the best advice.

Ericson shifted in his chair and looked at his colleague, who Lorna felt had taken an instant dislike to her from day one. The feeling, of course, was mutual.

'Lorna, now is your time to say anything else.'

'No comment.'

Lorna watched Ericson turn off the recording after stating the time of the interview. He stepped out of the interview room door, leaving Lorna with her solicitor. Within five minutes, the custody sergeant arrived to escort Lorna to the cell she had previously been held in. As she walked away with him, she sobbed, looking back at her solicitor like a puppy being separated from its mother.

# Chapter 54: DS Ronnie Ericson

Ericson and McCardle sat in the canteen. Ericson had chosen a slice of apple pie, claiming he was saving his appetite for the meal with Caroline and Kelsie that evening, that he would now almost certainly be able to go to. The file had been sent to the CPS, with further evidence due. Ericson was confident there was enough evidence to get two charges of homicide. They just had to wait for the green light. Everyone had worked so hard, but there had been something special about working with McCardle. She was an exceptional copper. But above that, she was an exceptional person.

'You need a few days off, McCardle. Spend some time with your lovely wife. You two must have been like ships in the night these last few weeks,' he said, stirring his cup of coffee.

'Yeah, it's not been easy, but Lisa understands. It'll be nice just to have dinner together and sit and chill out.' McCardle tilted her head.

Ericson smiled. The simple things make love successful. Comfort, contentment, companionship.

'You'll be looking forward to seeing your girls? Your Kelsie and her mam?' McCardle asked, finishing the last mouthful of her toasted sandwich.

'I am that, pet. I'm gonna give it my best shot. I've got nothing to lose and might gain the love of my life back. I'd be a fool not to try.' Ericson, normally a man who wouldn't open up easily, felt comfortable sharing his feelings with McCardle.

McCardle smiled and nodded, wiping her hands on the serviette by her plate. 'And I reckon Caroline would be a fool to not give you that chance, Boss.'

They got up, returning to the office to wait for the decision from the CPS. After what felt like a wait of decades, Ericson got the news that the evidence passed the threshold to charge Lorna Andrews with two counts of homicide.

'Flippin' brilliant!' he shouted as the team cheered.

Five minutes later, a meek and child-like Lorna Andrews was brought to the custody desk, where Ericson charged her on two counts of homicide. Ericson returned to the office, and the team gave a round of applause. He beamed and indicated a clap for everyone. He didn't like the credit and felt it was a team effort, just like it had been on so many operations over the years. Even the operations that had almost broken them all.

'We did it, Boss,' McCardle said as she passed him a cup of tea.

'We certainly did.' Ericson held his cup up in a cheer as the warm glow of pride for his team saturated him.

McCardle tapped the forearm of her superior. 'You're a legend, Boss.'

Ericson smiled. 'Don't be soft. Everyone played a blinder here, McCardle. You in particular.'

They sat in silence for a minute, absorbing their work over the last few weeks, but also thinking about their own personal lives. An hour later and the team briefing was done, finishing with more cheers and an applause louder than the crowds on match day, before it was time for everyone to go home for some much-needed rest.

Ronnie drove to his flat, observing the sky on his journey home turning into a beautiful carpet of pinks and purples as dusk began. Alongside it, the chill of winter dancing over the air. Turning up the heating, Ronnie thought about the night ahead, as he made his way home via the supermarket — picking up a bunch of Caroline's favourite flowers; yellow roses.

Ninety minutes later, Ronnie was waiting inside the entrance of the Thai restaurant. Alongside his nasal receptors having a party with the fragrant scents of pad thai and the nose-tickling spicy smell of tom yum goong, he felt those first date nerves. *Silly*, he thought to himself, but the electricity of excitement made him realise his life outside of work was important. A few minutes later, Kelsie and Caroline arrived. Kelsie came bursting through the door in a stunning red dress.

'Dad,' she exclaimed and put her arms around him.

She would never be too big for cuddles and Ronnie held his daughter, feeling his heart warm. She stepped back and Ronnie saw Caroline — for the first time in over six months — when it had been Kelsie's birthday, and a very strained affair.

Caroline looked breath-taking. Her thick dark hair curled and her aquamarine eyes looking more striking than he ever remembered, sparkling against her teal floral dress. For a few seconds, a cyclone of emotion engulfed Ronnie, and he felt he may cry. Ridiculous for a bloke like him, who was as hard as concrete at times, but in that moment, feelings overwhelmed him. Possibly the last few days, possibly the missing link of love in his life, or perhaps a combination of the two. He smiled at Caroline, uncertain of how to greet her as he handed over the yellow roses. He needn't have worried. Caroline stepped forward and gave Ronnie a hug.

Unsure if it was friendly or romantic, right then, in that five-second embrace, he didn't care. He just wanted to absorb her being. The elegance of her frame, the softness of her cheek as it briefly brushed his. The smell of her perfume and scent of her hair. It felt like home. She pulled away and smiled.

'C'mon man, I'm starving,' said Kelsie.

Ronnie laughed. 'Me too, pet.' He put his arm around his daughter and they walked to their table.

# Chapter 55: Lorna

The custody sergeant came to get her a few hours later. Lorna spoke with her solicitor, asking the same questions she had asked countless times about what could happen. The solicitor had repeated her knowledge and still she hadn't said the words Lorna needed to hear. As she was taken to another part of the building, Lorna knew what was happening. Trying to halt the inevitable, she pleaded to the officer who had become an emotionless robot.

She jerked her head. 'Please, please stop. You've got it wrong. You don't understand,' she shouted as tears fell down her pale face. She looked at her solicitor, who gave a weak smile, knowing what was about to happen.

Lorna saw the DS waiting in the reception. Someone like him could have been her own dad, had she been given half a chance in life. Now the DS was likely someone else's dad, and he was probably a great dad; loving, generous, and proud of his children. She let out a yelp, desperate for so much that would never be. Standing, she felt sure her legs would give way as her heart pounded and her mind screamed louder than a packed rollercoaster.

DS Ericson looked at her, no expression on his face. Another robot. 'Lorna Andrews, I'm charging you with the murder of Charlie Sinclair and Donald Armstrong. You do not have to say anything. But it may harm your defence if you do not mention now something which you later rely on in court.

Anything you do say may be given in evidence. Do you understand?' he said calmly.

Lorna glared at her solicitor again, who showed no signs of a rescue plan. Looking back at DS Ericson, she nodded to her fate, as the pain she had tried to manage all those years returned with full force. Lorna began sobbing like the child she still felt she was.

The solicitor sat with her as she cried until there were no more tears left and explained what would happen next. Although trained to be emotionless, Lorna absorbed the gentle way her solicitor explained, feeling it may be a long time before she receives any empathy from anyone else.

'Can I speak with James?' Lorna asked, wiping her eyes and almost gasping for breath.

'I'll ask,' replied the solicitor, tilting her head before she went to enquire.

A few minutes later, the custody sergeant advised Lorna she could make a phone call to James. It felt like the hardest thing she would ever do, but she had to speak with him. Lorna had played out what may happen with James a thousand times in the last few days. She'd put herself in his shoes, prayed to a God that didn't exist in her world, that he would stick by her, forgive her, understand her. That he would see she wasn't a bad person, just a damaged person who needed help, needed love — his love.

Dialling his number, her fingers trembled. She took a deep breath, feeling lightheaded. The phone began ringing.

'Hello,' he answered after four rings, and Lorna felt her heart may stop; it was pounding so hard.

'Hello,' James repeated. He sounded fraught, his voice unfamiliar in a way, and Lorna experienced a stabbing of guilt.

'James, it... it's m... me,' she stammered, crying as she clutched the phone with all her strength. Her legs were threatening to give way, as if she were standing in the path of a hurricane.

'Lorn, what the hell has happened? I, I can't get my head around it,' his voice crackled.

'I'm sorry, baby, I love you so much. I never meant for all this to happen.' Her voice was rushed, frantic, as she held her head with her free hand. 'It's all turned to shit. I wanted to do the right things, for the right reasons, and it's all gone wrong.' Lorna sobbed and dug her fingernails into her scalp.

She heard James crying on the other end of the phone. He could have been halfway across the world. That's how far she felt from him.

'Lorna, I love you but the police...' He stopped and gasp for breath as his voice became thick with emotion. 'The police, babe. I think they believe you killed those men. They've taken a shitload of things from the house. Our things, our fucking personal things. I don't understand.' He sniffed.

Lorna closed her eyes and pressed her lips together before speaking. 'I love you, James. I love you so much.'

'There was a load of... a load of notebooks under the kitchen kickboards. What the hell are they, Lorn? What's going on? I, I just don't understand. I don't know what to do. What the fuck is happening?'

She heard him sobbing. Her James, the love of her life. She had broken his heart. Betrayed his trust. She had to make it better.

'I love you.' Lorna couldn't say the words, the truth.

There was silence for a few seconds, then James spoke. 'I love you too, Lorna, but you've ruined it all. I don't understand. I can't get my head around all this. What have the police said?'

'I…' Lorna couldn't say it. She leant against the wall, needing some stability.

'What's happening?'

Still nothing.

'Lorna, are you there?' James shouted anxiously.

Life had always been so cruel to her and it felt like it was about to get a lot crueller.

'They've, the police, they've charged me with murder, James. I'm going to prison,' she almost spat the words out, thinking if they were said quickly, perhaps they weren't true.

Lorna heard a yelp from down the phone. Dropping the receiver, she slid down the white wall onto the cold grey lino floor of the police station. Sobbing, clutching herself in the foetal position, and knowing life would never be the same again.

# 12 Months Later

## Chapter 56: Stuart

The doors of the day centre creaked open, like they had the last few weeks. Stuart had reminded himself multiple times that he must get some oil on them. The thought dissolved once the working day began and the hustle and bustle, the cuppas, biscuits, meals, smiles, and complaints of the day centre started.

Stuart loved this time in the morning. Even after all these years, when it was cold and dark in the winter months and getting out of bed was a massive struggle. Harder with Teddy, his recently adopted rescue cat, who cuddled in beside him like a purring hot water bottle.

The last eighteen months had been turbulent for Homeless Helping Hands, after the murders and subsequent revelation that someone Stuart employed had killed vulnerable people. It had almost resulted in the centre closing down. Luckily, the police, the board, and most importantly, the team and people using the service had realised that Lorna Andrews acted alone. And in a way, everyone was taken in by her act, except for the police.

When it all came out, Stuart and the team were flabbergasted. Lorna was so meek at first, then became more confident but never cocky. Killing people, Lorna? It was too much to comprehend. But the more Stuart and the team heard, the more sociopathic they realised Lorna Andrews was. Stuart was angry with himself for not seeing it and putting people at risk. Vulnerable people at that.

Thinking about what happened still turned his blood cold. And if the police hadn't stopped her, well, it was too terrifying to contemplate — a real-life horror film. Stuart would take the guilt to his grave and carried it around like a suitcase full of bricks.

But he was reminded by Dot in particular — who he broke down in front of many times — that he took her for what they all thought she was, and that's why Stuart had such a good soul. The guilt remained. Stuart had learnt how to live with it, and he used the disaster to try to be the best he could be at Homeless Helping Hands.

He had just found out this last month that they had been awarded grant funding, which would keep the service going and help improve it. It felt like a turning point. A new start, a new focus. Stuart was ready for the challenge and knew everything would be okay. The charity would manage and keep getting stronger — just like he always had.

# Chapter 57: Mo

'Get up, you lazy lump,' Annie said playfully as she picked some earrings from her jewellery box. She looked over at Mo in bed, who smiled.

'Come back to bed, just for five minutes, love,' he pleaded, patting the mattress next to him.

'I can't! And you need to get up for work, else you'll be late.' She shook her head, raising her eyebrows.

Mo sighed, pushing the quilt back and yawning as he stood. He went behind Annie and, sliding his arms through hers, buried his head into her neck. He inhaled and let out a groan of attraction.

'I love you, Miss Joyce.' He kissed her cheek, and she spun around to face him.

'I love you too, you daft softie,' she said before kissing him tenderly on the mouth.

Mo had found his love, his Annie. And after navigating a few obstacles in the road, it had all worked out. She had stuck around when staff were getting questioned over the murders and when Mason's mam had created a stink, knowing Mo was happy.

Annie had put up with his mood swings, his fear and anger. She had encouraged and supported him to go back to counselling, working through his unresolved issues. She had stayed around, her roots firmly planted — she hadn't given up on Mo. He knew that made it real. Made it forever.

For years, Mo had closed off, limping with anger and resentment that made him volatile. He carried his own vulnerability, not wanting to be hurt. Not wanting to expose his heart to rejection and danger. Now Annie was his new addiction, for all the right reasons, and it made him feel good, so bloody good.

Everything was stable. For the first time in forever, Mo didn't feel a piece of the jigsaw was missing, well maybe one tiny bit. Mason was doing amazing. Mo felt seven feet tall with pride each time he saw his kid, and each week he witnessed his development.

'You're gonna be a genius, kidda, and you're a belter of a person,' he had said to a beaming Mason last week as they made pulled pork burgers, Annie joining them.

Life was good and after an unstable year or so, work had turned a corner. Homeless Helping Hands felt almost back to what it was. Stuart had struggled, understandably, shackled to the ghosts of guilt. There was a lot of talk in the centre, in Crosley, in the whole of Northumberland. There was a lack of trust in the charity and staff team. After all, if one of them could kill, what was to say the rest wouldn't? Lorna Andrews had the saint outfit washed, ironed, and sparkling each day — so it was understandable that people had reservations about the rest of the team.

Lorna had conned them all and inflicted the worst kind of abuse against a cohort of people who already carried the weight of prejudice on their shoulders. Through his counselling, Mo realised he had been part of the problem, and he continued to atone and try to be better; always a work in progress.

He had watched Stuart struggle after the news broke and

Lorna was remanded. At one point, Mo was really concerned about Stuart's mental health and he stuck to him like glue. They had helped each other and their bond had become stronger than ever, with Mo recently being promoted to deputy manager. Most importantly, Stuart had started to exorcise the ghosts that clung to him through no fault of his own.

That morning, as Mo got ready, he recalled his gratitude list — like he did each morning — which had always been part of his recovery. Getting his waterproof jacket out for work, he tapped the pocket of his smart winter coat that hung on the neighbouring hook. He and Annie were going for a meal that evening after work, to a cosy, romantic bistro in town. He felt it there, hidden in the pocket. The final piece of his jigsaw. Tonight was the night he would ask Annie to be his wife.

# Chapter 58: DS Ronnie Ericson

'This is it then, five more shifts,' Ericson said to McCardle, blowing out his lips as they sat in the canteen.

'What'll we do without you? You're part of the furniture. In fact, you are part of the bloody brickwork,' she laughed, tapping his forearm.

There were a few seconds of silence as the pair looked at one another across the table, both sets of eyes tinged with sadness as they smiled lightly at each other.

'I might come back and volunteer. You can always call me if you're struggling with a case,' Ericson said playfully, shrugging. The pair had grown closer after the Lorna Andrews case, continuing to work together on solving crime in Northumberland.

Their friendship was as crucial as their partnership work. It made them a phenomenal team and it was bittersweet that Ericson hadn't met Polly McCardle decades ago when he joined Northumbria Police. And now he was retiring. He had pushed her to go for promotion and it was likely McCardle would step into Ericson's old post soon.

Her face straightened. 'I'll miss you, Boss. It won't be the same.' She looked into her cup, then back up and swallowed. There was silence again, and Ericson sniffed.

'Seriously though, don't you go thinking I won't be popping in each day for an empire biscuit, and of course to see you,' she said, smiling as her eyes fixed on his.

'Well, don't let our canteen crew hear you say that. They'll be fuming,' Ericson joked.

The last year had been eventful for Ronnie, in a positive way. Thanks to Kelsie, Ronnie and Caroline had slowly gravitated back towards each other. Caroline had been doubtful, understandably. The last decade of their marriage was based on false promises and waiting for a day that never arrived. But the push from Kelsie and Caroline's birthday meal had been the catalyst for Ronnie.

He wasn't going to lose the only woman he had ever loved again. He had told her he would take his retirement and the shock on her face, followed by the biggest embrace, made Ronnie know his second chance would now be his number one focus.

They had talked, planned, talked more, planned more, and had come up with an idea which felt perfect. A lease had been going on a little coffee shop in town. Caroline had been a cook at a local school when Kelsie was little, to fit in with term times. She had baked over the years; cakes for people, the odd bit of catering, and was a natural. Ronnie knew that he couldn't give up work altogether, especially after a career that was often faster than a Formula 1 race. He always said if he stopped working, he would die or go mad. It was a truth he had seen all too often in the force, sadly.

The coffee shop idea had turned into a reality and The Cake Station had been cultivated. Caroline and Ronnie planned on working full time for a few years, building up a customer base and slowly employing staff so they could reduce hours and semi-retire. It was perfect. He had a new adventure with his Caroline; something to keep him busy but with the essential ingredient of love. And despite the end of an era at Northumbria Police, Ronnie felt a new lease of life from the fuel of his rekindled marriage. After a belly full of crime fighting, he was ready for the sweeter things in life. Well, for now anyway!

# Chapter 59: Lorna

It had been over two months since Lorna was sentenced at court, after pleading guilty to the murders of Charlie Sinclair and Donald Armstrong. She was sentenced to life imprisonment with a chance of parole after twenty years, of which she had served almost one on remand.

Lorna's solicitor said it could have been worse. The judge had commented that her crimes were abhorrent, that she had targeted vulnerable people, and tried to play the victim herself. A psychiatric assessment had ruled Lorna as being of competent mind, despite her challenging childhood.

Lorna had said little in court. It was pointless. In some ways, after feeling exposed to the world, she wanted to keep some things to herself. Sharing them would do no good, and no one had ever truly listened to her anyway. People could never understand how she felt as a child and how her feelings continued into adulthood. No one cared then, no one cared now.

Her grandparents had tried to support but they couldn't absorb what had happened. They would visit her, not knowing what to say, and failing to hide their horror behind a mask. It reminded Lorna too much of how it had been when her mam died, so she stopped them visiting, and felt they were relieved. Telling them to write instead — they did and it was some comfort.

James had kept in touch for a while, probably out of duty

or perhaps in case he worried Lorna would implicate him. She wasn't sure.

Then James's contact became less frequent until it stopped like a candle burnt out to the end of its wick. Lorna had to grieve all over again for her lost love, her happy-ever-after shattered and spat on. Chantelle was the only one who kept in touch; a true friend. She could see that Lorna wasn't a monster, well that's what Lorna hoped she thought.

The routine in prison was brutal at first and Lorna had made some enemies — whereas others thought she had done well, killing men who had mistreated women, and gave her respect. She had made some friends; they had each other's backs. It was sink or swim and she had at least nineteen years of battling against the tumultuous tide.

Absorbing the fact that she would be fifty years old when she could be released made Lorna want to end her life several times, and for the first two weeks, she was on suicide watch in a haze of tormented desperation. She still felt it, sometimes almost choking her. However, the increased medication dose was helping, and Chaplin Lawson provided a lifeline of compassion and empowerment to Lorna. Would she last? She wasn't sure. Time would tell.

Lorna got onto her bed that night, as the shouts of the inmates and the noises of the prison blared around her. She had almost perfected blocking out most of the constant background hum, but it was always there, just like her ghosts. Reaching for her pen that was certainly not fancy, but did the job, she opened her notebook and began to write,

Dear diary...

# Acknowledgments

Writing a book can be a long process of many highs and lows. Spoiler alert: it's not as glamorous as you may think! However, seeing the final product is a beautiful buzz. The process is never just one person, and I'm forever grateful for the support around me that enables me to write and create books.

Thank you, reader, for choosing this book. Readers are sunshine to an author's soul and I'm eternally grateful to each person who reads my work. The biggest thanks to Paul, my partner in love and life, who always makes me feel I can do it, even on days where I feel fragile. Thank you to my parents for always asking how it's going, and my mam and Auntie Carole, for supporting in the early days. To Sophie and Caroline for also reading. It's probably about a quarter of the same as the novel you read, showing just how long it takes to get it right! And massive thanks to Joanne and Carl, who were crucial in the development of Somebody's Nobody.

Additional thanks to my beta readers Mark, Kelsie, Elaine, Donna, and Claire. You were all a wonderful support and I'm so grateful for your feedback. And a big thanks to Rachel; a fellow author and cherished friend.

Somebody's Nobody was inspired by my own career in social care and developing and managing services for homeless people and those with multiple disadvantages. Offenders and victims of crime evoke a reaction from us and society. Often, this is around people who are deserving and undeserving of empathy, as well as a reaction what people look like, where they come from, and what their punishment should be. I hope that Somebody's Nobody made you perhaps think about this and that maybe some elements of the story raised a little awareness through the characters or plot. If you enjoyed the book, please do leave a review and tell people about it; this is the ultimate thank you to an author.

For more information, updates on the next book in the series, and news about my other publications and releases, please follow my website / socials and those of Write on the Tyne (CIC).

www.writeonthetyne.com
www.helenaitchisonwrites.com


| Instagram | @helen.aitchison_writes |
| Twitter / X | @aitchisonwrites |
| Facebook | @Helen Aitchison Writes |

| Instagram | @writeonethetyne |
| Facebook | @Write on the Tyne |

# The Dinner Club

Five people.

Five secrets.

Each needing healing, support and acceptance.

Derek's life has changed suddenly. His wife of the past few decades has left him, unable to live with his secret anymore. Inspired by a TV show, he decides to start a dinner club to make new friends, the kind that might accept him if he can be brave enough to tell them the truth.

Eddie is grieving, a widower, struggling as a single parent. The void in his life slowly destroying him and his relationship with his young daughter.

Florence, supported by her carer Jessie, craves one more adventure to round off the last 80 odd years.

Violet needs a focus, a new identity, until she has the confidence to escape her grim reality with abusive husband, Ben.

Cara is lost, with nowhere to call home and no one to go home to, now she's aged out of the care system.

Will this mishmash group fill each other's souls as well as their plates?

# The Life and Love (Attempts) of Kitty Cook

Kitty Cook may be a great school teacher, but learning the lessons of online dating is a harder subject than she first thought.

Finding herself alone again in her thirties, she decides to take her friend Sophie's advice and sign up for an online dating site. After recently leaving a failed five-year relationship, Kitty is hesitant to get her hopes up.

All she wants to do is graduate from the school of love, but will she ever find someone who will make the grade?

The Life and Love (Attempts) of Kitty Cook is an emotional yet heart-warming read that takes you on an unforgettable journey through the highs and lows of online dating and looking for love in your thirties.

# The 31 Days of May

In the wake of a devastating family loss, 24-year-old May finds herself adrift, her belief in love and happiness shattered. Struggling to navigate her new reality, May grapples with the persistent sensation of being a misfit in a world where she never quite belongs. But just as she begins to resign herself to this feeling of isolation, tragedy strikes once more, propelling May into action.

Determined to shield herself from further heartache, she concocts a radical scheme to safeguard against future abandonment. That is until May meets Mr. Parsley, a charming retiree who becomes May's unexpected neighbour. As May meticulously executes her plan, the presence of Mr. Parsley and his grown-up son, Sam, threatens to disrupt her carefully laid out path.

Will May stick to her meticulously crafted schedule, or will the warmth and kindness of the Parsley family lead her down an unforeseen, life-altering path? Join May on her poignant journey of resilience, love, and the transformative power of human connection in the face of life's most profound challenges.

## A Home for Every Cat

*All profits from the sale of this book are donated to New Beginnings Cat Rescue.*

Eric lives in a nice house with his parents, Helen and Paul. But his life wasn't always as safe and cosy. Eric was homeless as a kitten, walking the streets in search of food, friendship, and a loving home.

Thanks to some kind people, Eric found his forever home and the love he always wanted. After all, there is a home for every cat.

## Non-fiction includes:

In the Footsteps of Walker Women

Recovery Voices

Veterans' Voices

9 781739 488277